Andrew Carnegie

Round the world

Andrew Carnegie

Round the world

ISBN/EAN: 9783744730648

Printed in Europe, USA, Canada, Australia, Japan

Cover: Foto ©Andreas Hilbeck / pixelio.de

More available books at **www.hansebooks.com**

ROUND THE WORLD

BY

ANDREW CARNEGIE

NEW YORK

CHARLES SCRIBNER'S SONS

1884

TO MY BROTHER

AND TRUSTY ASSOCIATES,

WHO TOILED AT HOME THAT I MIGHT SPEND ABROAD,

THESE NOTES ARE AFFECTIONATELY INSCRIBED

BY THE

GRATEFUL AUTHOR.

BRAEMAR COTTAGE, CRESSON, July, 1879.

PREFACE.

It seems almost unnecessary to say that "Round the World," like "An American Four-in-Hand in Britain," was originally printed for private circulation. My publishers having asked permission to give it to the public, I have been induced to undertake the slight revision, and to make some additions necessary to fit the original for general circulation, not so much by the favorable reception accorded to the " Four-in-Hand," in England as well as in America, nor even by the flattering words of the critics who have dealt so kindly with it, but chiefly because of many valued letters which entire strangers have been so extremely good as to take the trouble to write to me, and which indeed are still coming almost daily. Some of these are from invalids who thank me for making the days during which they read the book pass more brightly than before. Can any knowledge be sweeter to one than this ? These letters are precious to me, and it is their writers who are mainly responsible for this second volume, especially since some who have thus written have asked where it could be obtained and I have no copies to send to them, which it would have given me a rare pleasure to be able to do.

I hope they will like it as they did the other. Some friends consider it better; others prefer the " Four-in-Hand." I think them different. While coaching I was more joyously happy; during the journey round the World I was gaining more knowledge; but if my readers like me half as well in the latter as in the former mood, I shall have only too much cause to subscribe myself with sincere thanks,

Most gratefully,

THE AUTHOR.

ROUND THE WORLD.

"Think on thy friends when thou haply see'st
Some rare, noteworthy object in thy travels,
Wish them partakers of thy happiness."

ROUND THE WORLD.

BANG! click! the desk closes, the key turns, and good-bye for a year to my wards—that goodly cluster over which I have watched with parental solicitude for many a day; their several cribs full of records and labelled Union Iron Mills, Lucy Furnaces, Keystone Bridge Works, Union Forge, Cokevale Works, and last, but not least, that infant Hercules, the Edgar Thomson Steel Rail Works—good lusty bairns all, and well calculated to survive in the struggle for existence—great things are expected of them in the future, but for the present I bid them farewell; I'm off for a holiday, and the rise and fall of iron and steel "affecteth me not."

Years ago, Vandy, Harry, and I, standing in the very bottom of the crater of Mount Vesuvius, where we had roasted eggs and drank to the success of our next trip, resolved that some day, instead of turning back as we had then to do, we would make a tour round the Ball. My first return to Scotland and journey through

Europe was an epoch in my life, I had so early in my days determined to do it; to-day another epoch comes —our tour fulfils another youthful aspiration. There is a sense of supreme satisfaction in carrying out these early dreams which I think nothing else can give, it is such a triumph to realize one's castles in the air. Other dreams remain, which in good time also *must* come to pass; for nothing can defeat these early inborn hopes, if one lives, and if death comes there is, until the latest day, the exaltation which comes from victory if one but continues true to his guiding star and manfully struggles on.

And now what to take for the long weary hours! for travellers know that sight-seeing is hard work, and that the ocean wave may become monotonous. I cannot carry a whole library with me. Yes, even this can be done; mother's thoughtfulness solves the problem, for she gives me Shakespeare, in thirteen small handy volumes. Come, then, my Shakespeare, you alone of all the mighty past shall be my sole companion. I seek none else; there is no want when you are near, no mood when you are not welcome—a library indeed, and I look forward with great pleasure to many hours' communion with you on lonely seas—a lover might as well sigh for more than his affianced as I for any but you. A twitch of conscience here. You ploughman bard, who are so much to me, are you then forgotten? No, no, Robin, no need of taking you in my trunk; I have you in my heart, from " A man's a man for a that " to " My Nannie's awa'."

PITTSBURGH, Thursday, October 17.

What is this? A telegram! " Belgic sails from San Francisco 24th instead of 28th." Can we make it? Yes, travelling direct and via Omaha, and not seeing Denver as intended. All right! through we go, and here we are at St. Louis Friday morning, and off for Omaha to catch the Saturday morning train for San Francisco. If we miss but one connection we shall reach San Francisco too late. But we sha'n't. Having courted the fickle goddess assiduously, and secured her smiles, we are not going to lose faith in her now, come what may. See if our good fortune doesn't carry us through!

OMAHA, Saturday, October 19.

All aboard for " Frisco!"

A train of three Pullmans, all well filled—but what is this shift made for, at the last moment, when we thought we were off? Another car to be attached, carrying to the Pacific coast Rarus and Sweetzer, the fastest trotter and pacer, respectively, in the world. How we advance! Shades of Flora Temple and " 2.40 on the plank road!" That was the cry when first I took to horses—that is, to owning them. At a much earlier age I was stealing a ride on every thing within reach that had four legs and could go. One takes to horseflesh by inheritance. Rarus now goes in 2.13¼, and Ten Broeck beats Lexington's best time many seconds. I saw him do it. And so in this fast age, second by second, we gain upon old Father Time. Even since this was written more than another second has been knocked off. America leads the world in trotters, and will probable do so in running horses as well, when we begin to develop them in earnest. Our soft roads are favorable for speed; the English roads would ruin a fast horse.

We traverse all day a vast prairie watered by the Platte. Nothing could be finer: such fields of corn standing ungathered, such herds of cattle grazing at will! It is a superb day, and the russet-brown mantle in which Nature arrays herself in the autumn never showed to better advantage; but in all directions we see the prairies on fire. Farmers burn them over as the easiest mode of getting rid of the rank weeds and undergrowth; but it seems a dangerous practice. They plough a strip twenty to thirty feet in width around their houses, barns, hay-stacks, etc., and depend upon the flames not overleaping this barrier.

Third night out, and we are less fatigued than at the beginning. The first night upon a sleeping-car is the most fatiguing. Each successive one is less wearisome, and ere the fifth or sixth comes you really rest well. So much for custom!

SUNDAY, October 20.

All day long we have been passing through the grazing plains of Nebraska. Endless herds of cattle untrammelled by fences; the landscape a brown sea as far as the eye can reach; a rude hut now and then for a shelter to the shepherds. No wonder we export beef, for it is fed here for nothing. Horses and cattle thrive on the rich grasses as if fed on oats; no flies, no mosquitoes, nothing to disturb or annoy, while the pellucid streams which run through the ranches furnish the best of water. There can be no question that our export trade is still in its infancy. The business is now fully organized, and is subject to well-known rules. At Sherman we saw the large show-bills of the Wycoming County Cattle Raisers' Association, offering heavy rewards for offenders against these rules, and the Cheyenne *Herald* is filled with advertisements of the various "marks" adopted by different owners. Large profits have been made in the trade—the best assurance that it will grow—but from all I can gather it seems doubtful whether the experiment of exporting cattle alive will succeed.

We saw numerous herds of antelope to-day, but they graze among the cattle, and are altogether too finely civilized to meet our idea of "chasing the antelope over the plain;" one might as well chase a sheep. As night approaches we get higher and higher up the far-famed Rocky Mountains, and before dark reach the most elevated point, at Sherman, eight thousand feet above tide. But our preconceived notions of the Rocky Mountains, derived from pictures of Fremont *à la* Napoleon crossing the Alps, have received a rude shock; we only climb high plains—not a tree, nor a peak, nor a ravine; when at the top we are but on level ground —a brown prairie, "only this, and nothing more."

<hr>

Desolation! In the great desert! It extends southward to Mexico and northward to British Columbia, and is five hundred miles in width. Rivers traverse it only to lose themselves in its sands, there being no known outlet for the waters of this vast basin. What caverns must exist below capable of receiving them! and whither do they finally go?

At the station we begin to meet a mixture of Chinese and Indians—Shoshones, Piutes, and Winnemuccas. The Chinamen are at work on the line, and appear to be very expert. At Ogden we get some honey grapes—the sweetest I ever tasted. It is midnight before we are out of the desert.

We are up early to see the Sierras. My first glimpse was of a ravine resembling very much the Alleghany Gap below Bennington—going to bed in a desert and awaking to such a view was a delightful surprise indeed. We are now running down the western slope two hundred and twenty-five miles from San Francisco, with mines on both sides, and numerous flumes which tell of busy times. Halloa! what's this? Dutch Flat. Shades of Bret Harte, true child of genius, what a pity you

ever forsook these scenes to dwindle in the foreign air
of the Atlantic coast ! A whispering pine of the Sierras
transplanted to Fifth Avenue ! How could it grow?
Although it shows some faint signs of life, how sickly
are the leaves! As for fruit, there is none. America
had in Bret Harte its most distinctively national poet.
His reputation in Europe proved his originality. The
fact is, American poets have been only English "with
a difference." Tennyson might have written the " Psalm
of Life," Browning " Thanatopsis," but who could have
written "Her Letter," or "Flynn of Virginia," or "Jim,"
or "Chiquita"? An American, flesh and bone, and
none other. If the East would only discard him, as
Edinburgh society did his greater prototype, he might
be forced to return to his " native heath " in poverty,
and rise again as the first truly American poet. But
poets, and indeed great artists as a class, seem to yield
their best only under pressure. The grape must be
crushed if we would have wine. Give a poet " society "
at his feet and he sings no more, or sings as Tennyson
has been singing of late years—fit strains to prepare us
for the disgrace he has brought upon the poet's calling.
Poor, weak, silly old man ! Forgive him, however, for
what he has done when truly the poet. He was noble then and didn't know it ; now he is a sham noble
and *knows it.* Punishment enough that he stands no
more upon the mountain heights o'ertopping the petty
ambitions of English life,

> " With his garlands
> And his singing robes about him."

His poet's robes, alas! are gone. Room, now, for the masquerader disguised as a British peer! Place, next the last great vulgar brewer or unprincipled political trimmer in that motley assembly, the House of Lords!

The weather is superb, the sky cloudless; the train stops to allow us to see the celebrated Cape Horn; the railroad skirts the edge of the mountain, and we stand upon a precipice two thousand feet high, smaller mountains enclosing the plain below, and the American River running at our feet. It is very fine, indeed, but the grandeur between Pack Saddle and San Francisco, with the exception of the entrance to Weber Cañon and a few miles in the vicinity, is all here; as a whole, the scenery on the Pacific Railroad is disappointing to one familiar with the Alleghanies.

At Colfax, two hundred miles from San Francisco, we stop for breakfast and have our first experience of fresh California grapes and salmon; the former black Hamburgs not to be excelled by the best hot-house grapes of England; and what a bagful for a quarter! We tried the native white wine at dinner, and found it a fair Sauterne. With such grapes and climate, it must surely be only a question of a few years before the true American wine makes its appearance, and then what shall we have to import? Silks and woollens are going, watches and jewelry have already gone, and in this connection I think I may venture to say good-bye to foreign iron and steel; cotton goods went long ago. Now if wines, and especially champagne—that creature of fashion—should go, what shall we have to tax? What if America, which has given to mankind so many political lessons, should be destined to show a government living up to the very highest dictate of political economy, viz., supported by direct taxation! No, there remain our home products, whiskey and tobacco; let us be satisfied to do the next best thing and make these pay the entire cost of government. The day is not far distant when out of these two so-called luxuries we shall collect all our taxes; and those virtuous citizens who use neither shall escape scot-free. Although these sentences were written years ago, now since we approach the threshold of fulfilment I am not sure that upon the whole the total abolition of the internal revenue system is not preferable. We should thus dispense with four thousand officials. In government, the fewer the better.

No greater contrast can be imagined than that from the barren desert to the fertile plains below; oleanders and geraniums greet us with their welcome smiles; grapes, pears, peaches, all in profusion; we are indeed in the Italy of America at last, and Sacramento is reached by half-past ten. Since the great flood which almost ruined it some years ago, extensive dykes have been built, walling in the city, which so far have proved a sufficient barrier against the rapid swellings of the

American River, that pours down its torrents from the mountains; but if Sacramento be now secure against flood, it is certainly vulnerable to the attacks of the not less terrible demon of fire. Such a mass of combustible material piled together and called a city I never saw before: it is a tinder-box, and we are to hear of its destruction some day. Prepare for an extra: "Great fire in Sacramento; the city in ashes;" but then, don't let us call it accidental.

What a valley we rush through for the hundred miles which separate Sacramento from San Francisco! It is about sixty miles wide, and as level as a billiard-table. Here are the famous wheat fields: as far as the eye can reach on either side we see nothing but the golden straw standing, minus the heads of wheat which have been cut off, the straw being left to be burned down as a fertilizer. Fancy a Western prairie, substitute golden grain for corn, and you have before you the California harvest; for four hundred miles this valley extends, and it is wheat from one end to the other—nothing but wheat. Granted sufficient rain in the rainy season—that is, from November till February—and the husbandman seeks nothing more; Nature does all the rest, and a bountiful harvest is a certainty. In some years there is a scarcity of rain, but to provide against even this sole remaining contingency the rivers have but to be properly used for irrigation; with this done, the wheat crop of the Pacific coast will outstrip in value, year after year, all the gold and silver that can be mined. Douglas Jerrold's famous saying applies to no other land so well as to this, for it indeed needs only "to be tickled with a hoe to smile with a harvest."

We reached Oakland, the Jersey City of San Francisco, on time to the minute; the ferry-boat starts, and there lies before us the New York of the Pacific: but instead of the bright sparkling city we had pictured, sinking to rest with its tall spires suffused by the glories of the setting sun, imagine our surprise when not even our own smoky Pittsburgh could boast a denser canopy of smoke. A friend who had kindly met us upon arrival at Oakland tried to explain that this was not all smoke; it was mostly fog, and a peculiar wind which sometimes had this effect; but we could scarcely be mistaken upon that point. No, no, Mr. O'B., you may know all about "Frisco," the Chinese, the mines, and the Yosemite, but do allow me to know something about smoke. We reached our hotel, from the seven days' trip, and, after a bath and a good dinner with agreeable company, were shown as much of the city as it was possible to see before the "wee short hour ayont the twal'."

PALACE HOTEL, SAN FRANCISCO,
Wednesday Evening, October 23.

A palace truly! Where shall we find its equal? Windsor Hotel, good-bye! you must yield the palm to your great Western rival, as far as structure goes,

though in all other respects you may keep the foremost
place.   There is no other hotel building in the world
equal to this.   The court of the Grand at Paris is poor
compared to that of the Palace.   Its general effect at
night, when brilliantly lighted, is superb; its furniture,
rooms and appointments are all fine, but then it tells
you all over it was built to "whip all creation," and
the millions of its lucky owner enabled him to triumph.
It is as much in place in San Francisco as the
Taj would be in Sligo; but then your California operator, when he has made a "pile," goes in for a hotel,
just as in New York one takes to a marble palace or a
grand railway depot, or in Cincinnati to a music hall, or
in Pittsburgh to building a church or another rolling
mill.   Every community has its social idiosyncrasies,
but it struck us as rather an amusing coincidence that
while we had recently greeted no less a man than Pot-
ter Palmer, Esq., behind the counter in Chicago as
"mine host of the Garter," we should so soon have found
ourselves in the keeping of Senator Sharon, lessee of
the Palace.   These hotels do not impress one as being
quite suitable monuments for one who naturally con-
siders his labors about over when he builds, as they are
apt apparently to prove rather lively for comfort to the
owners, and we have decided when our building time
comes that it shall not be in the hotel line.   We got to
bed at last, but who could sleep after such a day—after
such a week!   The ceaseless motion, with the click, click,

click of the wheels—our sweet lullaby apparently this had become—was wanting; and then the telegrams from home, which bade us Godspeed, the warm, balmy air of Italy, when we had left winter behind—all this drove sleep away; and when drowsiness came, what apparitions of Japanese, Chinese, Indians, elephants, camels, josses! passed through our brain in endless procession. We were at the Golden Gate; we had just reached the edge of the Pacific Ocean, and before us lay

> . . . "the wealth of Ormus and of Ind,
> Or where the gorgeous East, with richest hand,
> Showers on her kings barbaric pearl and gold.

To every blink the livelong night there came this refrain, which seemed to close each scene of Oriental magnificence that haunted the imagination:

> "And our gude ship sails ye morn,
> And our gude ship sails ye morn."

Do what I would, the words of the old Scotch ballad would not down. Sleep! who could sleep in such an hour? Dead must be the man whose pulse beats not quicker, and whose enthusiasm is not enkindled when for the first time he is privileged to whisper to himself, The East! the East!

> "And our gude ship sails ye morn."

HARBOR OF SAN FRANCISCO, Thursday, October 24.

At last! noon, 24th, and there she lies—the Belgic at her dock! What a crowd! but not of us; eight hundred Chinamen are to return to the Flowery Land. One looks like another; but how quiet they are! Are they happy? overjoyed at being homeward bound? We cannot judge. Those sphinx-like, copper-colored faces tell us no tales. We had asked a question last night by telegraph, and here is the reply brought to us on the deck. It ends with a tender good-bye. How near and yet how far! but even if the message had sought us out at the Antipodes, its power to warm the heart with the sense of the near presence and companionship of those we love would only have been enhanced. In this we seem almost to have reached the dream of the Swedish seer, who tells us that thought brings presence, annihilating space in heaven.

We start promptly at noon. Our ship is deeply laden with flour, which China needs in consequence of the famine prevailing in its northern provinces, not owing to a failure of the rice, as I had understood, but of the millet, which is used by the poor instead of rice. Some writers estimate that five millions of people must die from starvation before the next crop can be gathered; but this seems incredible. And now America comes to the rescue, so that at this moment, while from its Eastern shores it pours forth its inexhaustible stores to feed Europe, it sends from the West of its surplus to the older races of the far East. Thus from all sides, fabled Ceres as she is, she scatters to all peoples from the horn of plenty. Favored land, may you prove worthy of all your blessings and show to the world that after ages of wars and conquests there comes at last to the troubled earth the glorious reign of peace. But no new steel cruisers, no standing army. These are the devil's tools in monarchies; the Republic's weapons are the ploughshare and the pruning hook.

For three hundred miles the Pacific is never pacific. Coast winds create a swell, and our first two nights at sea were trying to bad sailors, but the motion was to me so soft after our long railway ride that I seemed to be resting on air cushions. It was more delightful to be awake and enjoy the sense of perfect rest than to sleep, tired as we were; so we lay literally

"Rocked in the cradle of the rude imperious surge,'

and enjoyed it.

To some of my talented New York friends who are touched with Buddhism just now and much puzzled to describe, and I judge even to imagine, their heaven, I confidently recommend a week's continuous jar upon a rough railway as the surest preparation for attaining a just conception of Nirvana, where perfect rest is held the greatest possible bliss. Lying, as I did apparently, upon air cushions, and rocked so softly on the waves, I had not a wish; desire was gone; I was content; every particle of my weary body seemed bathed in delight. Here was the delicious sense of rest we are promised in Nirvana.

The third day out we are beyond the influence of the
coast, and begin our first experience of the Pacific
Ocean. So far it is simply perfect ; we are on the ideal
summer sea. What hours for lovers, these superb
nights ! they would develop rapidly, I'm sure, under
such skyey influences. The temperature is genial, balmy
breezes blow, there is no feeling of chilliness; the sea,
bathed in silver, glistens in the moonlight ; we sit under
awnings and glide through the water. The loneliness
of this great ocean I find very impressive—so different
from the Atlantic pathway—we are so terribly alone, a
speck in the universe ; the sky seems to enclose us in a
huge inverted bowl, and we are only groping about, as
it were, to find a way out; it is equidistant all around
us ; nothing but clouds and water. But as we sail westward we have every night a magnificent picture. I have
never seen such resplendent sunsets as these : we seem
nightly to be just approaching the gates of Enchanted
Land ; through the clouds, in beautiful perspective,
shine the gardens of the Hesperides, and imagination
readily creates fairy lands beyond, peopled with spirits
and fays. It is not so much the gorgeousness of the
colors as their variety which gives these sunsets a character of their own ; one can find anything he chooses in
their infinite depths. Turner must have seen such in
his mind's eye. " I never saw such sunsets as these you
paint," said the critic of his style. " No ; don't you wish
you could ?" was the reply. But I think even a prosaic

critic would feel that these Pacific pictures have a spiritual sense beyond the letter, unless, indeed, he were Wordsworth's friend, to whom

> " A primrose by a river's brim
> A yellow primrose was to him,
> And it was nothing more."

He, of course, is hopeless.

THURSDAY, October 31.

We have been a week at sea. Can it be only seven days since we waved adieu to bright eyes on the pier? We begin to feel at home on the ship. The passengers are now known to each other, and hereafter the days will slip by faster. I went down with the doctor and Vandy to see the Chinamen to-day. What a sight! Piled in narrow cots three tiers deep, with passages between the rows scarcely wide enough for one to walk, from end to end of the ship these poor wretches lie in an atmosphere so stifling that I had to rush up to the deck for air. So far three have died, and two have become crazy. My foolish curiosity has made the voyage less satisfactory, for I cannot forget the danger of disease breaking out among this horde, nor can I drive the yellow, stupid-looking faces out of mind. The night of the day in which I had gone below we were playing a rubber of whist in the cabin when the port-hole at my head was pushed open, and a voice in broken English shouted, "Crazee manee; he makee firee, firee!" I jumped

round and saw a Chinaman. Such an expression—
Shakespeare alone has described it—

> " And with a look so piteous in purport,
> As if he had been loosèd out of hell
> To speak of horrors."

Fire! that epitome of all that is appalling at sea, the
danger each one instinctively dreads, but no one men-
tions. One ran one way and one another. The doctor
(a real canny Scot, who sings " My Nannie's awa' " like
Wilson) was over the rail and down the hold in a moment. I ran to Captain Meyer's room on the upper
deck and roused him. He too was down and in the hold
like a flash—brave fellows that they are, these " true
British sailors." I waited the result, knowing that if fire
had really started, a general stampede of Chinamen
would soon come from the hatches; but all was still.
How long those few moments seemed! In a short time
the captain returned, looking, in his night-clothes, like
a ghost. One of the crazy men had broken loose from
his chains, and the Chinamen were panic-stricken. The
watchman wanted the most startling alarm, and found
it, undoubtedly, in that word fire. It is all over; but
when he next has to sound an alarm let him " take any
form but that."

We have a reverend missionary and wife, with two
young lady missionaries in embryo, who are on their
way to begin their labors among the Chinese. They are
busily engaged learning the language. Poor girls! what

a life they have before them! But apart from all question of its true usefulness, they have the grand thought to sustain them, and ennoble their lives, that they go at the call of what seems to them their duty. We watch the Chinese eating and laugh at their chopsticks, but we forget that one reason why John Chinaman prides himself upon being at the pinnacle of civilization is that he uses these very chopsticks. (None of the races of Asia, and until recently he knew no other, have ever got beyond chopsticks, the use of which was first taught China, while most of them don't even have them yet.) Let us not forget that our ancestors were using their fingers—barbarians that they were—when the Chinese had risen, centuries before, to the refinement of these sticks, for the fork is only about three hundred years old. Shakespeare probably, Spenser certainly, had only a knife at his girdle to carve the meat he ate, the fingers being important auxiliaries. We must be modest upon this chopstick question. It costs the ship eleven cents ($5\frac{1}{2}d.$) per day a head to feed these people, and this pays for a wholesome diet in great abundance, much beyond what they are accustomed to.

While on the subject of the Chinaman I may note that of course we did not get through California without hearing the Chinese problem warmly discussed. It is the burning question just now upon the Pacific coast, but it seems to me our Californians' fears are, as Colonel Diehl would put it, "slightly previous." There

are only about 130,000 Chinese in America, and great
numbers are returning as the result of hard times, and
I fear harder treatment.   There is no indication that
we are to be overrun by them, and until they change
their religious ideas and come to California to marry,
settle, die, and be buried there, it is preposterous to believe there is any thing in the agitation against them
beyond the usual prejudice of the ignorant races next
to them in the social scale.

I met the owner of a quicksilver mine, whose remarks shed a flood of light upon the matter.   The
mine yields a lean ore, and did not pay when worked
by white labor costing $2 to $2.50 per day.   He contracted with a Chinaman to furnish 170 men at one-half
these rates.   They work well, doing as much per man
as the white man can do in this climate.   He has no
trouble with them—no fights, no sprees, no strikes.   The
difference in the cost enables him to work at a profit a
mine which otherwise would be idle ; and to such as talk
against Chinese labor in the neighborhood, he replies,
"Very well, drive it off if you please, but the mine
stops if you do."   The benefit to the district of having
a mine actively at work has so far insured protection.
This is the whole story.   Our free American citizen
from Tipperary and the restless rowdy of home growth
find a rival beating them in the race, and instead of
taking the lesson to heart and practising the virtues
which cause the Chinaman to excel, they mount the

rostrum and proclaim that this is a "white man's country," and "down with the nigger and the Heathen Chinee," and "three cheers for whiskey and a free fight!"
The Chinese question has not reached a stage requiring
legislation, nor, if let alone, will it do so for centuries to
come—and not then unless the Chinese change their religious ideas, which they have not done for thousands
of years, and are not likely to do in our time.

FRIDAY, November 1.

We saw flying-fishes to-day for the first time. The
captain had been telling us as we approached the 30th
degree of latitude that we should see these curiosities,
and, sure enough, while standing on the bridge this
morning, looking toward the bow, I saw three objects
rise out of the water and fly from us. One seemed as
large as a herring, the others were like humming-birds.
They have much larger wings than I had supposed, and
shine brightly in the sun as they fly. We have on board
a gentleman connected with the Dutch Government,
who visits their out-of-the-way possessions in the Malay
Archipelago. He has been where a white man never
was before—in the interior of New Guinea—and has
seen strange things. He tells us that the birds of paradise take seven years to develop. The first year male
and female are alike, but year after year the male acquires brighter feathers, until it becomes the superb
bird we know. Some one remarked that it is just the

reverse with the birds of paradise in man's creation.
Here our Eve puts on gayer plumage year after year
until finally she develops into a still more superb bird,
while the male remains the same sober-suited fowl he
was at first; but this was from a bachelor, I think.

We are in a new world, and the talk is all of
people and islands and animals we never heard of. Do
you know, for instance, that such a potentate as the
Sultan of Terantor exists? and, ambitious ruler that he
is, that he now claims tribute from the whole of New
Guinea? Then, again, let me tell you that the Sultan
of Burnei gets $6,000 per year tribute from Setwanak,
and, like a grasping tyrant, demands more; hence the
wars which rage in that quarter of the globe. The
Setwanaks have appealed to the "God of Battles," and
are no doubt shouting on all hands that " Resistance to
tyrants is obedience to God;" and "Millions for de-
fence; not a cent for tribute." Look out for their forthcoming declaration of independence; and why shouldn't
they have their " *Whereases* " as well as your even
Christian? The only trouble is that when monarchs
fight nothing is settled as a rule; what one loses to-day,
he tries to win back to-morrow, and so the masses are
kept in a state of perpetual war, or preparation for war,
equally expensive. If Herbert Spencer had never for-
mulated anything but the law underlying these sad con-
tentions between man and man, he would have deserved
to rank as one of our greatest benefactors. " When

power is arbitrarily held by chief or king, the military spirit is developed, and wars of conquest and dynasties ensue ; and just in proportion as power is obtained by the people, the industrial type is developed and peace ensues." Therefore the greatest thinker of the age is a republican. I quote from memory, but the substance is there, and it is because this law is true that there is hope for the future of the world, for everywhere the people are marching to political power. England is yet the world's greatest offender, because she is still ruled by the few, her boasted representative system being only a sham. When the masses do really govern, England will be pacific and make friends throughout the world instead of enemies, " and sing the songs of peace to all her neighbors."

The Dutch have 35,000,000 under their sway in Java and the other Malay Islands; as many as Great Britain has within her borders. The world gets most of its spices and its coffee from these people. So the Dutch are not to be credited only with having taken Holland, you see.

Another Chinaman is reported gone to-day : all have to be embalmed, of course, and the doctor gets as his fee $12.50 for each corpse. He complained to me the other day that these people would not take his medicines, and, Scotchman-like, didn't see the point I made— that they might naturally hesitate to swallow the potions of one whose highest reward arose from a fatal result. The Heathen Chinee is not a fool. The coffins of the dead on the wheel-house begin to make quite a show ; they are covered with canvas, but one will sometimes see the pile. Not one of these men could ever have been induced to leave his home without satisfactory assurance that in case of death his remains would be carried back and carefully buried in the spot where he first drew breath. I remember reading in MacLeod's " Highland Parish " that so strongly implanted is this sentiment in the Highlanders that even a wife who marries out of her clan is brought home at her death and buried among her own kith and kin. I confess to a strange sympathy with this feeling myself. It seems to agree with the eternal fitness of things, that where we first saw day we should rest after the race is run. Yes, the old song is right :

> " Wherever we wander in life's stormy ways
>   May our paths lead to home ere the close of our days,
>   And our evening of life in serenity close
>   In the Isle where the bones of our Fathers repose."

One of our company has kindly shown me " some things in waves " which I have always passed over before. Hereafter they will have a new interest and a new beauty for me. I now watch by the hour for some rare effect and colors to which I was before stone-blind. Some of the rarest jewels are rated by comparison with the emerald and aqua-marine tints shown by the pure waves of the ocean. Thanks, my fellow-traveller, for a new sense awakened.

The albatrosses, which follow us in large numbers, are a source of pleasure. These are not the sacred birds of the Ancient Mariner, but are of the same species. They excel all other birds, I think, in power and gracefulness of flight. It is rather a glide than a fly, as they appear scarcely ever to flap their wings, but sail on as it were "by the sole act of their unlorded will." No wonder such woe befell the Ancient Mariner through killing one. They are too grand to destroy. Last evening I had a treat in seeing these birds gathering for the night on the waters in the hollow of a deep wave. A dozen were already in the nest as our ship swept past, and others were coming every moment from all directions to the fold; probably thirty birds would thus nestle together through the long night in the middle of this waste of waters. I was glad for their sakes, poor wanderers, that their lonely lives were brightened at night by the companionship of their fellows.

Our second Sunday at sea. As I write, the bell tolls for church. Our missionary will have a small congregation, for there are only twenty-two passengers. I trust he will be moved to speak to us, away in mid-ocean, of the great works of the Unknown, the mighty deep, the universe, the stars, at which we nightly wonder, and not drag us down to the level of dogmas we can know nothing of, and about which we care less.

The sermon is over. Pshaw! He spent the morning attempting to prove to us that the wine Christ made at the marriage feast was not fermented, as if it mattered, or as if this could ever be known! and I was in the mood to preach such a magnificent sermon myself, too, if I had had his place. No; I shall never forgive him—never!

It is an even chance that this missionary will one day inflict such frivolous stuff upon the heathen as part of the divine message ; for of the majesty, the sweetness, and the reforming power of Christ's teaching and character, he seems to have not the faintest conception. To the enquiry one constantly hears in the East—why churches send forth as missionaries such inferior men as they generally do, whose task is to eradicate error and plant truth—there is this to be said : churches must take the best material at their disposal, and men who have the ability to influence their fellows through the pulpit find their best and highest work at home. This leaves the incapables for foreign service. The other class from which missionaries must be drawn are the over-zealous, who have plenty of enthusiastic emotional fervor, but combined in most cases with narrow, dogmatic views—the very kind of men to irritate the people to whom they are sent, and the least likely to win their hearts or reach their understanding. There are notable exceptions, able men who still go at duty's call ; but such generally see that they can be ill spared from more pressing home work.

MONDAY, November 4.

Our course is the southerly one, 5,120 miles to Yoko-hama, some five hundred miles farther than that of the great circle ; but for the increased distance we have full compensation in the delightful weather and calm seas we experience. The water is about 72°, the air 73°, so that it is genial on deck. We are really in summer weather—something so different from Atlantic sailing that I get accustomed to it with difficulty. Last night at ten o'clock we passed the half-way point ten days and eight hours out. The captain showed us his chart to-day, and it was reassuring to see that to-mor-row we shall pass within 120 miles of land—the Mid-way Islands. Upon one of this coral group the Pacific Mail Company has deposited 3,000 tons of coal and a large amount of mess pork as a reserve supply in case any steamer should be disabled. We passed the Sand-wich Islands, not more than 450 miles to the southward, when one quarter of the way over, and the Bonin Islands occupy about the same relative position in our course to the eastward, so that the immense distance between San Francisco and Yokohama is finely pro-vided for in case of accident. You have but to sail southward and find a port of refuge. Indeed, there is along this entire parallel of latitude a new strip of land under process of manufacture. A good chart shows islands dotting the South Pacific Ocean, all of coral formation ; these millions of toilers are hard at work, and it is only a question of time when our posterity will run by rail from the Sandwich to the Philippine Islands, always provided that the work of these little builders is not interfered with by forces which destroy. Thus the grand, never-ending work of creation goes on, cycle upon cycle, revealing new wonders at every turn and knowing no rest or pause.

Gone, November 5th, 1878, a *dies non*, which never was born. Lost, strayed, or stolen—a rare diadem, composed of twenty-four precious gems—some diamonds bright, some rubies rare, some jet as black as night. It was to have been displayed at midnight to an admiring few who nightly gaze upon the stars, but when looked for it was nowhere to be found. A well-known party, familiarly known as Old Sol, is thought to be concerned in the matter, but chiefly is suspected a notorious thief who has stolen many precious jewels—Old Father Time. Oh! many an hour has that thief stolen, but this gobbling up of a whole day and night at one fell swoop seems out of all reason. Yet he has done it! We have no 5th of November. An amusing story is told of some clergymen returning to America, in which case a day is gained, and it is necessary to have two days of the same date instead of omitting one, as in our case. The line was crossed on Sunday, and the captain, never thinking, called out to the chief officer to make another Sunday to-morrow. One of the clergymen was Scotch, and Presbyterian at that.

"Mak a Sawbath—mak the holy Sawbath; ma conscience!" The order had been given, however, and two Sundays were observed; but our scandalized friend could never be reconciled to the captain who had presumed to have a holy Sabbath of his "ain making."

THURSDAY, November 7.

These nights were not made for sleep, nor these days either, for that matter; but of all the nights I have ever seen I think this one excels. The moon is overhead and at the full, casting her mellow light around, suffusing with a soft glory the heavens above, and lending to the dancing, foaming waves a silvery shimmer. Jupiter is on the western horizon, fading out of sight, but how lustrous! Lyra, Arcturus, Aldebaran, seem of gigantic size. All sails are set, and a fair, balmy wind from the sweet south makes the Belgic glide through the rushing waters. We are only twenty miles from the Morrell Islands. How I long for a deckful of my friends to exult with me in this delight! Nothing but Byron's lines will do it justice. They are too long to quote here, but here are a few lines, which I must repeat:

> . . . . "for the night
> Hath been to me a more familiar face
> Than that of man; and in her starry shade
> Of dim and solitary loveliness
> I learned the language of another world."

One does feel in such moments, when beauty and sublimity are so overpoweringly displayed, that there are worlds and life beyond our ken, or should be such, for this short day on earth surely should be but the foretaste of a sublime existence which such moods indicate as our congenial home.

FRIDAY, November 8.

I know I went to bed some time early this morning, but after reading last night's effusion in the cold, sober light of day, it strikes me I must have been rather enthusiastic. However, as I intend these notes to be an honest record of my feelings, I shall not attempt to modify the outburst. I know I recited poetry all the evening as I trod the deck, and therefore was in the mood for anything. The captain told me to-night that in all his voyages at this season he had never had one so fine as this. Of course he hadn't. Just our luck, you see. He never had one who enjoyed a trip more—that he is free to confess. I fairly revel in the sea, and pity poor Vandy, who is never quite up to the mark on shipboard. Some far-away ancestor, some good Scotch "deil ma care," who took to smuggling instead of the more fashionable occupation of cattle-stealing, for most of the carles

> "Found the meat that made their broth
> In England and in Scotland both,"

must have implanted in the Carnegies the instinct of

the salmon for the sea. I should have been a sailor bold, and sailed the " sawt, sawt faeme," a pirate with a pirate's bride captured *vi et armis*, and all the rest of it.

I am up late again to-night, but, fortunately, there wasn't a soul on deck to hear me trying to sing

> " Up, up with the flag; let it wave o'er the sea,
> I'm afloat, I'm afloat, and the Rover is free !"

The officer on the bridge halloaed to me once, and asked if I wanted any thing; but I forgave him. He could only hear my roaring at his distance; had I been nearer, the melody would no doubt have reached his ears, and he would have known I was singing a tune. Still I thought it politic to affect not having heard him, and quietly stepped down to bed. I shall avoid friend Ryan in the morning, as it would be embarrassing to be asked, especially before the young ladies, who or what I was howling at last night. Some people have no tact, and he might be one of these and fail to comprehend. With the exception of the officers, our crew, sailors, stewards, and all, are Chinese, and in all and each of these capacities they excel. They stand the heat of the furnaces better than any other people, and as stewards are models.

SUNDAY, November 10.

Our third Sunday at sea. The past week has been unbroken sunshine, moonlight, and smooth seas. So far not a ship has been seen. I have read carefully eleven of Shakespeare's plays during the spare hours of the voyage, and have enjoyed those most with which I was least familiar, while some passages in even the best known I wonder greatly at not having long ere this committed to memory, to live there with the rest, and come at my call to minister to me. They are such gems. I have them now, and feel as if I have made new friends, whose angel visits will do me good in days and nights to come. Byron affected to disparage the master, but I note two other gems, beside many I knew of before, for which he stands indebted. The idea in his celebrated lines in " Mazeppa "—

> " Methought that mist of dawning gray
> Would never dapple into day "—

is from *Two Gentlemen of Verona*, and the " Bright, particular star" from *All's Well that Ends Well*. But of course I do not intend any reflection upon Byron. Such was, and is, the all-pervading, transcendent nature of Shakespeare's genius; it was, and is, and shall be for ages yet to come, simply impossible for any writer to avoid drawing from that fountain, for every thing has its " environment," and Shakespeare is the environment of all English-speaking men.

***

WEDNESDAY, November 13.

Four hundred and fifty miles from land ! To-day we have had the only taste of Neptune's power he has favored us with: it began to blow at midnight, and to-day we have a grand sea. I have just come from the deck after witnessing the Pacific in its fury, and no one would believe that one ocean could differ as much from another as this does from the Atlantic. The waves here move in immense masses. It is an acre of water in motion, as one solid lump, instead of a few feet square dashed into foam. One says instinctively,

"What care these roarers for the name of king?"

I have noticed that even in the smallest waves cast aside by the ship formations are different from those of other seas. It is midnight, and we are only 125 miles from Japan. Not a passenger except myself on deck, but I cannot sleep. Vandy would be with me, I know, poor fellow, were he able to crawl, but the storm has settled him for the present. How strange that none feel sufficient interest to stay awake and watch with me! They would be amply repaid. The phosphorescent sea shows forth its wonders now—not alone in the myriads of small stars of light, which please you in the Atlantic, but at every turn of the foam dashed from the bow and sides of the ship masses of glittering phosphorescence as large as my travelling cap. What creatures these must be which can emit light in such clusters! I leave the deck with the cheery "All's well!" ringing in my ears as the ship dances before the wind which brings to a close our long flight across the Pacific. How we have longed for this last night, and yet how often in after life are we to sigh for a return to the glorious nights we have lived at sea! Where we have

> " Mingled with the universe to feel
> What we can ne'er express,
> Nor cannot all conceal."

Good-night, my band of dear, dear friends, now in the midst of your daily toil—for it is yet day with you—racking your brains that the holiday wanderer may revel as he is now doing. In the earnest hope that the day may not be far distant when to you may come similar enjoyment when he is the toiler, he goes at last to bed.

FRIDAY, November 15.

Land ahoy! The islands of Japan are in sight, and the entrance to the bay is reached at 4 P.M. The sail up this bay is never to be forgotten. The sun set as we entered, and then came such a sky as Italy cannot rival. I have seen it pictured as deluging Egypt with its glory, but this we have yet to see. Fusiyama itself shone forth under its rays, its very summit clear, more than 14,000 feet above us. The clouds in large masses lay east and west of the peak, but cowering far below, as if not one speck dared to rise to its crown. It stood alone in solitary grandeur, by far the most impressive mountain I have yet seen; for mountains, as a rule, are disappointing, the height being generally attained by gradations. It is only to Fusiyama, and such as it, that rise alone in one unbroken pyramid, that one can apply Schiller's grand line,

" Ye are the things which tower,"

Fusiyama *towers* beyond any crag or peak I know of; and I do not wonder that in early days the Japanese made the home of their gods upon its crest.

It was nine o'clock when the anchor dropped, and in a few minutes after small boats crowded alongside to take us ashore. Until you are rowed in a sampan in style, never flatter yourself you have known the grotesque in the way of transportation. Fancy a large, wide canoe, with a small cabin in the stern, the deck in front lower than the sides, and on this four creatures, resembling nothing on earth so much as the demons in the *Black Crook*, minus most of the covering. They stand two on each side, but not in a line, and each works a long oar scull-fashion, accompanying each stroke with shouts such as we never heard before; the last one steers as well as sculls with his oar, and thus we go propelled by these yelling devils, who apparently work themselves into a state of fearful excitement. We land finally, pass the Custom House without examination, and with sea-legs which are far from steady reach our hotel. A bite of supper—but what fearful creatures again to bow and wait on us! More demons. We laugh every minute at some funny performance, and wonder where we can be; but how surprisingly good every thing is which we eat or drink on land after twenty-two days at sea!

———

TUESDAY, November 19.

We have been three days in Japan, and all we can tell you is that we are powerless to convey more than the faintest idea of that which meets us at every turn. Had we to return to-morrow, we should still feel that we had been fully compensated for our journey. Though we have seen most of the strange and novel which Europe has to show, a few hours' stroll in Yokohama or Tokio has revealed to us more of the unexpected than all we ever saw elsewhere. No country I have visited till now has proved as strange as I had imagined it; the contrary obtains here. All is so far beyond what I had pictured it that I am constantly regretting so few of my friends will probably ever visit Japan to see and enjoy for themselves. Let me try to describe a walk. We are at the hotel door, having received the repeated bows, almost to the ground, of numerous demons. A dozen big fellows rush up, each between the shafts of his " ginrikshaw " like a cab-horse, and invite us to enter, just as cabmen do elsewhere. But look at their costume, or shall I rather say want of costume? No shoes, unless a mat of straw secured with straw strings twisted around and between the big toe and the next one may be called a shoe; legs and body bare, except a narrow strip of rag around the loins; and such a hat! it is either of some dark material, as big as the head of a barrel (I do not exaggerate), to shelter them from sun and rain, or a light straw flat of equal size. These are the Bettoes, who will run and draw you eighteen miles in three hours and a quarter, this being the distance and time by "ginrikshaw" to Tokio. We decline their proffers and walk on. What is this? A man on stilts! His shoes are composed of a flat wooden sole about a quarter of an inch thick, on which the foot rests, elevated upon two similar pieces of board, about four inches high, placed crosswise about three inches apart. On the edges of these cross-pieces he struts along. A second has solid wooden pieces of equal height, a third has flat straw shoes, a fourth has none. Look out behind! What is this noise? "Hulda, hulda, hulda!" shouted in our ears. We look around, and four coolies, as naked as Adam, one at each corner of a four-wheel truck, pushing a load of iron and relieving themselves at every step by those unearthly groans. Never have we seen that indispensable commodity transported in that fashion before. But look there! A fish-monger comes with a basket swinging on each end of a bamboo pole carried over the shoulder—all single loads are so carried—and yonder goes a water-carrier, carrying his stoups in the same manner, while over his shoulders he has flung a coat that would make the reputation of a clown in the circus. The dress of the women is not so varied, but their painted lips and whitened necks, and, in the case of the married women, their blackened teeth, afford us much cause for staring, although I cannot bear to look upon these hideous-looking wretches when they smile; I have to turn my eyes away. How women can be induced to make such disgusting frights of themselves I cannot conceive, but Fashion—Fashion does anything. The appearance of the children is comical in the extreme. They are so thickly padded with dress upon dress as to give them the look of little fat Esquimaux. The women invariably carry them on their backs, Indian fashion. Here are two Japs meeting in the middle of the street. They bow three times, each inclination lower and more profound than the preceding one, infinite care being taken to drop the proper number of inches befitting their respective ranks, and then shake their own hands in token of their joy. We soon reach the region of the shops. These are small booths, and squat on the floor sit four or five men and women around a brazier, warming their hands while they smoke. All the shops are of wood, but a small part is constructed of mud, and is said to be fire-proof. In this the valuables are instantly thrown when one of the very frequent fires occurs. The floors are matted, and kept scrupulously clean. No one thinks of entering without first taking his shoes off. The shop floors are raised about eighteen inches above the street, and on the edges purchasers sit sidewise and make their bargains. The entire street is a pavement, as no horses are to be provided for.

We visited the tea factories at Yokohama. Japan has become of late years an exporter of tea to America, no less than five thousand tons being shipped last year. Tea when first gathered is tasteless, but after being exposed to the sun it ferments like hay. It is then curled, twisted, baked, and brought to the dealers, who again pick it over carefully and roll it into the form in which it reaches us. We saw many hundreds of women and girls in the establishment of Messrs. Walsh, Hall & Co. rolling rapidly about with their hands a quantity of the leaves in large round pots under which a small charcoal fire was burning. And now, for the benefit of my lady friends, let me explain that the difference between black and green tea is simply this: the former is allowed to cure or ferment in the sun about fifty minutes longer than the latter, and during this extra fifty minutes certain elements pass off which are thought to affect the nervous system; hence green tea has a greater effect upon weak nerves than the black, but you see the same leaf makes either kind, as the owner elects. But here comes in a strange prejudice. Green tea of the natural color could not be sold in the American market. No, we insist upon having a "prettier green," and we are accommodated, of course. What can a dealer do but meet the imperious demands of his patrons? The required color is obtained by adulterating the pure tea with a mixture of indigo and gypsum, which the most conscientious dealers are compelled to do. But we saw used in one case Prussian blue, which is poisonous—this, however, was not in Messrs. Walsh, Hall & Co.'s—and I was told that ultramarine is sometimes resorted to. These more pernicious substances produce even a "prettier green" than the indigo and gypsum, and secure the preference of ignorant people. Moral—Stick to black tea and escape poison. For all of which information, and many kind attentions, I have to thank Mr. Walsh, our banker.

One hears very often in Japan during the night a long, plaintive kind of whistle, which, upon inquiry, I found proceeded from blind men or women, called shampooers, who are employed to rub or pinch those suffering from pain, and who cure restlessness by the same means. It is a favorite cure of the Japanese, and some foreigners tell us they have employed it with success. I suppose, this climate being productive of rheumatism and kindred pains, the people are prone to fly to anything that secures temporary relief: but it is a new idea, this, of being pinched to sleep.

We live well at the hotels here. Japan abounds in fish and game in great variety. Woodcock, snipe, hares, and venison are cheap, and all of excellent quality. The beef and mutton are also good, as are the vegetables. Turnips, radishes and carrots are enormous, owing, I suppose to the depth and fineness of the soil. Vandy measured some of each, and reports: "Radishes, eighteen inches, and beautifully white; carrots, twenty inches, and splendid."

We started this morning from Yokohama for Tokio, the great city of the Empire, which contains 1,030,000 inhabitants, according to a census taken last year. Until within a few years past Japan had two rulers—the Mikado, or spiritual, and the Tycoon, or secular ruler, although, strictly speaking, the former was theoretically the supreme ruler, the latter obtaining his power through marriage with the family of the former. The seat of the Mikado was at Kioto, a fine city near the centre of the island, while the Tycoon resided at Tokio, or Yeddo, as it was then called. The Mikado was invisible, being the veritable veiled prophet, none but a privileged few being ever permitted to gaze upon his divine person. A few years ago it was decided to combine the two powers, and make Yeddo the only capital. The Mikado was carried to Yeddo closely veiled, in triumphal procession, and the vast crowds, assembled at every point to see the cavalcade, prostrated themselves, and remained with eyes bent upon the ground as the sacred car approached. An eye-witness describing the entry into Tokio says that few dared to look up as the Presence passed. Lately, the same Mikado has made a royal progress through the country, meeting the principal men in each district, and travelling in view of the entire population, so rapidly have manners changed in Japan. When the Mikado was elevated to supreme power, the feudal system, which had existed up to that time, was abolished, and we now see no more of the Samuri, or two-sworded men, or of the Daimios, the petty princes who formerly promenaded the streets in gorgeous dresses, accompanied by their military retainers. The soldiers, sailors, policemen, and all the official classes are dressed in European style. It is the reigning fashion to be European, and even furniture after our patterns is coming into use. It is the same with food. The hotel where we are rejoices in a French cook, expressly imported, and every night we have parties of wealthy Japanese dining at this Tokio Delmonico's. Last night we had a party of the most celebrated actors enjoying a dinner to commemorate the successful completion of a new piece which had enjoyed a great run. I amused myself trying to select the Montagu, Gilbert, Becket, and Booth of the party, and succeeded well, as I afterward heard. Actors are held in estimation in Tokio, and these attracted great attention as they dined. Matters are much as with us, I fancy. Our interpreter, in his broken English, told us in regard to the two young lovers, "Very high thought by much high ladies—oh, very high!" I do not think European dress improves the appearance of the Japanese gentlemen; they are very short, and—I regret to report it—generally quite crooked in the legs, and their own flowing costumes render them dignified and graceful. Indeed, after a residence in the East for a while one agrees with the opinion he hears often expressed there that our costume is the most unpicturesque dress in the world.

We were fortunate in having as shipmates Captain Totaki, of the navy, and a young lady, Mlle. Rio, who had been in America several years, and had acquired an English education. They were excessively kind to us during our entire stay, and much of the pleasure derived is due to them. The captain gave us one evening an entertainment at a fashionable tea-house, and introduced us to the celebrated singing and dancing girls of Japan, of whom all have heard. We were shown into a large room, the floor of which was covered with bamboo matting laid upon some soft substance. Of course our shoes were laid aside at the door of the house. There were neither chairs nor furniture of any kind, but subsequently chairs were found for us. The salutations on the part of the numerous women servants were most profound, each prostrating herself to the floor, and touching the mat with her forehead every time she entered or left the apartment. Velvet mats were carried into the room by a servant and placed around a brazier of charcoal. In a few minutes servant after servant entered, prostrating herself to the ground, and placing before us some Japanese delicacy. One served soup in small lacquer bowls, another fish, a third cakes, a fourth tea in very tiny cups, and others various things, and finally saki, the wine of the country, was produced, served in small cups like the tea. Then came the girls. Seven approached, each carrying a musical instrument of queer construction. They bowed profoundly, but I noticed did not touch the mat with their foreheads, their rank being much superior to that of the servants, and began to play and sing.

No entertainment is complete without a troop of these Gahazi girls, and such entertainments form about the only social amusement of the Japanese. And now for the music. Please understand that the Japanese scale is not like ours, and nothing like melody to our ears can be produced by it. They have a full tone between each first and second note, and a semitone between each third and fourth, and yet the same feelings are awakened in them by their music as in us by ours, so that harmony itself is simply a matter of education after all, and the glorious Fifth Symphony itself, "Lohengrin," or "Scots wha hae," played or sung as I have heard them, would convey no more meaning to these people than so much rattling of cross-bones; but imagine the Fifth Symphony on any scale but ours! I cannot reconcile myself to the idea that we have not the only scale for such a theme; but one has to learn that there are different ways for every thing, and no one who knows much will assume that he has the best. Owing to the change of the scale, I suppose I missed the sentiment of every piece performed. When I thought they were giving us a wail for the dead it turned out to be a warm welcome, and an assurance on the part of those pretty maidens of their happiness in being permitted the great honor of performing before such illustrious visitors. Our companion, Mlle. Rio, took one of the instruments and played and sang a piece for us, but I was not more fortunate in my guess with her. It was a wedding chorus, which I was willing to wager was the Japanese "Miserere"; but this error may have its significance after all. To us, in short, the music was execrable. A falsetto, and a grinding, sing-song falsetto at that—the most disagreeable sound I ever heard in music—is very common, and highly esteemed. The instruments resemble banjos, and there is a harsh kind of drum accompaniment; but there is one larger string instrument, the Japanese piano, upon which much older women play, the younger girls not being sufficiently skilled to perform upon it.

After a few songs had been sung, several of the girls laid down their banjos, and after obeisance prepared to dance. Instead of being a sprightly performance to lively music, "first ae caper syne anither," Japanese dancing is a very stately and measured performance, the body instead of the feet being most brought into requisition. With the aid of the indispensable fan the girls succeed in depicting many different emotions, and all with exquisite grace. It is the very poetry of motion. Each dance illustrates a story, and is as well known by name as is the " Highland Fling " or the " Sailor's Hornpipe." Here there was no difficulty in following the story. Unlike music, acting is a universal language, and in its domain "one touch of nature makes the whole world kin." There are no different scales for the expression of feeling. Love, in some of its manifold forms, as was to have been expected, is the theme of most of these dances. I redeemed my reputation here as a guesser, I think. I could give a very fair report to Mlle. Rio of most that took place in the dances, and we enjoyed this portion of the entertainment highly. To a Japanese, how stupid our people must appear whirling round a room until fatigued or dizzy, all for the fun of the thing!

The dresses of the girls were of the richest and most fashionable description, the quietness of the colors surprising us, and their manners those of high-born women. Indeed, they set the fashions, and are the best educated and most accomplished of their sex. These girls are sent for to furnish entertainment for an evening just as we would engage a band for a party. They are said to be highly respectable as a class, invariably reside with their parents, who educate them at great expense, and often make, we were told, very favorable marriages. The contrast between them and their less accomplished sisters is so great as to strike even us, who have been here only a few days, and must be held ignorant of style.

The most wonderful sights of Tokio are the temples and the famous tombs of the Tycoons. There is much similarity in the latter, but that of the sixth Tycoon, at

Shibba, is by far the most magnificent. It has been rendered familiar by photographs and engravings, and at any rate no description would convey a just idea of it. It is gorgeous in color, and the extreme delicacy of the gold is surprising; upon it, too, are found the finest known specimens of the old lacquer. But these tombs totally failed to impress me with any feeling akin to reverence; indeed, nothing in Japan seems calculated to do so—the odor of the toyshop pervades everything, even their temples. As for their religious belief, it is hard to tell what it is, or whether they have any. One thing is sure, the educated classes have discarded the faith of the multitude, if they ever really entertained it, and no longer worship the gods of old. The ignorant classes, however, are seen pouring into the temples with their modest offerings, and asking for prayers in their behalf. It is in Japan as it was in Greece—one religion for the masses, and another, or rather none in the ordinary sense, for the educated few.

As in Catholic countries, some shrines are esteemed more than others. The Temple of the Foxes is the most popular in the Empire. It is adorned with statues of Master Reynard in various postures. His votaries are numerous, for the sagacity of the fox has passed into a proverb, and these people hope by prayers and gifts to move the fox-god to bestow upon them the shrewdness of the symbol. The fox may be justly rated as the most successful preacher in Japan: he draws better than any other, and his congregation is the largest; but he has a rival not without pretensions in the favorite goddess "Emma." We found her to be a large, very fat woman, sitting in Japanese style, and surrounded by images of children. Babies cluster like cherubs around the principal figure, while an attendant sells for a cent apiece ugly painted ones made out of clay, many of which have been placed by worshippers before the goddess. As we approached, a young woman—married, for her teeth were black, and respectably but not richly dressed—was on her knees before the goddess so earnestly engaged in prayer that she appeared wholly unconscious of our presence. There was no mistaking that this was sincere devotion—a lifting up of the soul to some power considered higher than itself. I became most anxious to know what sorrow could so move her, and our interpreter afterward told us that she asked but one gift from the goddess. It was the prayer of old that a man-child should be born to her; and, poor woman! when one knows what her life must be in this country should this prayer remain unanswered, it saddens one to think of it. A living death; another installed in her place; all that woman holds dear trembling in the balance. How I pitied her! I also saw men praying before other idols and working themselves into a state of frenzy. Indeed I saw so much in the temples to make me unhappy that I wished I had never visited any of them. It gives one such desponding hopes of our race, of its present and of its future, when so many are so bound down to the lowest form of superstition.

At one of the principal Shinto temples I saw the sacred dance with which that great god is propitiated. In a booth two stories high, in front of the temple, was a small stage upon which sat three old priests. One beat a drum, the second played a flute, while the third fingered a guitar. To this music a very pretty young daughter of a priest, gorgeously arrayed in sacred robes, postured with a fan, keeping time to the music. This was all. But, like the tom-tom beating of the Buddhist which we heard at the same moment from an opposite temple, the dance is thought to dispose the gods to receive favorably the gifts and prayers of the devotees. We saw at the same temple a large wooden figure which is reputed able to cure all manner of diseases. So much and so hard had this figure been rubbed by the poor sufferers that the nose is no longer there; the face is literally rubbed smooth. The ears are gone, and it is only a question of time when all traces of human form will have vanished. It reminded us of the toe of St. Peter, in the cathedral at Rome, which has been worn smooth by the osculations of devout Christians.

Japan is rapidly adopting the manners and customs of European civilization. There is at present a cry for representative government, and one need not be surprised to hear by and by of the Parliament of Japan.

War-ships are building at the arsenal, which are not only constructed but designed by native genius. A standing army of about 50,000 men is maintained. Gas has been introduced in some places, and railroads and telegraphs are in operation ; and, not to be behind their neighbors, a public debt and irredeemable currency (based upon the property of the nation, of course,) have been created. The currency is now at 22 per cent. discount as compared with gold, and further depreciation is apprehended. (It has since reached 50 per cent. discount.) It is modelled on our American paper money, and is actually printed in New York. Let us hope that Japan may soon be able to follow the Republic farther by making it convertible—as good as gold. Notwithstanding its wide " base "—in short, our greenbackers' " base "—it doesn't seem to work here any better than at home.

Art in Japan is utilitarian ; in no other country are articles of common use so artistic. The furniture of a Japanese house is scanty. We see no walls hung with pictures with showy gilt frames, no portières or curtains, none of the sofas, chairs, tables, brackets, chandeliers, etc., which give our rooms so crowded an appearance. The bareness of the rooms strikes one at once upon entering, but when one examines the utensils in daily use even by the poorer classes he sees that they are of uncommon beauty. Surely this is of more moment than to have art confined to the few, both as to articles and to persons. In Japan, art may be said to be democratic; all classes are brought under its sway.

One thing must be said, however, about art throughout the East, in China and in India as well as in Japan: up to this time it has been content to remain solely decorative. The higher creative and imaginative power has yet to be reached. Why this should be so is an interesting question, and I resolve to read up the authorities when opportunity offers and see how they account for it. May not the poverty of the East have much to do with it? So very few are rich; indeed, scarcely any are opulent in our sense, six thousand dollars (£1,200) a year being considered a fortune in Japan, I am told, and very few, even of the higher classes, possess as much. In China and India it is much the same, a few rajahs in the latter country excepted.

The start which religion gave to art in Europe is wanting in the East, for the temples are mean and destitute of costly works. Rich commercial and manufacturing classes do not exist in the East—as wealth does not run into "pockets" as it does in Europe—especially in England—and in America. I fear, therefore, that art in the East will not advance much beyond the decorative stage for centuries to come.

SATURDAY, November 23.

Vandy and I walked to-day through the principal street of Tokio from end to end, a distance of three

miles. It is a fine, broad avenue, crowded with people and vehicles drawn or pushed by men. There
is also a line of small one-horse wagons running as
omnibuses on the street—a novel feature, unknown
anywhere else in the Empire. Our appearance attracted such crowds whenever we stopped at a shop,
that the police had to drive the gazers away. The city
is built upon a plain, and supplied with water by wells
only. Fires are of frequent occurrence. Japanese cities are such piles of combustible material that I wonder
they exist at all. But fires are little used—only a brazier
of charcoal now and then for cooking purposes; and as
most of the people eat at cook-shops, there is never any
fire at all in many of the houses. Long ladders are
erected as fire-towers, and upon these watchmen sit
through the night to give the alarm. It is only by
tearing down or blowing up surrounding houses that
the progress of a fire can generally be stayed. There
is no such thing as insurance in Japan, the risks being
much too great.

The Japanese go to the theatre early in the morning
and remain until five o'clock in the evening. Doors
open at five A.M., but the rich classes do not appear
before six or seven o'clock, at which hour the performance begins. Breakfast is served in the theatre about
noon. The audience smoke, eat, sip tea, and enjoy
themselves as they choose. No seats are provided,
but a small mat is put down for each person as he

enters, and beside it a box filled with sand, in the middle of which are two pieces of glowing charcoal, at which pipes are lighted. Ladies, as well as gentlemen, be it remembered, invariably smoke in Japan. Every one carries a small pipe with a long stem, and a tobacco-pouch attached to it. At short intervals a little tobacco is put into the pipe—just enough to give two whiffs of smoke—after which the tobacco is knocked out and the pipe again replenished. In no case have I ever seen more than two very small whiffs taken at one time. Even young ladies smoke in this manner, and to one who detests tobacco, as I instinctively do, it may be imagined this habit did not add to their attractiveness. A sweetheart who defiled her lips with tobacco! "Phew!" Neither is it considered disrespectful in any degree to begin smoking in the presence of others. Deferential as the singing girls were, when at leisure they lighted their pipes as a matter of course, wholly unconscious that they were taking a liberty.

The marriage ceremony differs greatly from ours. The priests have nothing to do with it, nor is there any religious ceremony. The parents of a young man select a proper wife for him when he is about twenty years of age, and manage the whole affair. They consult the young lady's parents, and if the match is a satisfactory one to them, writings are exchanged between the parents of the young couple, the day is appointed, and the bride and groom drink saki from the same cup; feasting and rejoicings follow, sometimes continued for several days if the parents are wealthy, and the marriage is consummated. In all cases the bride goes to reside with the husband's parents, to whom, much more than to the husband, it is necessary she should continue to be satisfactory. Very often three generations live together, and an amount of deference is paid to the oldest such as we have no conception of.

The custom of blacking the teeth by married women, is the most revolting practice I have yet seen. I have been in the houses of fine people of Japan, and seen women, otherwise good-looking, who had only to open their lips to convert themselves into objects of disgust. I rejoice, therefore, to hear that fashion is setting in against this abomination, and that some of the more recent brides have refused to conform to the custom.

One readily gets used to anything, earthquakes included, and Japan has many of these unruly visitors. One night we had three shocks at Tokio, one sufficiently strong to wake me from sleep. My bed shook violently, and the house threatened to fall upon us. The same night we had a large fire in the city, and a hundred shrill, tinkling bells, like so many cows in the woods, were rung to give the alarm. The clapping of the night watchmen about our street assured me, however, that it was all right with us, and I lay still. The night watchmen here use two small square pieces of hard wood which they strike frequently against each other as they go the rounds as their " All's well " signal ; but I think strangers, as a rule, fail to appreciate the point in being awakened every now and then simply to be assured that there is not the slightest occasion for their being awake at all.

———

MONDAY, November 25.

To-day we took a small steamer and visited the arsenal upon the invitation of our friend Captain To-taki, Mlle. Rio being of the party. It is finely situated on the bay about fifteen miles below Yokohama, and is quite extensive, having good shops filled with modern tools. Several ships have already been built here, and two men-of-war are now upon the stocks—another evidence of so-called civilization. Japan, you see, is ambitious. All the officials, foremen, and mechanics, are natives, and these have proved their ability in every department. The wages paid surprise us. All branches are about upon an equality. Painters, moulders, blacksmiths, carpenters, machinists, all get the same compensation—from 25 to 40 cents per day, according to their respective value as workmen ; common labor, outside, 18 cents; shop labor, inside, 25 cents; foreman of department, $80 per month. Work, nine hours per day, every tenth day being a day of rest corresponding to our Sunday. In addition to the two men-of-war under construction, the machinery for which is all designed and manufactured here, the Emperor is having built for his private use a large side-wheel yacht, which promises to be magnificent. However poor a nation may be, or however depreciated its currency, if it set up an emperor, king, or queen, improper personal expenditure inevitably follows. Even as good a woman as Queen Victoria, probably the most respectable woman who ever occupied a throne—such a character as one would not hesitate to introduce to his family circle, which is saying much for a monarch—will squander thirty thousand pounds per annum of the people's money on a private yacht which she has used but a few times, and which is one of three she insists upon keeping at the State's expense. It is the old story: make any human being believe he is *born* to position and he becomes arbitrary and inconsiderate of those who have exalted him. Serves the foolish ones right, I suppose is the proper verdict. But one is not indignant at the worship of their emperor by the Japanese: he is a real ruler, has power, and stands firmly upon divine right. The Japanese are yet children politically; but the English should be out of their swaddling-clothes, surely.

The captain being high in command, and this being his first visit to the arsenal since his return from a tour round the world, he was received by the officials with manifestations of delight. We had another opportunity of seeing the bowing practice in its fullest development. The various foremen as they approached bowed three times almost to the ground, and in some cases they went first upon their knees and struck the floor three times with their foreheads. We were afterward informed that only a few years ago these would have added to the obeisance by extending the arms to their full length and placing the palms of the hands flat upon the ground; now this is omitted, and I have no doubt, as intelligence spreads, less and less of this deference will be exacted. But up to this date it may safely be said Japan is in the condition of Sir Pertinax MacSycophant, who, it will be remembered, admitted that his success came from "booing." He "never could stand strecht in the presence of a great man;" no more can a Japanese.

My writing has just been interrupted by another earthquake shock. My chair began to tremble, then the house; I could not write, and looking up I saw Vandy standing in amazement. For a few moments it seemed as if we were rocking to pieces, and that the end of all things had come. I shall never forget the sensation. The motion of a ship rolling at sea transferred to land, where you have the solid earth and heavy stone walls surrounding and threatening to fall upon you, is far from agreeable; but it passed away, and old Mother Earth became steady once more.

The way to buy in Japan is not by visiting the shops, for there nothing is displayed, and a stranger has infinite difficulty in learning where certain articles are to be found; but just intimate to your "boy" what you wish, and at your door in a few minutes stand not

one or two merchants, but five or six, all bowing as you
pass in or out, and awaiting master's pleasure to examine their wares. They leave any articles you may wish
to decide upon, and the result is that one's rooms become perfect bazaars. The most unpleasant feature
connected with purchasing is that everything is a matter of bargain. A price is named, and you are expected
to make an offer. Vandy is a great success at this
game, and seems to enjoy it. I am strictly prohibited
from interfering, and so escape all trouble. It is always
comforting to know that one's interests are in much
abler hands than his own, and I always have this pleasure when Vandy is about.

Wherever we go, Fusiyama looks down upon us.
What a beautiful cone it is, and how grandly it pierces
the heavens, its summit clad with perpetual snow! No
wonder that the Japanese represent it on so many of
their articles. Thousands of pilgrims flock to it annually from all parts of the Empire, for it is their sacred
mount and the gods reward such as worship at this
shrine. It was once an active volcano; but there has
been no eruption since about 1700, when ashes were
thrown from it into Yeddo, sixty miles away. The
crater is nearly five hundred feet deep. Fusiyama
stands alone among mountains, a vast pyramid rising
as Cheops does from the plain, no " rascally comparative " near to dispute its sway.

WEDNESDAY, November 27.

We sail to-day for Shanghai, leaving Yokohama with sincere regret; nor shall we soon forget the good, kind faces of those who have done so much to make our visit to Japan an agreeable one. Had it been possible to remain until Saturday I should have been greatly tempted to do so to accept an invitation received to respond to a toast at St. Andrew's banquet. It would surely have stirred me to hold forth on Scotland's glory to my fellow-countrymen in Japan; but this had to be foregone. At Kiobe the steamer lay for twenty-four hours, and this enabled us to run up by rail to Kioto, the former residence of the Mikado, reputed to be the Paris of Japan. The city itself deserves this reputation about as well as Cincinnati does that of our American Paris, which I see some one has called it. Kioto is only a mass of poor one-story buildings, but its situation is beautiful, and cannot probably be equalled elsewhere in the Empire, and this one can justly say of Cincinnati as well, while the beauty of Paris is of the city and not at all rural. There are more pretty toy villas embowered in trees upon the little hills about Kioto than we saw in all other parts of Japan. The temples at Kioto are much inferior to those at Shibba. Our journey enabled us to see about seventy miles of the interior, and we were again impressed by the evidences on every hand of a teeming population. Gangs of men and women were everywhere at work upon small patches of ground, six or seven persons being busily engaged sometimes on less than one acre. It is not farming; there is in Japan scarcely such a thing as farming in our sense; it is a system of gardening such as we see in the neighborhood of large cities. Compared with that prevalent throughout the whole country, I have seen nothing equal to it in thoroughness, not even in Belgium.

We are upon the old steamer Costa Rica, now belonging to the Japanese Company, which recently purchased this and other boats from the Pacific Mail Company. Among our cargo is a large lot of live turkeys which some pushing Jap is taking over to Shanghai for Christmas; and listen, you favored souls who revel in the famous bird at a dollar a head, your fellow countrymen in China have to pay ten dollars for their Christmas turkey. It is said the Chinese climate is too damp for the noble bird; but it flourishes in Japan. I wish the exporter who thus develops the resources of his country much profit on his venture. But it strikes me that, instead of the eagle, the more useful gobbler has superior claims to be voted the national bird of America. "A turkey for a dollar!" repeated the shipper as I told him our price; "a turkey for a dollar—what a country!" The climate of Northern China is not favorable for Europeans, and many take a run over to Japan to recuperate, a fact which argues much for the future of Japan. Although our ship belongs to the

Japanese, the servants are generally Chinamen, and the agent explains this by informing us that while the former do very well until they arrive at the age of manhood, they then begin to develop more ambitious ideas and cannot be managed, while with the Chinese a "boy" (a servant throughout the East is called "boy") is always a boy, and is constantly on the watch to serve his master. Again, the Japs are pugnacious, a race of little game-cocks, always in for a fight, especially with a Chinaman. The captain told us the other day a great big Chinaman had complained to him that one of the Japs had abused him. Upon calling up the belligerent, he proved to be such a small specimen that the captain asked the sufferer why he hadn't picked him up and thrown him overboard. The complaint was dismissed: served the big fellow right. But some missionary should expound the civilized doctrine to him, per revised edition, which reads: "When smitten on the one cheek, turn to the smiter the other also, but if he smites you on that, *go for him.*" To-morrow is to be one of the great days of our trip, for we shall enter the famous inland sea of Japan at daybreak. Will it be fine to-morrow? is the question with all on board. The signs are earnestly discussed. The sun sets favorably, and I quote Shakespeare to them, which settles the question :

> " The weary sun hath made a golden set,
> And by the bright track of his fiery car
> Gives token of a goodly day to-morrow."

Let to-morrow be fair, whatever we may miss here-after. This is the universal sentiment.

What a day this has been! Many a rich experience which seemed grand enough never to fade from the memory may pass into oblivion, but no mortal can ever sail through the inland sea of Japan on a fine day and cease to remember it till the day he dies. It deserves its reputation as the most beautiful voyage in the world; at least I cannot conceive how, taking the elements of earth, water and sky, anything more exquisitely beautiful could be produced from them. Entering the narrow sea at sunrise, we sail for three hundred and fifty miles through three thousand pretty islands,

> "Which seem to stand
> To sentinel enchanted land."

These divide the water, making, not one but a dozen pretty lakes in view at once. It is the Lakes of Killarney, or the English or Scotch lakes, multiplied a hundred-fold; but instead of the islands and mountains being in pasture, they are cultivated to their very tops, terraced in every form, in order to utilize every rod of ground. On the shores cluster villages, nestling in sheltered nooks, while the water swarms with the sails of tiny fishing boats, giving a sense of warm, happy life throughout. These sail-boats add greatly to the beauty of the scene. I counted at one time from the bow of our steamer, without looking back, ninety-seven sails glistening in the sun, while on the hills were seen everywhere gangs of people at work upon their little farm-gardens. It is a panorama of busy, crowded life, but life under most beautiful surroundings, from beginning to end, and we all vote that never before have we, in a like space of time, seen so much of fairy-land as upon this ever-memorable day. We begin to understand how the thirty odd millions of the Japanese exist upon so small an area. The rivers and seas abound in fish; the hills and valleys under irrigation and constant labor grow their rice, millet, and vegetables. A few dollars per year supply all the clothing needed, and a few dollars build their light wooden houses. Thus they have everything they need, or consider necessary, and are happy as the day is long, certain of one established fact in nature, to wit, that there is no place like Japan; and no doubt they daily and hourly thank their stars that their lines have fallen in pleasant places, and pity us— slaves to imaginary wants—who deny ourselves the present happiness they consider it wisdom to enjoy, in vain hopes of banquetting to surfeit at some future time, which always comes too late.

On emerging from this fairy scene, we encountered a gale upon the China Sea, which lasted for the few hours we were upon it before reaching Nagasaki, the last port of Japan. Here, two hundred years ago, the Dutch secured a small island, from which they traded

with Japan long before any other nation was permitted
to do so. The Catholics also had their headquarters
here. They were so successful in converting the natives
that the government became alarmed, and several
thousand Christians were driven to the island and all
massacred. This was in the sixteenth century; but it
is only a few years ago that seven thousand native
Catholics were banished from this region. To-day all is
changed. These fugitives have been permitted to return, and there is entire freedom of religious worship.
Last month a return was made of professing Christians
(Catholics) in this district, and thirty-five thousand
were reported. Protestants are very few indeed.

As far as I saw in the East, here is the only real and
considerable advance made toward christianizing a people. At other stations throughout my journey I saw
only a few ignorant natives who professed Christianity
—sometimes a dozen or two, rarely more. European
residents invariably told me that these were the depend-
ants or servants of foreigners who held their places
mainly because of their conversion to the new faith. If
dismissed, they relapsed. One can readily see that the
lowest and most unscrupulous would be the first to fall
before the almost irresistible temptation, for a means of
comfortable livelihood seems the one serious concern of
life in all the East to a degree difficult for us in America,
at least, to imagine.

I remember the dear, kind Catholic Bishop of Canton

telling me with such delicious simplicity that every workman engaged in building the Cathedral—a work of many years and yet unfinished—had by the grace of God been converted to Holy Mother Church. The hotel-keeper told me afterward this so-called conversion was a source of much amusement among the natives. Well, be it so. I believe, myself, that the holy father is the victim of misplaced confidence. But here in Nagasaki nothing like this can be said. Thirty-five thousand professing Christians in a district where there are not a hundred foreign Christian families, if half so many, and where to be a Christian is to declare one's self of the minority and so out of fashion, surely this does prove that the Church has succeeded, and justifies it in hoping that ere long this part of Japan at least will one day enter the fold.

One great reason for this undoubted success is probably that neither the Government nor the people have the slightest objection to missionaries, for their own religion sets but lightly on the Japanese. With the Chinaman it is totally different. His own religion is sacred to him, a vital force, and his gods must not be defamed. He stands by his faith like a Covenanter. It touches the most sacred feelings of his nature, and is everything to him. Mrs. D. O. Hill's celebrated statue of Livingstone in Prince's Gardens, Edinburgh, therefore, represents too truly the attitude of our missionaries in the flowery land as well as in other so-called heathen lands:

the Bible in one hand and the pistol in the other. In Japan the pistol is wholly unnecessary. The man of Japan regards missionaries as harmless curiosities, and if not disposed to trouble himself about their new ideas, he has not the least objection to their being expounded.

There is now no established religion in Japan, Buddhism having been abolished in 1874. The temples and priesthood are maintained by voluntary contributions. The poor laws are simple: government gives nine bushels of rice to every person over seventy or under fifteen years of age, who cannot work, and the same to foundlings under thirteen. Out of the total population of thirty-six millions, there are only ten thousand and fifty paupers, and of these more than a thousand are at Tokio in the workhouse.

———

HARBOR OF NAGASAKI, MONDAY, December 2.

Vandy and I were off early this morning for the shore, and did not return to the ship until late in the afternoon, having walked over the high hills and down into the valleys beyond. We had a real tramp in the country. It is here just as elsewhere, terrace upon terrace, every foot of ground under cultivation; water carried by men in pails, or on the backs of oxen, to the highest peaks, which it is impossible to irrigate, and every single plant, be it rice, millet, turnip, cabbage, or carrot, watered daily. What good Mother Earth can be induced to yield under such attention is a marvel. The bountiful earth has another meaning when you see what she can be made to bring forth. Although we are in December, the sun shines bright, and it is quite warm. I sat down several times under the hedge-rows, and heard the constant hum of insect life around me. Butterflies flitted about, the bees gathered honey, and all looked and felt like a day in June. The houses of the people which we saw were poor, and the total absence of glass causes them to look like deserted hovels; but closer inspection showed fine mats on the floors, and everything scrupulously clean. I counted upon one hillside forty-seven terraces from the bottom to the top. These are divided vertically, so that I think twenty-five feet square would be about the average size of each patch; and as the division of terraces is made to suit the ground, and hence very irregularly, the appearance of a hillside in Japan is something like that of a bed-quilt of irregular pieces. The terrace-walls are overgrown with vines, ferns, etc., so that they appear like low green hedges: and this adds much to the beauty of the landscape. No wonder the cultivators of these lovely spots never dream of leaving them. Animal food is not half as important to the Japanese as the supply of fish—indeed the former is said to be comparatively little used, while fish of some kind or in some form is ever present at meals. The favorite fish is the *tai*, which is red when taken from streams with sandy bottoms, but black when caught at the mouths of the same streams, where the dark soil of the sea begins. A curious parallel case is seen in the black and red pines of this country: in sandy soils they grow red, while in the softer black soil they are dark. Transplant the two varieties and they change color. The same law, you see, with fish and plant. We are all creatures of our environment. Therefore let us choose our companions and surroundings well. To know the best that has been said and done in the world is no doubt much; to be planted and to grow among those who have done the greatest work and who live up to the best standard in our day and generation is surely equally important.

We had an alarm of fire on the Belgic in mid-ocean, but this morning we had the real article. I had just parted from the captain at the stern of the ship, intending to go ashore, when, walking forward, I saw dense volumes of smoke issuing from the walking-beam pit, and in a few moments I heard the cry of fire from below. All was in a bustle at once, but the crew got finely to work. Fortunately, although there was no steam in the main boilers, the small donkey boiler was full, and the pumps were put to work. Meanwhile boats from the various men-of-war in the harbor with hand fire-engines came to our assistance. The steamer is an old wooden craft, and I knew her cargo was combustible. Were the smoke ever to give place to flame, panic was sure to ensue, and not one of the small native boats that had until now been clustering around us could then be induced to approach ; indeed, they had already all rowed off. There was one lady on board, Mrs. McK., a veritable Princess of Thule from the Island of Lewes, and I decided that she had better be taken off with her sick child at once; so, bribing a greedy native by the immense reward of a whole dollar (a large fee here, small as it seems at home) to come alongside, I grasped the baby and followed the mother down the gangway, and remained at a safe distance until the danger was over. A few minutes more, and the Costa Rica would have followed her sister ship, the America, which some years ago took fire under similar circumstances in the harbor of Yokohama, and was completely destroyed. Fortunately we are about done with wooden steamships; otherwise they should not be permitted to run as passenger vessels.

The post-office department of Japan is of recent origin, having been established in 1871 ; yet in 1881, after only ten years' growth, it carried ninety-five millions of letters, newspapers, books, etc. Thirty millions of these were post-cards. Three millions of telegrams were also transmitted in that year. Perhaps no statement will give one a clearer idea than this of the rapid progress of this strange country in the ways of the West.

Japan has only two short lines of railway for thirty-six millions of people—a population nearly equal to that of Great Britain: one eighteen miles from Yokohama to Tokio, the other seventy miles from Hiogo to

Kioto. This seems a scanty allowance; nevertheless it is not probable that more than a few hundred miles of rail will be built for centuries. The habits and poverty of the people, and in many districts the topography of the country, are such as to render railways unsuitable. The main highways are, however, kept in admirable order. I was amused with the classification of these. Those of the first class are such as lead from the capital to the treaty ports; of the second class those lines leading to the national shrines. Commerce has thus usurped the first place. Both the first and the second class roads are maintained by the General Government as being national affairs. Various grades of roads follow, some being maintained by large districts; others, of local importance, by taxes upon a smaller area; but all under the strict supervision of central officials at Tokio.

Not the least surprising feature in the revolution going forward so peacefully in Japan is the prompt adoption of the newspaper as one of the essentials of life. A few years ago the official Gazette, read only by officials and containing nothing of general interest, was the only publication in the Empire; to-day several hundred newspapers are published, many of them daily. A censorship of the press still exists, however, and leads to the usual mode of evasion. Pungent political articles are conveyed under cover of criticisms ostensibly upon the blunders of lands not so enlightened as Japan. Here is a specimen: " In America during the Civil War paper currency was issued and made legal tender. At every successive issue the premium rose higher and higher till the currency was not worth more than a third of its face. The Southern States followed in the same path, but they kept on till their issues were found to be good for about one purpose only—to line trunks withal—such fools these Americans be. Happy Japan! blessed with rulers of preëminent ability, who keep the finances of our land in such creditable form."

The fact was that Japanese currency was then at 22 per cent. discount and rapidly declining in value under successive issues, just as it had done in America. Such articles are no doubt far more effective than open, undisguised assaults could possibly be, for the cleverness of the evasion gives additional zest to the attack. The Press is a hard dog to muzzle, and, like dogs in general, only vicious when muzzled. The Japanese will soon find it safer to " let Truth and Error grapple" in the full face of day, for they are not slow to learn.

———

Tuesday, December 3.

The turbulent China Sea has passed into a proverb. The Channel passage in a gale, I suppose, comes nearest to it. We started to cross this sea at daylight, and surely we have reason to be grateful. It is as smooth as a mirror, the winds are hushed, and as I write the shores of Japan fade peacefully from view. I cannot help thinking how improbable that I shall ever see them again; but, however that may be, farewell for the present to Japan. Take a stranger's best wishes for your future.

Our cargo shows something of the resources of the country. It amounts to eight hundred tons, comprising seaweed—a special kind of which the Chinese are fond —ginseng, camphor, timber, isinglass, Japan piece-goods, ingot copper, etc. Every week this line takes to China a similar cargo, and the trade is rapidly extending. This steamship company is worth noting as an evidence of what Japanese enterprise is doing. The principal owner, the Commodore Garrison of Japan, had a small beginning, but now runs some thirty-seven steamers between the various Japanese ports. Under the management of Mr. Krebs, a remarkable Dane, this company beat off the Pacific Mail Company from the China trade, and actually purchased their ships. There are many things found on these vessels which our Atlantic companies might imitate with advantage.

I believe I mentioned that Japan, not to be behind her Western neighbors, had created a public debt, which now amounts to about $300,000,000, but $250,000,000 of this was used in payment of the two hundred and sixty-six daimios and their numerous retainers, when government took over the land to itself. Each of these potentates had vested rights in a certain proportion of the yield of the soil of his district, and this was commuted by the government into so much in its bonds, a fixed land tax being substituted for the irregular exactions of former landlords. On every side I hear that this has greatly improved the condition of the population—made the people more contented, and at the same time vastly augmented the products of the soil. Not less than three millions of the population shared in this operation.

The nationalization of the land is under discussion in England, and it is conceded that some change has to be made. Here is Japan proving the results of nationalization, while Denmark shows what private ownership of small pieces of land can do under a system of cumulative taxation in proportion to the size of the estate held. One of these two systems is likely to prevail in England some day. Meanwhile, here is food for thought for the British tax-payer: out of seventy-five million yens (£15,000,000) of revenue raised by Japan, forty-three million comes from the land tax. The tax on alcoholic liquors yields about seventeen millions more.

Since my visit to Japan an imperial decree has been published, promising that a national assembly shall meet in 1890; so we have the foundations of representative government almost at hand. Surely no other nation ever abandoned its traditions and embraced so rapidly those of a civilization of an opposite character. This is not development under the law of slow evolution; it seems more like a case of spontaneous generation. Presto, change! and here before our very eyes is presented the strange spectacle of the most curious, backward, feudalistic Eastern nation turning into a Western one of the most advanced type.

That Japan will succeed in her effort to establish a central government, under something like our ideas of freedom and law, and that she has such resources as will enable her to maintain it and educate her people, I am glad to be able to say I believe; but much remains to be done requiring in the race the exercise of solid qualities, the possession of which I find some Europeans disposed to deny them. They have travelled, perhaps, quite fast enough, and I look for a temporary triumph of the more conservative party. But the seed is sown, and Japan will move, upon the whole, in the direction of progress. And so, once more, farewell, Japan; and China, now almost within sight, all hail!

CHINA.

In one respect at least pilgrims from other lands must bow to the empire we are about to visit. It is the oldest form of civilized government on earth. While the English monarchy boasts its uninterrupted course of eight hundred years, and America has just celebrated its first century of existence, this remarkable people live under a government which has been substantially un-

changed for four thousand long years. The first au-
thenticated dynasty dates from 2345 B. C., and what is
now China has been under one central government for
nearly two thousand five hundred years. Even the
Papacy, the most venerable of existing Western institutions, is young compared to this. There was
something in the reply of the mandarin to the boast of
one of our people as to the superiority of our system :
" Wait until it is tried ! " To a Chinaman a thousand
years or so seems too short to prove anything. Theirs
alone has stood the test of ages. That the Chinese are
a great race goes without saying. Four hundred millions (nearly one-third of the human race) existing for
thousands of years under one unchanging government,
riding out the storms which have overwhelmed all other
nations; nay, even absorbing into themselves the Tartar
hordes, who came as conquerors, and making them
Chinese against their will. Such a record tells a story
indeed ! At a date so remote that Egypt and Assyria
were the great Western powers, when Athens and Troy
had just been founded, and Rome was not even thought
of, these people were governed much as they are now,
and since A.D. 67 have published a daily Peking *Gazette*,
of which (thanks to our intelligent " host of the Garter,"
Mr. Janssen) we have secured a copy. We are all but
of yesterday compared to the Heathen Chinee, and it is
impossible to sit down and scribble glibly of such a people. In Japan there is no record. It is a new race ap-

pearing almost for the first time among civilized nations. It has given the world nothing, but how widely
different here! It is to China the world owes the compass, gunpowder, porcelain, and even the art of printing, and to her also alone the spectacle of a people ruled
by a code of laws and morals embracing the most minute particulars, written two thousand four hundred
years ago, and taught to this day in the schools as the
rules of life. It is an old and true saying that almost
any system of religion would make one good enough
if it were properly obeyed; certainly that of Confucius
would do so. I have been deeply impressed with his
greatness and purity. Dr. Davis writes in his work on
China: "Confucius embodied in sententious maxims
the first principles of morals and of government, and
the purity and excellence of some of his precepts will
bear comparison with even those of the Gospel." In
Thornton's History of China I find this noteworthy
passage: "It may excite surprise, and even incredulity,
to state that the golden rule of our Saviour had been
inculcated by Confucius five centuries before almost in
the same words." If any of my readers wish a rare
treat, I advise him to add at least the first volume of the
Rev. Dr. Legge's Life of Confucius to his library immediately, and let him not entertain the idea that the
sage was a heathen or an unbeliever; far, very far from
that, for one of his most memorable passages explains
that all worship belongs to Shangti (the Supreme Ruler);

no matter what forms or symbols are used, the great God alone being the only true object of worship. But I must resist this fit of Confucianism, reserving, however, the privilege of regaling you with more of it by and bye, for really it is too good not to be scattered among you. Meanwhile, remember well what Matthew Arnold says:

" Children of men ! the unseen Power, whose eye
    For ever doth accompany mankind,
  Hath look'd on no religion scornfully
    That men did ever find.

  Which has not taught weak wills how much they can ?
    Which has not fall'n on the dry heart like rain ?
  Which has not cried to sunk, self-weary man :
    Thou must be born again ! "

THURSDAY, December 5.

We reached Shanghai Thursday morning, and found excellent accommodations at the Astor House, in the American settlement. The Chinese Government has set apart for the accommodation of foreigners a strip of land, about six miles long and one mile wide, fronting the river. This is divided among the English, French, and Americans. During the Taeping rebellion a few years ago, thousands of natives flocked into this territory and found a refuge under the foreign flags, and to-day it contains more than seventy thousand Chinese, who do most of the retail business of the city. The foreign population does not exceed two thousand. The streets are broad, and as well cared for as in an English town, and it is lighted with gas, has a fine steam fire organization, and is thoroughly drained. It is here the natives of this district are learning their first lesson of Western civilization, and at length some impression has been made upon this hitherto immovable mass and it begins to move. Mandarins come from the country to enjoy a drive in the streets, for, let it not be forgotten, there is not a street or road in the region, outside of the reservation, in which a horse can travel; only footpaths, where a wheelbarrow pushed by a man is the only possible vehicle. Now several wealthy Chinese have set up their carriages, and may frequently be seen driving; and I learn from many that when any are compelled to visit their former residences elsewhere, they return to Shanghai declaring that they could not live any longer in the old style. But think of one-third of the race living at this late day without a mile of railroad or of telegraph, or even of macadamized roads! Communication in China is solely by means of the rivers, canals, and small branches which have been led from the main channels to every acre of ground for irrigating purposes, and by narrow footpaths between the fields. But some of us will live to see this changed. I saw in a newspaper an official notice permitting the first telegraph line to be built. True, it is to be only a few miles in length, extending from the sea to the port of Peking (Tien-Tsin), but this is of course only a beginning. The question of railroads is more serious, and what think you is the one obstacle to their introduction? Graves—the "tombs of our ancestors." China is one vast cemetery. Go where you will, in any direction, the mounds of the dead intrude themselves upon you at every step. There are no cemeteries or places set apart for burial purposes; on the contrary, the Chinaman seems to prefer having his dead buried on his own land, and as near to him as practicable. In this neighborhood their mode of sepulture is revolting. The coffins are not put into a grave at all, but are laid directly on the surface of the ground and covered with but a few inches of earth ; and it is not at all uncommon for them to be wholly exposed, simply laid out in the fields, and so close to the roadside —I mean to the main roads built by Europeans near their settlements—that you can almost touch them with the end of your walking-stick as you pass. The stench from such coffins became so offensive last year at the rifle range that the European authorities had to enter complaint to the Chinese Mandarin. I was, like all others, at first much shocked at the sight of these evidences of mortality. One day I stood and counted a hundred and thirty-four different mounds and exposed coffins within sight. I am glad to say that in other parts of China this custom does not prevail, the dead being buried in graves, and walls built above them in the shape of a horseshoe. As is well known, the Chinese worship their ancestors, and believe that much of their happiness depends upon the respect shown to those to whom they owe their lives. Cases have been known where successive afflictions have been attributed to some defect in the resting-places of the dead; their ancestors, "after life's fitful fever," were not sleeping well, and at great expense the bones have been removed to another place; but it is an extreme case when they venture to disturb the dead. Every true son of the Empire of the Sun echoes the anathema of Shakespeare,

"And curst be he who moves my bones."

One special feature of the Flowery Land is, I think, the repugnance of the people to debt, or to credits in any form. As I have remarked, they have no banks of issue; no promises to pay for the Celestials; they deal only in the coin itself. All debts must be paid at the beginning of each year. The Chinaman who does not settle every account and enter upon the new year without an obligation is accounted either very unfortunate or very regardless of the duties of life. This aversion to debt, perhaps, accounts for the fact that these four hundred millions of people had not a penny of national debt until four years ago. But they have just made a loan of $12,000,000, I believe, the first ever made by China in all its thousands of years' history. This may be taken, perhaps, as

another proof that the empire is influenced by Western ideas, but one cannot help regretting that her
long reign of freedom from debt should at last be
stained, even for so paltry an amount. If I were a
Chinese statesman, I would never rest until the last
farthing of this debt was paid off. The fashion nowadays in America is to urge that it is paying off its debt
much too fast. I am sorry for this. What an example
to all lands we shall give when the last bond of the
nation is cancelled at Washington amid public rejoicings! A republic's part is to give less advanced nations,
still under the influence of feudal institutions, such lessons as this will be. Do not let us, however, underrate
England's part in such a work. She has reduced her
public debt wonderfully, and the next twenty years is
to see seventy millions sterling more extinguished, unless legislation now existing for this end is interfered
with.

The general government of China is a very economical one, its total revenue being only about $125,000,000
(£25,000,000). Of this $15,000,000 is spent upon the
army, a sum which for 400,000,000 people compares
very favorably with that expended by other nations.
China has outgrown the so-called heroic age, in which
England still dwells, and has little need of armies.
A government not worth thirty cents (fifteen pence)
per year for each inhabitant, which is the cost in China,
is not worth having.

In our stroll to-day Vandy and I came upon one of
the gates of the old city, of which there are six in a
wall three miles in circumference, and entered. It contains 300,000 people. We walked some distance through
its filthy, narrow alleys, and saw the poor wretches in
their dens working at all kinds of trades, from the forging of iron to the production of Joss-money, but the
villainous smells soon overpowered me, and I had to get
Vandy to escort me out. He can go through anything
of this kind without flinching, and means to return; but
I have seen enough of it, and am sorry that human
beings have to exist under such conditions. The Chinese
have no coined currency except a small bronze piece
worth one-tenth of a cent, called "cash." It has a hole
in the centre, and when a native goes to market he puts
several lots of them on strings, fifty or a hundred on
each string, and throws them round his neck; think of it,
one thousand pieces, ten strings of one hundred each, to
make a dollar! Sometimes they are carried in the
market-basket. In larger operations Mexican and
American dollars are used, but away from the coast
people decline to take even these, insisting upon silver
cast in the form of a horseshoe and called "sice."
This silver is hoarded here, and also in India, and were
it not for this its value would probably fall to a point
which would rule it out of the list of precious metals.
The evils of a silver currency are obvious to all here.

Its value has changed three times in one day since we have been in the country. Business is seriously disturbed, and suffers from this cause, and it is to such a plight that our misled silverites at home would reduce us!

———

To-day we walked through the fish and vegetable markets. It was funny to see the people making their purchases. Each one carries a small stick with a weight attached to it. This serves as a weighing-beam, and every fowl, fish, and vegetable is carefully weighed by the customer. No cheating of a brother Celestial by the seller. We pass now and then a shop where nothing is dealt in but Joss-money; hundreds in every place are engaged in its manufacture. It is made out of thin gold and silver paper, in the horseshoe ingot form of genuine " sice." I bought a box containing eight pieces for thirty cents. Some of it also is made in imitation of silver dollars. This bogus money is laid upon the altars of the temples as offerings to the gods, who are supposed to find as much use for it as if it were genuine; and no doubt this is the case. It would therefore be a great pity, says the Heathen Chinee, to waste the real article, although I doubt not the priests would infinitely prefer it.

We attended a " paper-hunt " in the afternoon. Between forty and fifty riders, all Europeans, on small horses, started across country, the route having been previously laid down by means of small pieces of white paper scattered at every point where one of the innumerable little creeks was to be crossed. The finish was a rare sight. The banks of the creeks were very muddy, falls were numerous, and several of the riders came in besmirched from head to foot. Europeans take to horses here, and a race-course is maintained. The animals are a small breed from the north, which are now known as Shanghai ponies. I do not think I could enjoy the sport of paper-hunting here. The exposed coffins and graves one has to gallop over from end to end of the hunt are not calculated to enhance one's pleasure; but perhaps one would in time get used even to them, though I doubt it.

It was sad to see the roadway which had been prepared for the railroad from Woosung, at the mouth of the river, to this city, a distance of about twelve miles. The rails had actually been laid in some places when a decree from Peking ordered their removal. No better location in the empire could have been found to prove the advantages of railway travel, and I believe, if it had been finished, the Chinese would have quickly appreciated the benefits to be derived from it. Britain will some day find in China its best field for railway enterprise. By the time we next visit Shanghai we expect to see not only the rails restored to this line, but also many other miles in successful operation.

MONDAY, December 9.

We visited the ship-yard of Messrs. Boyd & Co., and found none but native workmen employed. Blacksmiths receive about five dollars per week, machinists six dollars; carpenters, sixty to sixty-five cents per day. But this concern pays high wages, and requires its men to equal Europeans, which I am told they do. Common gang labor is contracted for with a head man, who engages to supply day by day the number of coolies wanted at twenty cents a day per man. Mr. Grant, the senior partner, told me he was buying Belgian iron in large lots, assorted sizes, for £4 10*s.* per gross ton—just about one cent per pound; ship plates at £6, equal to $29 per gross ton, free on ship at Antwerp. Such figures prove the severity of the struggle for existence among the iron manufacturers of Europe.

The servants at the hotel pay a contractor two dollars per month for food, they not being permitted to eat anything at the hotel. A coolie's board costs about five cents per day. For this he gets an abundance of coarse rice and cabbage spiced with pieces of dried fish and pickles, and upon such a diet lives from year to year. Clothing is estimated at two to three dollars per year. This is the country of low prices, where one eschews luxuries and comes down to first principles. Cab fare is five cents per mile for ginrikshaws, which have been introduced from Japan, and are generally used in Shanghai. At Tokio I remember cab fare was even cheaper. We paid only eight cents per hour for a man and his carriage, or seventy-five cents for the entire day. European society here is quite extensive, and very pleasant and hospitable. We are indebted to kind friends for numerous attentions. As General Bailey, our worthy Consul-General, is a public official, I may be permitted to express to him my special thanks. He was unremitting in his efforts to render our visit agreeable. It is from such men that America is to draw its trained diplomatists when Civil-Service Reform has done its needed work.

We attended last night a very good amateur theatrical performance. Shanghai society was present in force, and in full evening dress. The preponderance of fine-looking young men, and the almost total absence of young ladies, was most marked. The number of married ladies was not great. In answer to my inquiry where the young ladies were, I was informed that there were but few in town. One was pointed out, but as she was engaged she scarcely counted. If ladies will only be contented with unremitting attentions from a crowd of handsome beaux, this is their paradise; but, as our lady friend explained, none of these fine fellows can afford to marry: they are clerks and assistants in the European houses, the partners of which unfortunately are married already. I think it but fair to mention this for the benefit of any of my fair young friends who might otherwise think of visiting the East. The absence of young ladies renders the taking of female parts by the opposite sex a necessity. A splendid "singing chambermaid" of this kind, dressed and looking the part to perfection, but with a deep bass voice, caused peals of laughter every time he spoke. During the evening there was a song cleverly introduced and sung by a brawny Scot—a parody upon "May I like a soldier fall," beginning,

> " Oh! may I like a Scotchman fall
> Upon St. Andrew's Day."

It appears the Scotch residents had just been celebrating that memorable night, having brought up from Hong Kong no less a personage than the head piper of the Highlander Regiment to grace the festival. But the pipes proved too much for the more enthusiastic of the party, and capturing the piper about three o'clock in the morning, they compelled him to march at their head playing through the town. It may be readily surmised that

> " If no fou, they just had plenty."

As long, however, as the martial strains continued, they managed, arm and arm, to keep upright and together, but, unfortunately, from some cause or other not clearly explained, at the turn of the street Donald himself lost his footing, the bagpipes ceased, and then, surging one against the other, without the music to keep them in step, the mass was laid low, yelling to the last, however, the "March of the Cameron Men." "Oh, what a fall was there, my countrymen!" The Central Hotel was fortunately not far off, and by the aid of wheelbarrows they were safely conveyed thither and taken care of until morning. Ah, well, let the censorious take note. This is not the first time, as the world knows, when the sound of the pibroch has kept Scotchmen shoulder to shoulder, "one stepping where the other fell," when upon them lay the issue of the fight; nor shall it be the last. Burke pardoned something to the spirit of liberty, and shall we do less to the august shade of St. Andrew? Heaven forbid!

While bemoaning the absence of foreign young ladies here and in Japan, I may as well tell those at home something of the marriage customs of the East, for Japan, China, and India all have much in common here. First and foremost, then, please understand that the couple about to be married have nothing whatever to do with the affair. The match has been made by the parents, and as a rule neither has seen the other until after the contract has been closed; and in many cases it is thought advisable that they should meet for the first time when the ceremony begins. It is considered one of the most important duties of a mother to select a wife for each of her sons as he arrives at maturity, as a failure to do this might involve the fearful catastrophe of a break in the worship of the family's ancestors, and indeed of her own and her husband's ashes, for there might be no men to perform the sacred rites over them. The parents of the young men take the initiative, but how to propose is said to be even more embarrassing than it would be to the son himself, as a refusal implies that the lady's parents consider the proposal much beneath them. There exists, therefore, a class of "marriage brokers," who keep themselves informed of the eligible sons and daughters in their circle, and can sound the parents, name the *dot* to be given or required, and suggest and finally bring about a satisfactory alliance without wounding the family pride upon either side. The Chinese are very superstitious, and no union takes place without the astrologer's sanction. He must consult the stars and see that there is proper conjunction. If all is favorable, the marriage takes place.

But now, my lady friends, don't imagine that the happy pair set up a separate establishment, as you expect to do when you marry. No; the wife goes in every case to reside with her mother-in-law, to whom, as also to her husband's father, she renders implicit obedience. This obedience to parents is the most conspicuous duty in their religion. Should the daughter-in-law be disrespectful, even, to her husband's parents, these would be upheld in putting her away, even against the wish of her husband; and unless the son happened to have an independent income or means of support, which is very rarely the case, his parents would select for him another wife who knew her duty better. The deference exacted and bestowed not only by children but by grown men and women to their parents, is wholly inconceivable by Americans; but, remember, their religion teaches them that those from whom they derive existence are entitled to their worship. No priest is required at a marriage. The ceremony always takes place at the man's house, the bride coming from her parents in grand procession through the streets in a sedan chair with its blinds closely drawn, the presents being ostentatiously displayed by men carrying them in front. We saw several of these processions. I cannot give a tithe of all the customs observed; they would fill pages. But one is significant; the bride is required to kneel before the husband's family tablet, and to worship his ancestors, her own being from that moment apparently of no account to her, and her father gives her, as his parting injunction, the command to yield hereafter to her new parents the obedience and reverence hitherto his due.

When the entire day has been spent in the ceremonies required, dinner for the couple is announced, and they are left alone with each other for the first time in their lives; but she may not partake one morsel of the feast, and, harder still, perhaps, not one syllable must she speak. Etiquette demands that she " sit in silence, grave and dignified," and she cannot break fast upon her wedding day. The woman's chief study is a book giving minute instructions for her guidance through life.

In this are prescribed the three great duties of woman:
1, obedience when a child to her parents; 2, obedience
when a wife to her husband; 3, obedience when a widow
to her eldest son.   The government of man is thus secured for the weaker vessel from the cradle to the
grave.   No Eastern man could be made to believe that
the influence of the masculine intellect is not absolutely
essential for the well-being of the female; and so it undoubtedly will be in the East as long as woman is un-
educated.   It is in America we find woman in her
highest development, higher even than the English
standard, simply because in the best circles she receives an education nearer to that of man than is given
her elsewhere.

By many such curious customs is secured the entire
absorption of the woman, her total eclipse as a separate individuality; there is nothing left of her as far as
law and usage can destroy her rights.   This is the
Eastern idea.   But she has her triumph later.   As
a wife she knows there is little for her.   Divorce
is almost sure unless she bear a son; but when, in
the language of Scripture, "a man-child is born"—
presto change! she is a mother, supreme, invested with
a halo of sanctity which secures rank and reverence
from all.   She becomes by this the equal of her lord,
and must be worshipped like him, and jointly with him,
by succeeding generations, for Confucius enjoins upon
every son the erection of the family tablets, to father

and mother alike. Nor is her rule confined to her own children, but, as before stated, to their children as well to the latest day of her life, and the older she becomes the more she is reverenced as being nearer to heaven, dearer to the gods; and it is considered of much moment to any family to be able to boast a great-great-grand-mother living.

Do not mourn too much over the sad fate of a young Chinaman compelled to marry one whom he has never seen, for indeed there seems little difference between the young ladies of China. Thousands of years of seclusion, of unvarying customs, have at last moulded women into the same form, mentally and physically, and anything like individuality can exist only to a small degree, and in exceptional natures. They are as like as peas, and one may as well marry one as another. If the husband has not the joys of love, neither has he the anxieties pertaining to that super-sensitive condition; for she is not to be his constant companion, nor his companion at all if he has not drawn a prize.

The position of woman would seem, therefore, to be almost entirely different from what it is with us: in youth she is nothing there, in old age everything; with us it is the opposite. The "just mean" between the two would probably yield better results than either. In China a man may marry more than one woman, but the first only is recognized as his legal wife; all others are her servants, and bound to wait upon and obey her;

and should there be children, these are considered as children of the legal wife only, and it is her they must worship, and not their real mother. Among the masses wives are invariably bought from the parents, about ninety dollars being a fair market price among poor people. This sum is supposed to recompense them for the outlay involved in rearing the young girl. But this custom is valuable in this, that the possession of so large a sum by a young workingman is the best possible guarantee that the son-in-law has acquired steady habits, and is competent to provide for his family. If a test of this nature could be applied with us, I think paterfamilias would not regard it as the worst of institutions. These Chinese have ideas that are sometimes worth thinking over.

Friday, December 13.

Our intended trip up the Yang-tse has been inter-fered with by a storm of rain and dense fog, but the days never seem long. We get a little time to read up. Our book-table shows seven important works on China and its people—all interesting. To-day is marked by a notable invitation to dinner extended to us through General Bailey. We are to have the honor—one not often bestowed upon globe trotters—of dining with the Mandarin.

The dinner lasted more than three hours, and was composed of I don't know how many courses. I de-pended upon Vandy to keep count, but he found so much to wonder at that he lost the run when in the teens. From birds'-nest soup, which, by the way, is insipid, to shark's fin and bamboo shoots in rapid succession, we had it all. I thought each course would surely be the last; but finally we did get to sweet dishes, and I knew we were approaching the end. Then came the bowl of rice and tea, which are supposed to be able to neutralize the mess which has gone before. Our host pressed all to drink frequently of a celebrated native wine, the champagne of China, grown in his district, of the quality of which he seemed very proud. Whenever he showed the bottom of his cup, guests were expected to empty and replenish theirs. I did the best I could, both as to tasting the compounds and drinking the wine, but I fear I was voted not a great success in either. The natives were quite hilarious, and smoked at intervals during the feast. They played the ancient game of digits like Romans, and also a Japanese game with the hands and arms, the loser in every case being compelled to drain his cup. When tea was served, the Mandarin, through his interpreter, addressed General Bailey, as the principal dignitary present, thanking him for the great honor conferred upon his humble self by those present having condescended to sit at his table. The general's reply was equally polite and very happy, and appeared to please our host greatly, who then hoped that the illustrious travellers from America would be pleased with China and return safely to their great country from their journey round the world, adding that, having now got the telegraph, America and China and all countries were brought nearer to one another, and would know each other better. I replied that this was happily true, and ventured to express the belief that as we knew each other better we should also like each other more, and that as we, and all modern nations, had learned so much from his country in the past, I hoped that in return we might be able, to some extent at least, to repay that debt by perhaps showing China some things which she could adopt with advantage. To this sentiment there was a most cordial response.

Before rising from table the photograph of the host was presented to each guest. I requested that his autograph be put upon ours, that we could insert it in our albums among the eminent men we met. He replied that he must then go at the very end, because he had not on his Mandarin hat. But I asked the interpreter to assure him that we in America did not care about the hat; "it was the head that was in it" which had raised him so high. This appeared to please the company inordinately, and we got the autograph, and so ended our first, and, in all probability, our last, Mandarin dinner. Vandy ate and drank of everything offered him, and this morning, when I fully expected him to be as sick as a dog, and with a head like to split, he surprised me by reporting himself as all right, and telling me that in some respects Mandarin cooking beats the world. I should mention that the politeness of our host was overpowering. The first course he served himself to each guest, his servants following him round the table and handing him the dishes ("and I my-self shall be your servant, sir, says good Uncle Toby"), and upon entering, as well as upon retiring, he stood in the open court outside of his threshold to welcome and to bid farewell. The shaking of one's own hands instead of grasping those of your friends is soon learned; but what a world of pleasure the Chinaman misses by his mode!

Of course we saw none of the ladies of the household, nor were they inquired for or referred to by any of us. If a Chinese gentleman were asked how many children he had, he would probably not count the girls at all, but at all events he would distinguish thus: two children and a *girl.* When a boy is born the father is overwhelmed with congratulations, presents are sent, and rejoicing takes place. If the little stranger happen to be a girl, the event is hushed up. No reference is ever made to the great misfortune which has befallen the expectant father. Friends are apprised of the result by advertisements carried through the streets. Yellow strips of paper are used if the child is a boy; *any other color* means a girl. Among the poorer classes girl babies are frequently drowned. Some estimate that in the Shanghai district one-third are so destroyed; the excuse given by the parents is that they cannot afford to rear a girl. Men monopolize most of the occupations here, and a woman can earn little or nothing; besides, a husband for every girl must be provided upon some terms. After a certain age an unmarried woman is regarded as disreputable, entailing something of disgrace upon her family; and so China lacks that most useful, and, as far as my experience goes, most unjustly maligned class—old maids.

A universal sameness prevails in China which soon becomes monotonous. One street looks precisely like another. If a traveller were set down in any city of China, he would be at a loss to tell where he was. It might be Shanghai, Canton, or Peking. There are the same rows of one-story, or, at most, one-and-a-half-story huts, without the slightest attempt at ornament or variety. There are no grand mansions scattered throughout the land, no city halls, colleges or commercial exchanges, as with us, but one dead flat level of low structures wherever you go. Probably the exactions to which wealth is subject here has much to do with this; all are concerned to hide their resources, but I am told the Chinese educated mind has really reached the stage in which ostentatious display is regarded with contempt. It seeks escape from ceremony and show, in sweet simplicity of living, as most truly great men have done and are doing more and more.

Life *"en grand seigneur"* has never been the foible

of the rich American, but as the seigneur is a species of recent growth and has not yet had time to blossom into flower and show us just to what his nature turns, we must watch his movements hereafter with interest. So far, he seems endued with quiet tastes, as far as personal parade is concerned. A few have built grand mansions, but still live plainly in the matter of retinue and ceremonial.

Even in England one notes nowadays a general expression of disappointment at the result of living up to one's rank, according to the old standard. It is not altogether from lack of means to maintain great style, although this is the real reason with the majority, perhaps, who have abandoned former habits. Another cause is operating, even with such as are wealthy : the squire or his lordship is not the all in all of his district any more; and he is educated now, in many cases, to enjoy intellectual pleasures, which he finds incompatible with so much society and numerous establishments with their endless staffs of servants to maintain. Many of the stately homes of England, therefore, are for rent, and their owners live more within themselves and in simpler manner than before.

———

SHANGHAI, Saturday, December 14.

We leave for Hong Kong, eight hundred miles south, by the mail steamer which sails at daylight. Our usual good fortune attends us. The monsoon blew us to port one night sooner than we expected. A night saved was quite an object, as the Geelong is a small craft, and her rocking means something. Vandy was very ill, but I managed to report regularly at table as usual. We slept on shore Tuesday night, and the morning revealed one of the prettiest places we have ever seen in the East. Hong Kong is an island about twenty-six miles in circumference, situated one mile from the mainland of China, and just at the mouth of the river leading to Canton. There is scarcely an acre of level ground upon it except one little spot which does duty as a race-course, and is not level either by any means. A narrow strip fronting the water is occupied by the city of Victoria, which extends about three miles, but back of this the ground rises rapidly, and houses cluster upon the steep sides of the mountain. Nevertheless, public gardens have been laid out with exquisite taste and skill upon the hillside, and excellent walks reach to the very top of the peak, more than eighteen hundred feet high. So closely does this crag overhang the town below that a stone could be dropped into the settlement from its crest.

It is the thing in Hong Kong to do the Peak, and we did it, but not in a manner very creditable to our staying powers, I fear. The fact is, we had been tossed for some days upon a small ship. It was exceedingly warm. We were very tired (conscience suggested another word for tired); in short, there were a dozen reasons—good, bad, and indifferent—why two strong, lusty fellows should, under the circumstances, be carried up instead of attacking the Peak on foot; and so each of us, in a sedan chair, borne by four strong coolies, managed to get to the top and enjoy the splendid view, coming down in the same novel manner. It was surprising, after we had returned, to find how decided a misunderstanding had arisen between us on the subject. I had not pressed walking up on Vandy's account, while he had only denied himself that wished-for pleasure in deference to my supposed inability. You see, had this point been made clearer before we started, we might have had the walk after all. As it is, the credit of both is fairly maintained, and I do think that neither of us regrets the unfortunate misunderstanding; one gets so lazy in these latitudes!

More than a hundred thousand Chinese have come from the main land to reside in Hong Kong and enjoy the benefits of British rule, and the population, which in 1841 was only five thousand, is now a hundred and forty thousand. So the good work of reforming China goes forward by the surest of all means, good example. It is at such points as Hong Kong—one of the keys of the world—that England does her real work and lifts up mankind.

———

Thursday, December 19.

We took the steamer for the Paris of the East, far-famed Canton, distant ninety-five miles. The steamer is just an American river boat, and we enjoyed the trip very highly. And here let me note two strange customs which prevail in China. First, your passage money generally embraces all the liquor, beer, or wine you choose to consume on the trip. Such was the case to-day, and passengers were free to call for anything they wished to drink at any time (champagne excepted). The other custom is universal. There is no coin in circulation but silver, and it is so heavy that Europeans have adopted the habit of carrying none, giving for any debt incurred I. O. U.'s, called "chits," which are sent in at the end of each month for payment; a vicious custom, which leads to deplorable excesses, especially in drinking and in gambling. Men drink and gamble more freely when immediate payment is not required, or when the chances of a lucky turn may recoup their losses; besides, many who have no means to pay incur debts. Indeed, so many cases of this kind have happened since "hard times set in" that I am encouraged to hope the end of "chits" approaches. The rule at the clubs now is that no chits can be given beyond a trifling amount each month, and that they must be promptly redeemed. Canton was reached by four in the afternoon, and such a swarm of small boats as surrounded us was never seen elsewhere. When we were a full mile from the wharf I saw the mass begin to stir, and such a stir! and almost all rowed by women, yelling and striving, and dashing one boat against another, in their efforts to be first. One of the most active scrambled up the guards and reached us on the upper deck almost before the boat had stopped, and secured us as her spoil. How she and a young girl handled our trunks, carrying them over intervening boats and then coming back for us, giving us her hand to convey us to her craft! No mistaking her business capacity, nor her ability to cope with the strongest and most active man and capture two passengers to his one. John is no match for a Canton boatwoman on water, whatever he may be on land.

CANTON, **Friday, December 20.**

We have just returned from our first stroll through the narrow, crowded alleys of Canton. Pictures and descriptions had prepared us for what we were to see, but, as is usual in the East, we knew nothing until we had seen for ourselves. In most cases the more one reads or hears about a certain locality the more confused he is when he visits it. He was a traveller who first said, " The eye and the ear are close together, but what a distance between hearing and seeing!" This recurs to me constantly. But to revert to Canton. We decided to walk instead of following the custom of Europeans, who generally take sedan chairs and dash through, seeing nothing in detail. We cross the river by one of the innumerable boats rowed by women, and are in the city. For five hours we are guided through streets varying from six to ten feet in width through one continuous mass of Chinamen. As for Chinawomen, they are rarely or never seen. A few men are in silks; numbers of coolies, with loads, are almost naked, but more, of a slightly higher order, are in rags; for the Chinese, unlike their scrupulously clean brethren of Japan, appear to pile on one tattered, greasy cloth rag over another until they are a bundle of filth, against which you fear at every step lest you may be pushed. The shops or booths on each side of the narrow streets are resplendent just now, preparatory to the New-Year celebrations, and those which make temple decorations a specialty are brilliant in the extreme. As every shop, house or boat contains an altar, which, as well as those in the public temples, must be freshly decorated at the beginning of every year, the extent of this trade is surprising, and all that tinsel can do with the most gorgeous coloring imaginable is seen in this branch to perfection. One thing appears very strange: even in the principal streets various manufactures are carried on, the workmen being so close that you can touch them from the pavement with your cane. We saw to-day glass-making in a space not more than fifteen feet square, iron-forging and shaping, cloth-weaving, the making of coffins (such massive affairs these are, too, in China!), of Joss-sticks and Joss-money, fire-crackers, and many other articles. The front part of the building is usually occupied by the shop for the sale of the product, the ornamental shrine serving as a kind of screen to shut off the manufacturing department; but by stepping behind you see crowds of almost nude workmen, hard at work, making by hand with the aid of the rudest appliances almost every article known. The wages of a tradesman—a carpenter, for instance—is fifteen cents per day; in addition the master has to give him three times per day his rice, etc., estimated to cost six to eight cents more. The workmen are fed by the employer, and allowed to sleep in and about the premises somewhere or somehow. We saw freely exposed for sale dogs, rats, and mice, all nicely dressed and hanging upon spits to tempt the hungry passers-by, while above a large pot from which the steam was issuing was a card, which, being translated by our guide, read, " A big black cat within; ready soon." The dogs which are eaten are fed especially for the purpose, and are hung up in state with labels setting forth their superior merits. As far as I should have known, they might have passed for delicious young roasting pigs, delicate enough in flavor to have satisfied gentle Elia himself.

Our guide, in answer to numerous questions upon the subject, informed us that some of his countrymen had acquired a taste for dogs, while others had succumbed to the sweeter attractions of cats; others again found rats their favorite morsel, but in all cases these penchants are indulged in on the sly. Upon no account would a Chinaman think of taking either of these peculiar delicacies home, for it appears that mesdames, much to their credit, have serious objections to their use. They draw the line here, and the husband must confine the indulgence of his uncanny longings to restaurants, and say nothing about it, or his lady friends might mark him as one of whom " 'twas said he ate strange flesh." Contrary to the statement of travellers, I find this food is not confined to the poorer classes. The price of it is about the same as that of pork, and far beyond that of hare or deer. How strange these people are! The price of a black dog or cat is fully double that of a white one, the superstition being that the former makes blood much faster than the other, while rats are supposed to make the hair grow.

We returned to our hotel in time for luncheon, and in the afternoon called upon Captain Lincoln, the United States Consul, to whom General Bailey had given us letters which secured us a cordial reception. The European settlement at Canton is very pretty, with its broad, well-shaded avenues, exquisite flower-garden, and lawn-tennis and croquet grounds. Its club-house is a gem, comprising a small theatre, billiard-room and bowling-alley—everything complete. The colonel took us for a stroll about the settlement, and pressed us to join a party he was just about taking over the river to visit the best flower-gardens of the city. We could not decline such a treat, and this gave us the pleasure of meeting Mrs. Lincoln, who is so well known in China as to be regarded somewhat in the light of an historical character. Her collection of teapots promises to render her famous. She boasts already of more than two hundred, no two alike in form, and the record grows day by day; and the melancholy feature is that there is no end for the passion save in death, a mania for "a bit of the blue" ranking first in the list of diseases for which *materia medica* boasts no antidote.

Almost everything seems to have been tried in China during its thousands of years of national life. We read for instance that in A.D. 841 the emperor, seeing the evils of monasteries and nunneries, suddenly closed them all and sent the inmates back to their families. So far, perhaps, so good; but he also shut up all the temples and told the priests to turn their faces in the direction from which they came. He was far too "thorough," and when the next emperor was so favored by heaven as to become the discoverer of a veritable bone of Buddha and brought it to the capital with many solemn ceremonies, the people were quite ready for the inevitable reaction, and Buddhism was again restored. This is a comparatively modern instance. Away back two hundred and more years B.C., we find the famous builder of the Great Wall attempting an impossible task with no better result. He was a great reformer—indeed the first universal emperor of all existing China, which was consolidated by his genius.

The privileged classes, of course, opposed his reforms and gave him much trouble by holding up to the admiration of the people the feudal times of the past, and extolling the heroes of those days to the disadvantage of those of the present. At last the emperor resolved to break with the past altogether, and ordered that all books should be burned except such as referred to his own reign, that all who even spoke of other books should be put to death; that those who spoke of the past as superior to the present should be put to death, and their relatives as well. Soon after this order, more than four hundred who had disobeyed it were ordered to be executed. Even the books of Confucius were not exempt; indeed these were chief offenders, for the sage was remarkable for such worship of the past as has scarcely a precedent in history.

Of course such an order could not be carried out. The condemned books were secreted and all the more venerated from the dangers which surrounded their possession. To-day we are thankful that so many books exist telling truthfully of the past—those good old times which were very bad times indeed. The history of the past should be studied carefully that we may learn not what to copy, but what to avoid. Let all the records be preserved.

I take it that to many blessings for which we have to thank the Heathen Chinee may be added our axiom: " Resistance to tyrants is obedience to God." The

Emperor of China is in theory the most absolute of rulers, and holds in his hands the power of life and death—" whom he wills he slays, and whom he wills he keeps alive." So runs the edict. It is the duty of the subject to render implicit obedience. But here follows another duty no less imperative: He is bound to resist the emperor's authority if he " ceases to be a minister of God for the good of his people." Confucius distinctly teaches " the sacred right of rebellion," and the next highest authority, Mencius, puts it in even stronger terms. This seems a striking anomaly, for the whole theory of government to-day, as thousands of years ago, is the patriarchal one: as the emperor is the Son of Heaven, so his people are the sons of the emperor, and he alone can intercede between his children and heaven. It is his prayers and sacrifices to which supreme importance is attached. Notwithstanding all this, as we have seen, the Chinaman believes it to be his duty to dethrone a bad emperor and even to put him to death. You see, my friends, a Chinese emperor can do wrong, which follows from his having power direct from heaven to do anything; therefore the right to decapitate him upon occasion must be reserved to the people. It is only in England that the doctrine that the king can do no wrong can safely be accepted. It is quite true there, for these Islanders have so managed matters as not to allow that ornamental appendage to do anything beyond opening fancy bazaars or laying foundation stones, where even an hereditary monarch cannot go very far astray.

On the 8th day of the 12th month, in the reign of Man-Ti, A.D. 593, occurred one of the most remarkable events in the history of our race. An edict was issued that the various texts then in circulation should be collected and engraved on wood, to be printed and published. Here began the art of printing, but it was not till a blacksmith named Pe-Ching, three or four hundred years later, invented movable types that the astounding possibilities of the invention were seen. Off hats to the memory of that learned blacksmith! Tall oaks from little acorns grow; but surely never before nor since has the world seen such stupendous results from so small a change as that of substituting little pieces of wood, each with one character upon it, for larger pieces which contained many. That blacksmith has revolutionized the world. I shall never pass one of the craft again without honoring him as distantly related to Pe-Ching by virtue of his calling. Vulcan has done much in the past in his smithy, forging the thunderbolts of war, but put all such weapons together and I will back the movable types of Pe-Ching for victory.

China carries the principle of home rule to a greater extent even than the United States do, for each province not only manages its own local affairs and levies its own taxes, but also supports its only army and navy. This would seem fatal to the organization of solid, vital forces; but as the Chinese have passed farther beyond the barbarous thirst for so-called "glory" (disgrace, rather) than western nations, it is not essential that either army or navy should be efficient. Indeed, the less so the better.

I trust, however, the Chinese cannot rob the Republic of the credit of having the poorest navy and smallest army among the nations, for this I consider perhaps the foremost evidence that America gives to the world that she is worthy to lead our race to nobler issues than those which have so largely occupied it in the past.

SATURDAY, December 21.

To-day has been devoted, like yesterday, to Canton sights; but as we had several distant places to visit, we took sedan chairs, and went shouting along, four coolies each, Indian file, through the town, forming quite a cavalcade, with our guide in front. It was the same interminable maze of narrow, crowded thoroughfares, crammed with human beings, that we had seen for the first time yesterday. A great commotion was seen ahead at one place, out of which emerged several men in crimson robes, bearing banners, clearing the way and shouting out the name and dignities of a mandarin who was approaching. An ornamented chair, borne aloft, came into view, on which his lordship, an official of the third or fourth button, sat in state, followed by two servants on ponies, the only species of horseflesh we have seen in Canton. It is with considerable difficulty that even these small animals get through, and their use is confined to escorting high officials.

At almost every corner we pass crowds of poor wretches gambling in various modes, from fantan down to dice and dominoes. Children participate, and stake their "cash" with the elders; indeed, a young Celestial rarely spends his stray coppers in candy without tossing with the stall-keeper, double or quits; the little scamps begin early, and at every counter we noticed the dice lying ready to facilitate the operation. Is it any wonder that the vice of gambling seems inherent in the Chinese character? We saw rather a funny illustration of this practice, at which we couldn't help laughing. A class of venders keep a large pot boiling on the pavement in some partially secluded place, in which is an assortment of odds and ends. Such a mess of tidbits—pieces of liver, chicken, kidneys, beef, almost every conceivable thing! These the owner stirs up, taking care, I thought, to bring the largest bits adroitly to the surface. You should see the longing faces of the hungry beggars around. One risks a cash (one-tenth of a cent), a rattle of the dice—the customer has won. The fork is handed to him, and he has two dabs in the pot. What a prize! Down go the *bonnes bouches* one after the other, and back goes the fork to the pot-boiler, who again uses it to stir up in the pot prizes to tempt the lucky owner of funds sufficient for the indulgence of this piece of extravagance. I really believe the poor, miserable, hungry wretches lounging around the pot derived satisfaction from the odor emitted. And as the lucky gamester gobbled his prizes, I imagined every one around involuntarily went through the motion of smacking his lips, as if he shared in the inward satisfaction of his lucky neighbor. Vandy almost overwhelmed one of these people by handing him a cash to try his fortune; but he thinks his man was too hungry to risk the dice, and took the sure thing. He probably considered one bite in the mouth worth two in the pot; but he wasn't a representative Chinaman by any means.

At one point our guide in advance called a halt, and upon our dismounting he led us into a walled enclosure, and startled us with the information that we were in the execution grounds. He pointed out spots still damp with the blood of criminals, several jars containing the heads of victims, the protruding hair matted with the lime used to decompose the flesh more rapidly, and a rude cross still remaining upon which a woman had recently been crucified and cut to pieces while alive. Her crime was the gravest known to Chinese law: she had murdered her husband. Poor wretch! probably he had not illy deserved his fate were the whole story known, for the provocation which would nerve a woman in China to rise against her husband and owner must be beyond human endurance. Instead of this spot being

set apart and shunned by man, woman and child, as
defiled by the horrors enacted within its walls, the area
was filled with large clay jars, used as stoves, the product
of a manufactory adjoining, set out there in rows to
dry. Men moved in and around them unconcernedly,
and at the entrance and within the enclosure there was
a temporary fantan gambling shop, composed of bamboo poles and mats, in full operation, surrounded by
crowds of people. Of a surety the Heathen Chinee is
peculiar. The grounds are of course cleared of everything upon " execution days," and I suppose the swarm-
ing masses of Canton see no reason why even this acre
of notorious ground should be permitted to lie useless
several days in succession. There is nothing which is,
not put to use in China.

Our next visit was more to our taste; it was to the
place of the literary examinations, which are held every
third year. Here the grounds are kept in good order,
and exclusively devoted to this noble use. It is well
known that each province in China has public examinations for its students. Those who are successful become
eligible for the higher examinations, which are held at
Canton and at two or three of the other great cities.
Candidates who pass at these are permitted to enter for
the final struggle at Peking, where success brings rank,
honor, and fortune. At Canton the ten acres of grounds
are covered with long rows of brick sheds, divided into
stalls about six by four feet, with neither door nor win-

8

dow, and open at the back; a narrow footway permits entrance, and a blank wall forms the front of the succeeding row, and so on. The stalls contain no furniture, but a board extending from the front, half the length of the stall, and working backward and forward in grooves in the wall, is used as a seat; a smaller one higher up at the foot of the stall makes a writing-table, and these combined made a bed. A small lamp is furnished, and the aspirant remains for three days and nights writing upon subjects given to him after he has entered the stall. No chance for cramming here. Out of ten thousand six hundred who competed last year, only eighty-two were found worthy to appear at Peking. I believe only a certain number can succeed throughout the whole Empire, and the standard is, therefore, kept very high.

Amid much which causes one to mourn for the backwardness of this country, here is the bright jewel in her crown. China is, as far as I know, the only nation which has advanced beyond the so-called heroic age when the soldier claims precedence. England and America must be content to claim that

> " Peace hath her victories
> No less renowned than war,"

while here the triumphs of peace are held in chief esteem. No general, no conqueror, be his victories what they may, can ever in China attain the highest rank.

That is held only by successful scholars who have shown the possession of literary talent. When the news reaches a town or village that a townsman has been victorious at Peking, a general rejoicing takes place, and triumphal arches are built in his honor to witness for centuries how deeply they appreciate the honor conferred upon the town by their illustrious fellow-citizen. Upon his return the whole population turns out to meet and welcome him, and his career inspires other young men to emulate his virtues. Henceforth his life is one of honor, for from this class the rulers of China are taken. These are the Mandarins, and there is no other aristocracy in China. Nor are his honors hereditary. His sons, if they would be ennobled, must outstrip their fellows in knowledge, as their father did before them. An aristocracy founded upon learning, and composed of those who know the most, is an institution with which we have no serious quarrel. It is claims from birth which make my blood boil. These are an insult to every commoner, and we must not rest until every trace of hereditary privilege is swept from the earth. Neither king, queen, prince, nor lord should live in our native isle to insult us if I had my way—and my way may come ere I depart if I get the three score and ten allotted to mortals by the psalmist.

Our trip to-day had another surprise for us. We were taken to the city court and prison. A poor naked wretch was on his knees as we entered, his back a mass of blood caused by the blows just inflicted with the bamboo which an officer, standing close behind, still held over the victim, ready to use again at a word from the judge. What a quivering, miserable spectacle the culprit was! As I write this I can see him tremble. His reputed crime was stealing, but he had denied it, and the judge, not getting satisfactory answers to his questions, had ordered the bamboo to be applied. Another poor soul sat under torture, laced by ropes against a large flat board in some diabolical manner so that his features were distorted by pain, while at a short distance from the door many hardened-looking criminals, all chained to large balls of iron, awaited trial and sentence. The most enlightened of the judges here still urge that it would be impossible to administer justice without torture or physical punishment in order to force replies from the accused. If you can compel a culprit to answer every question which a trained examiner is allowed to put, it is not difficult to convict the guilty. With us we forego that advantage by requiring no man to convict himself. Here he has to prove his innocence in a measure; at least he must tell a straight story; and this he would never do, it is said, in China, unless he were held in fear of bodily chastisement or torture. It is an effectual mode of getting answers, as I can testify. The judge asks a question which goes to the very root of the matter. The wretch hesitates an instant. I thought I could see from his supplicating gesture that he felt the true answer would expose his guilt. "Bamboo, attend— ready!" Another instant, and the blow descends, the trembling man stammers out his reply, and his sentence is pronounced. Another, who has been cleverly allowed to witness the manner in which recusant parties are dealt with, is dragged before the judge, his back bared, and he falls on his knees to make answer. No skilful lawyers here to defend and throw around the prisoner the safeguards of the law; but neither is there any upon the side of the prosecution. The accused has only to satisfy the judge by giving a true account of himself and his doings. I should say an innocent man would prefer this mode, a guilty one detest it; and this seems a strong argument in its favor.

My room fronts on the river, and is upon the second story of this strange little hotel. This gives me fine views of the unceasing traffic of the stream, but it is not without its disadvantages as a place of rest at night. The Chinese gods, or devils rather, have a strong fondness for fire-crackers, and these are set off at all hours of the night by the more devout of the boat-women right under my windows. I waken with a start every now and then, as an unusally large bunch is fired. It occurred to me last night that some of the extra fees bestowed upon our woman and her bright little sister may be responsible for part of this species of devotion. It is very likely that some part of their extra earnings is considered due to their gods. I write this at nine in the morning, and there are two boats busily engaged in their prayers just now, one battery of crackers responding to the other. One would almost think a naval war upon a small scale was raging. I must plead ignorance till now of this strange manner of propitiating the supernatural powers. If I ever read of it, it has passed away and been forgotten, like a thousand things one reads of. Another custom which interferes with slumber is the noise made by the night watchman, who walks backward and forward beating a tenor gong with a hard stick. One, two, three, slowly, followed by two quick taps, is the signal that all is well. Extraordinary precautions have to be taken in the cities against theft. Almost every block has its watchman, and gates short distances apart are shut at nine o'clock, after which only those known personally to him are allowed to pass. One provision struck me as putting an effectual check upon mischief of all kinds: no one is allowed to walk after night without carrying a lantern, and one found disregarding this law would be held " suspect." Our landlord told me that the watchman would be sternly dealt with if a robbery occurred, as he is held responsible for the safety of his block.

The boat population of Canton is famous as being something unique, but it exceeds all ideas I had formed of it. It is said that three hundred thousand people live in boats ranging from the size of a skiff to that of a yawl. I have seen a family of six huddled together in one of the former size, but these were the poorest of the poor. The usual passenger boat is twenty feet long by four and a half wide—the size of the hotel boats we use. We got into one this morning, and as the crackers were going off from numerous boats on all sides, our woman explained that the unusually vigorous fusilade was owing to this being " Joss day." "All people go Jossee Temple this day." "Do you go?" "No ; have got Jossee here on boatee." "Where? Show us." With that one of the girls at the stern pushed aside two small sliding-doors in the extreme end of the boat, and revealed a little shrine with a lamp ever burning, and Joss sticks in the incense bowl. The entire family burst into laughter at our surprise, evidently tickled with the idea that it was a decidedly cute thing to have their Joss cooped up " Jack-in-the-box" style. Yesterday the Emperor, at Peking, after fasting all the previous day, would ascend into the Temple of Heaven, accompanied by two thousand of his highest officials, and worship, while his subjects celebrate the event by this fire-cracker carnival.

I was curious to see how a small yawl could be the residence of a family, and examined several of them. The centre of the extreme stern is occupied by the Joss temple, on either side of which small dishes, cans, etc., are arranged; then comes an open space extending across the boat, about four feet long, over which is thrown a light board about six inches wide, upon which stands the woman who sculls and steers the craft. A permanent bamboo roof is built over about the next six feet of the boat, and around the walls are hung a few ornaments, generally old-fashioned plates and cheap prints from the English illustrated papers, while on a shelf are those indispensable articles, the smoking pipes of the family—large and curious affairs, with richly ornamented square brass bowls about four and one-half by two inches in size. A tiny china tea-set and various little "curios" are found in the best boats. The next portion, where passengers sit, has nicely cushioned seats running across the boat, and on each side as well, and is also covered by the roof. Next to the bow is a platform three feet deep, upon which stands the second woman, who rows or poles the boat, as may be necessary. Under her feet is the kitchen, and she has only to lift a board to show a small square covered with clay, upon which a fire can be built. Pots and pans are seen snugly stowed away around this, so that, by means of movable platforms, trap-doors, etc., the entire boat is rendered available to its very keel. At night, when the business of carrying passengers is over, all the boards are made into a fine flush deck, which is divided, in a very few minutes, into sleeping apartments by means of bamboo poles and mats; and so it comes to pass that what I was before disposed to believe almost impossible is accomplished with a degree of comfort quite surprising. These boat people live for less than ten cents a day. Rent there is none; food costs about five cents per day for each person; clothing does not cost two. From the child of eight to the great-grandmother, all do something. When not otherwise engaged, they sew, make Joss-sticks, slit bamboo, or do something or other, the baby being strapped on the mother's back that her capacity for work may not be interfered with; and her stepping backward and forward as she sculls must be a soothing lullaby, for we haven't heard a child crying yet in China. Upon such boats as I have here attempted to describe, and many far smaller and destitute of ornament, millions of the people of China live, move, and have their being. Children are born, old men die, upon them, and many thousands of their occupants have never slept a night upon shore.

I was surprised to hear that there is no theatre at Canton. The government had some time ago to prohibit night performances, as they were constantly the scenes of disorder. The only amusement is furnished upon large gayly decorated boats, where feasts are given, at which girls belonging to the boats appear and sing. We saw one of these, but it was a poor performance compared with our experience in Japan.

———

SUNDAY, December 22.

We allowed our guide to leave us for to-day, and strolled about alone. In the early part of our walk we heard music—a harmonium and a well-known old hymn tune—and on entering a building found Rev. Dr. Hopper preaching in Chinese. We had entered at the wrong door, and were among the women, who are separated from the men by a high, solid wall; but Mrs. Hopper rose and conducted us to the other side, and after service the Doctor came and greeted us cordially. We spent an hour in their house, and were surprised to hear that both were old Pittsburghers. There were at church that morning about thirty Chinamen, all of the poorer classes, principally servants and dependents of Europeans. In the afternoon we stumbled upon the large Catholic cathedral, which is now almost ready for use. It is a magnificent granite structure, three hundred feet long and eighty-eight feet wide. If anything can impress the Chinese mind it must be grand mass in such a temple, with its vaulted roof, stained windows, the swelling organ, and all the "pride, pomp, and circumstance" of Catholic worship. As we stood admiring, the saintly bishop approached and greeted us with exquisite grace. He could not speak English, but his French was the easiest to understand of any I ever listened to, and my little knowledge of the language enabled us to carry on an interesting conversation. When I told him I had been in St. Peter's at Rome, and had seen the Pope when the assembled thousands fell prostrate before him as he advanced up the aisle, carried upon his palanquin, he seemed much affected, and pressed us to visit his quarters, apologizing, as he showed us into a poor one-story building, for the poverty of his apartments, but adding that the true *prêtre Catholique* must needs dwell in poverty among the poor of the earth. I asked if he did not expect to return to France to die; but, laying his hand upon his heart, he answered that he must not allow himself to think of France, since it had pleased God to place him here. For thirty years he had labored among these people, and among them he must die; it was the will of God. There were only a table and a few chairs in this bishop's palace, not even a mat or carpet on the floor; but he ordered a servant to bring wine, of which he only tasted, while we drank "*sa santé.*" He subsequently took us to the orphanage, where we saw eighty boys being educated. About an equal number of little girls are in a separate building. If the Chinese are ever to be reformed, this is the way to do it—get control of the young, and teach them. As for the older generation, I fear it is too late to do much with it. There are in and around Canton about five thousand Chinese Catholics, mostly recruited, I understand, from among the young, taken by these sagacious workers into their schools and orphanages and other institutions, and educated as Christians from their youth up.

When I told the good Bishop we spent our summers at Cresson, very near Loretto, and often drove to Count Gallitzin's tomb, he grasped my hand and gave me his benediction.   Oh, blessed man! a grand Catholic, Father Gallitzin!

Every one has heard of the great wall of China, which stretches across the northern frontier from the sea to the westernmost province, a distance of twelve to fifteen hundred miles. It is fifteen to thirty feet high, with brick towers about forty feet high at intervals along the whole route. This gigantic work was begun in the third century before Christ by one of the greatest rulers of men the world has ever seen, the Emperor Che Hwang, who hoped that it would prove an insuperable barrier to the inroads of the Tartar hordes. But a still greater warrior than he, Genghis Khan, leader of the Mongols, showed in 1212 that it could be overcome. To this day the Chinese dynasty is Tartar, but the four hundred millions of people remain the same, having assimilated the foreign element. The Tartars are fast becoming Chinese, although a difference between the races is still clearly discernible. The Heathen Chinee changes not. The Jews and the Scotch are perhaps the races in Europe who preserve their types with the greatest tenacity, but compared with the Chinese they must be considered plasticity itself. Apart from their overwhelming numbers, which, being of one unvarying type throughout, constitute a mass upon which it is almost impossible to make much impression, one sees how climate and conditions of life in China operate to bring

to the Chinese type all foreign elements, and to retain
them there. Mrs. McC. has just been explaining to me
to-day how much trouble she has to keep her children,
for instance, from becoming young Celestials. They are
of pure Scotch parentage upon both sides, yet are constantly alarming their fond mother by developing tastes
wholly opposed to hers in food, dress, habits, manners,
language, everything. It is just the same in India:
the child of foreign parents there must be taken home
for years before he is seven or eight years old, or he becomes a Hindoo. We have just such differences at home
in a less degree. If two brothers leave Boston with
their families, one for New Orleans, another for Chicago, the differences in their grandchildren will be very
noticeable. The dream of some dreamer, that Englishmen can be grown in Hindostan or Australia, or even
in America (or in Ireland, for that matter), will be
rudely dispelled by a few weeks' residence in China or
India. The opening gowan transplanted from its Scot-
tish glen loses its modest charm and grows rank upon
the prairies of the West even in its second year. The
shamrock pines away in exile beyond the borders of its
own Emerald Isle. Man, the most delicately touched
of all to fine issues, is also the creature of his surroundings, even to a greater degree.

MONDAY, December 23.

Now for a frank confession. Like Mark Twain's
preacher with the car rhyme, "I have got it, got it

bad"—the "curio" malady in one of its most virulent types. Ever since we were dropped upon that uncanny land of Japan the symptoms of forthcoming disorder have not been wanting. I had to succumb occasionally, but rallied in time to preserve a tolerably clean bill of health. But if I have one weakness more than another, it is for the harmony of sweet sounds, and this the tempter knew right well. I met my fate in the famous Temple of Hoonan, in which is the most celebrated "gong" in China. I struck it, and listened. For more than one full minute, I believe, that bowl was a quivering mass of delicious sound. I thought it would never cease to vibrate. In Japan I had counted one that sounded fifty seconds, and its music rang in my ears for days. I asked "Ah-Cum" why the temple would not sell this gong and buy another far cheaper; for my opinion is, and my experience too, that there is nothing in China that money will not buy. However, this was an exception. Well, does the priest know where there are any temple gongs that can be bought? Yes, three that belonged to a temple destroyed by the rebels some years ago, and which were still in the hands of curio dealers. The address was obtained, and off we set to see them. I wish I could describe the places we visited in our search, the collections of curios we saw! No antiquary outside of Canton ever saw a tithe of the strange old things we examined. One might stumble upon a magic mirror, or an Aladdin's lamp, in some of these recesses, and scarcely wonder at it; all is so strange. But to the gongs. There is a little bit of history connected with one of them which is significant. We found we had to get from one of the priests a certain ticket before the article could be delivered. I thought a moment, and then:

"Oh, my prophetic soul, *my uncle!*"

It was even so. The priest had seen "his uncle," the curio dealer, and in some moment of want or dire temptation had pledged the gong of the temple for an advance. I got those which had a fairer record, and told our guide I wanted the other if he could get it; but this was impossible. Judge of my surprise, however, when the identical gong reached me at Hong Kong. I have it, with the pawn mark fortunately only partially obliterated, but so that the name of the guilty priest is no longer legible. Ah-Cum must have bargained for that ticket, the rogue, knowing I would pay the price; but really, had that gong reached me while in Canton, and had it been possible for me to return it to the right temple, I should not have thought, under the circumstances, of carrying it off. It seems as if I were in some degree a receiver of stolen goods; but as it only came to me after we had reached Hong Kong, and I knew neither priest nor temple, what could I do but decide to hold it myself until claimed by the rightful owners? Therefore, my friends, one and all of you, please take notice: whatever you may take a fancy to among my curios, don't ask me for that gong. I don't feel my title quite as clear as I could wish it, but I shall ease my conscience by agreeing with myself to act as temporary custodian—only that and nothing more. There are others beside temples' gongs, and I have to confess to several (genuine "sous chows," all of them). Indeed to-day was the curio day throughout. I cannot give even a partial record of the spoils as our procession marched hotelward in the evening. I burst into loud laughter as I eyed our party. In the advance was Ah-Cum, the guide, bearing aloft a fearful idol, "the ugliest I could find in China," this being Sister Lucy's characteristic commission; Vandy followed with his pockets stuffed with "birds'-nests," "Joss-sticks," "temple money," and etceteras too numerous to mention; then came two coolies, one after the other, naked as Adam after he donned the fig-leaf, carrying the gongs, while I brought up the rear with fans, vials, ivory carvings, and what-not. I cannot tell what part of this maze of shops we had been in, but the curio shops were so far from our hotel that not a man about them knew where it was, although there is but one European hotel in the city, consequently the coolies had to follow us. Vandy has just reported that it will take nine boxes to hold our spoils from here. I exclaim, Vandy, for goodness' sake let us get out of this immediately and try to regain our good, hard common sense, and be sound, practical men once

more. Give me a *Pittsburgh Commercial* and let me see
the price of pig metal, and what is said of steel rails and
coke and manufactured iron, and all the rest of it ; and
that monthly report of the Lucy Furnaces and of
the Edgar Thomson, both the largest upon record.
Thanks ! Ah ! now I feel better. How is it with thee,
my friend ? Fortunately Vandy felt the necessity for
keeping an eye upon me, and he never was in such danger himself. But if any one can pass through Canton
and escape a touch of the Toodleian malady, which
prompts one to buy everything one sees, I warrant him
sound to the core.

———

HONG KONG, Christmas Eve.

We returned this afternoon from Canton. After retiring I heard a well-known sound—the ubiquitous mos-
quito. It was rather odd to be compelled to rise and
ring for our " boy " to put up mosquito-bars on Christmas evening, but it had to be done. We talked till late
of home, and speculated upon what our friends would
all be about away up there almost above our heads—
" topside," as John Chinaman always expresses it. So
far we have only one paper from home ; no letters,
these having been missed at Shanghai. The news of the
triumph of hard money views rejoiced us greatly, as
proving once more that in grave emergencies the good
sense of the people of America can always be depended
upon. One has only to visit the East to see what evils
the silver basis entails upon a nation.

The economy practised in China is striking. A sweet potato is sold in halves, or even in quarters, if required; ferriage across the river in a boat—a stream as wide as the Ohio at Pittsburgh—costs one-fifth of a cent, and you can engage an entire boat for yourself for a cent, if you wish to be extravagant; poultry is sold by the piece, as we sell a sheep, the wings, breast, legs, all having their price, and even the very feet of a chicken being sold for soup. Common iron nails are laid out in lots of six each; these have been used and used again, no one knows how often; we see the people at work straightening old nails at every turn. You can buy one-tenth of a cent's worth (1 cash) of either fish, soup, or rice. Verily things are down to a fine point here!

In one of our strolls we came upon a string of ten blind beggars wandering through the narrow, crowded street, the hands of each upon the shoulders of the one in advance, the leader beating with his cane upon the stone pavement, and all beseeching alms. It was a strange sight. The Chinese Government gives to every blind person a small monthly pittance, and well-dressed passers, I observed, generally bestowed a cash upon the gang.

I have not said much about the temples of Canton or of China, as they are poor affairs compared with those of Japan; besides, one becomes sated with temples which are for the most part copies of one another; the pagodas are much more picturesque at a distance than when closely inspected. The Chinese actually prefer all their places to smack of age, and repair them reluctantly, so that all have a dilapidated air, which gives a very unfavorable impression to a stranger. At best, China has nothing whatever to boast of in the way of architecture. We did not see a structure of any kind which would attract a moment's notice, a few pagodas and temples, perhaps, excepted ; but even these are poor and mean affairs.

The only temple worthy of mention I saw in any part of China is that of the Sages. In it we were shown tolerably good busts of five hundred of the most famous characters known to Chinese history—all the writers, statesmen, and rulers who have distinguished themselves for thousands of years. Among them, curiously enough, Marco Polo has by some means found a place. Compared with the hideous monsters worshipped in other temples, I regarded this deification of the illustrious dead with sincere satisfaction. No man can erect a house superior to what his rank or station in life justifies. A public officer prescribes the limit of expenditure, after investigating the affairs of the intending builder, as every one in China tries to conceal his wealth, fearing unjust exactions by the State. It is easy to see why no palaces are forthcoming. This is not " liberty ;" but I suspect several of my friends who have erected palatial structures of late years have seen reason to wish that such a safeguard had existed when they began to build.

Christmas Day.

Yesterday's papers announced that the Hallelujah Chorus was to be performed in the English Cathedral this morning at eight o'clock. I had been so long out of the region of music that I rose early and went to church. The Japanese and Chinese music grated so on my ears, I longed to hear an organ once more. I enjoyed the service very much. The music was well performed, and as for the sermon—I had to be back for breakfast, you know. It was specially pleasing to see at church the detachment of British soldiers, the more so as they were Highlanders. My heart will warm to the tartan. One strange feature I shall not soon forget. Several soldiers, in their scarlet uniforms, sang in the choir. I scarcely ever see soldiers without being saddened by the thought that the civilization of the race is yet little better than a name when so much must still be done to teach millions of men the surest way to destroy their fellows; but I take hope from this omen—these mighty men of war engaged this morning chanting the seraphic strains which proclaim the coming of the better day when there shall reign "on earth peace, good-will toward men."

Whatever old China may be doing, young China is progressing, for I saw in the park this morning several youthful Celestials, with their pigtails securely tied and out of the way, hard at cricket and baseball. Nor were they "duffers" either, although our wee Willie and his nine could no doubt, in the way of a "friendly" inning or two, show the lads a sweet thing, especially in the "underthrow," for which my little nephew, I hear, is famous.

We are all creatures of prejudice, of course, but I could not help being somewhat shocked on Sunday, as I strolled about the Cathedral, to see some thirty odd sedan chairs on the one side, and I suppose as many on the other, each with two, three, and some with four coolies in gorgeous liveries in attendance, all waiting the closing of prayers, lying in the shade, and some of them improving the opportunity to enjoy a quiet gamble with dice this fine Sunday morning. It did not seem to me to be quite consistent for some of my Scotch friends who stand so stoutly for Sabbath observance to keep so many human beings on duty, say three for one who worshipped, just to save them from walking a few short squares to and from church, for the town is small and compact. But custom has much to do with one's prejudices, for, after all, how is this worse than to roll in one's carriage to our Fifth Avenue temples? Yet this never struck me as so much out of the way before, and I think, unless the future Mrs. C. seriously objects, we shall walk to church as a rule— when we go. Really, three men kept at work that one may pray seems just a shade out of proportion.

I astonished Vandy this morning by getting up early; but I did not care to explain the reason for this phenomenon, which was that I had to catch the Canton boat to send a note back to Ah-Cum asking him to get me certain additional curios after all. While at Canton I had manfully resisted the temptation, but the thought of leaving China without the treasures proved overwhelming, and now my only fear is lest Ah-Cum should fail me. I confessed to Vandy, after we had had a glass of good wine at tiffin, and I shall not soon forget his quiet smile. "You've got it bad, haven't you?" 'Twas all he said, but you should have heard the touch of infinite pity in his tone. Yes, I have got it bad, I know, but to-morrow we shall escape from this old curiosity shop forever.

The fire-bell rang just after we retired, and from eleven o'clock until now (two this afternoon—fifteen hours) a disastrous conflagration has raged, often threatening to consume the entire settlement; indeed, nothing could have saved it but the splendid conduct of the 74th Highlanders. They were everywhere, and fought the fire the whole night long. The singers of the morning were the intrepid firemen of that tempestuous night. It was only by blowing up row after row of buildings that the flames were confined to one district. I saw the brave fellows march into the buildings upon the edge of the swirling flames to lay the fuse. A moment after their return the bugle would sound; then came the explosion, and the men were off to another building to repeat the work. All was done by bugle call, with military precision. Ten thousand times more " glory " in this march to save than in all the charge at Balaklava. Had equal pluck been shown on the field of battle, the flag of that splendid regiment would have blazoned with another war-cry. Let them place this record on their banners, instead of the name of a city destroyed: December 25th, 1878. Hong Kong *Saved!* They have no prouder triumph to commemorate, even in their glorious history.

I have not yet mentioned that slavery, in its mildest form, exists in China; but the children of a slave are free, and custom, which is all-powerful there, requires a master to give up his servant if the latter can repay the amount originally paid for him; and those who own a woman-servant are expected to provide a husband for her when she becomes of age. The purchase of boys and girls is, as a rule, confined to those who wish in this way to be provided with servants who shall become part of the household and can be relied upon. In no case can a master or mistress require a slave to engage in any disreputable calling unless the purpose for which the sale is made is clearly set forth, in which event the cost is fully doubled. Without special provisions in the bill of sale, it is understood that the servant is to perform a servant's ordinary duties and to be fairly treated, and to be required to do no wrong thing.

The firing of firecrackers caused me to speak to our

boatman one day, as I was annoyed by the noise, having always had a dislike for sudden explosions. "Why don't you worship something good and beautiful," I said; "some god that would detest such things as fire-crackers?" "So we do," said he, "in our hearts, but this is not worship; it is sacrifice to the bad gods, so they will be pleased and do one no harm." "But won't the good god be displeased and do you harm?" "No, the good god would never harm any one." His words were, as near as I can recollect them, "He no do badee; no can; always likee he; much goodee; by-by kill bad Jossee may be;" and so they go, good lord, good devil; no saying into whose hands one may fall, as the sailor had it. I gave it up, as the business woman came on board and took command, the husband going off to his work elsewhere. This woman Susan—Black-eyed Susan, as we have dubbed her—and her bright young sister-in-law continue to interest us more and more, they are such active, intelligent women. The girl is orna-mented with bangles and heavy anklets, and her ear-rings are of blue-bird feathers; her hair is banged, and everything about her evinces the care of really good, respectable people. I told Susan if I were a boatman I should try hard to save money enough to buy her sister-in-law, and asked her price. "No sellee you; sellee goodee Chinaman two hundred dollars." This was said as a great boast, as the ordinary price for one in her station is only ninety dollars. Our guide turned up his lip in scorn and whispered to me, "She talkee with mouthee too muchee ; ninety dollar plenty." Perhaps he had his eye upon the maid for his son. If so, I put in a good word for her, telling him I was reputed one of the best judges of young ladies in America, that I could tell their qualities at a glance, and that it was certain she would make an excellent wife ; and, what I thought would weigh as much with him, I added that for a business woman who could please travellers and get lots of money I did not believe she had her equal in Canton. One always likes to help on a match when he can, and something may come of this ; who knows?

I wish to bear my testimony to the grand work which is going forward at various places in China by means of the medical departments of missions. There are four teen hospitals of this kind in the country, and patients from all parts flock to them. In diseases of the eye unusual success seems to have been achieved, and stories are told of mandarins almost blind who have been restored to sight ; and in dealing with cutaneous disorders, which are very common, the doctors have also done wonders. A small mission hospital established in the Island of Formosa only a few years ago has already treated ten thousand patients, and I am informed that the Canton establishment numbers its beneficiaries by the hundred thousand. Whatever objection the people make to missionaries, doctors are ever welcome, and regarded as benefactors. Nor must we forget that the entire credit of this indisputably grand work is wholly due to those who consider it a sacred duty to endeavor to force their religious views upon the consideration of the Chinese. One can hardly find terms strong enough to speak fitly of the good missions are performing in this department of their labors; and while upon this subject we should remember that it is also to missionaries alone we owe almost all we know of China and its literature. Even Confucius was given to the world in English by a missionary. I take special pleasure in saying all I justly can for those who are so universally decried throughout the East. With scarcely an exception—indeed I do not remember one—every European or American engaged in the East speaks disparagingly of missionaries and their labors. I believe, myself, that trying to force religious views upon those who only tolerate them because the cannon stands behind ready to support the preaching is not the better way, and that many more converts would be made by " the word spoken in season " by ministers of the European congregations now scattered throughout the East, and by doctors and others with whom the natives are daily brought in contact, if the paid propaganda were withdrawn; but this should not prevent us from crediting the missionaries with the collateral advantages which are now flowing from another branch of their efforts. They are on the right track now; the M.D. is the best pioneer of the D.D. There is another powerful lever at

work in the *Herald*, a weekly paper published in
Shanghai and distributed throughout the Empire. It is
obtaining an immense circulation. It gives each week
an epitome of the most important events occurring in
every country, and America, I saw, headed the list. A
Mr. Allen, formerly connected with missions, is the pub-
lisher, and he is probably doing more to revolutionize
China than all others combined.

China, as everybody knows, grows a great deal of
tea, but few are aware how great a proportion of this
indispensable article she produces, and how much of it
she uses herself. Here are the figures I see printed:
Total production of the world, 1,300,000 net tons;
China's portion, 1,150,000 tons, being about nine times
more than all the world beside. But what is more
wonderful is that China uses 1,000,000 tons per annum,
and exports only 150,000 tons. But every one in
China, upon all occasions, partakes of the cup which
cheers and does not inebriate. Neither sugar nor
cream is used in it ; a little tea is placed in the cup and
boiling water poured over it and it is drunk immediately.
The strength of the tea is drawn in a few moments
after the water is poured upon it. The coloring matter
leaves it later. It is therefore a great mistake to use a
teapot and allow tea to remain in it, and equally to use
either sugar or cream—at least such is the verdict of
those here who should know best. We quite agreed
with them, and recommend our readers to try the

Chinese plan, always provided they are so fortunate as to have a good sound article of pleasant flavor. With most of the tea found in England, and especially so with that generally used in America, the sugar and cream are no doubt necessary to drown the "twang." A Chinaman would put this practice on a par with putting sugar in Chateau Lafitte. Tea is the wine of the Celestial. A mandarin will "talk" it to you as a gourmet talks wine with us; dilate upon its quality and flavor, for the grades are innumerable, and taste and sip and sip and taste as your winebibber does—and smack his lips too. We are told of teas so delicate in flavor that fifty miles of transportation spoils them.

It is popularly supposed that a small-footed woman must be one of rank, but this is an error. It is a matter of family ambition, even among the poor, to have in the family at least one such deformity. Gentlemen marry only small-footed women, and their child might make a good match. If large-footed, this would be impossible; but such hopes are sometimes doomed to disappointment, or after marriage reverses may ensue; and so it happens that many small feet stamp about in poverty and try to eke out a living under disadvantages from which their less genteel neighbors are free. The most remarkable feature in the streets is the total absence of women of any class except such as drudge alongside of men, and even these are not numerous, for man appears to monopolize most of the work, at least in the cities.

Occasionally we pass a sedan chair, or one passes us, closely covered up, which no doubt contains a lady of position compelled to visit some temple or relative; but I do not recall seeing in China any woman in a costume above that of the working classes, so jealously do Chinamen sentence their ladies to seclusion. A curious illustration of this occurred on our passage out. On our ship was one of the leading Chinese merchants of San Francisco with his wife. Rather than have her seen, even among the few cabin passengers, he engaged a portion of the steerage, had it closely boarded up and confined her in it, and she was never seen by any of us during the entire voyage. He and she took their meals together in the box. It was said that now and then at night she was carried secretly on deck for a breath of air; of course with her small feet she could not walk.

The steerage had to be fumigated at intervals and every soul was ordered on deck before the process began. This necessity had evidently not been taken into account by the exclusives, and much difficulty did our good doctor encounter with them. The husband declared that rather than be exposed to the gaze of the crowd, his wife would run the risk of being fumigated to death. The operation was postponed until a small cabin could be provided and the veiled beauty taken secretly to it.

A Chinese woman in China would hold it disgraceful

to expose her face to a strange man. Queen Victoria, sober, sage matron and pink of propriety as she is reputed, would not consider a lady properly dressed for her levee—where the more strange men to gaze the better—who did not expose her face and neck and shoulders to full view. Education, my boy, education! all things right and all things wrong within a very wide range of affairs. Chinese women pinch the feet, ours pinch the waist, and each pities the other for their woful lack of knowledge and their wickedness in marring God's image—and for their bad taste, which is, I fear, equally heinous to the female mind.

Our visit to the Celestial Empire is now at an end. We sail at noon by the French mail steamer Pie Ho for Singapore, fourteen hundred miles south. The more we see of China the greater it grows. A country much larger than the United States, with eight times the population, and not one mile of telegraph or railroad in it, in many districts not even one mile of public road broad enough for anything wider than a wheelbarrow— and yet a reading and writing people, a race of acknowledged mental power, with a form of settled government the oldest in the world—how inconsistent all this seems to us! But the reason for this paradoxical condition of affairs is, I think, that the unequalled resources of the country, which give to the people every necessary of life and almost every luxury, encouraged them in early days to eschew intercourse with the poorer lands around them, and then their superiority as a race to all their neighbors led them quite justifiably to conclude that all beyond were outside barbarians. They rested content with the advanced position attained, and as each successive generation copied the past, change became foreign to their whole nature, and in this path they have stubbornly persisted until the once inferior races of the West have far outstripped them. Among these outside barbarians must be ranked our noble selves, for it isn't one thousand years, let alone two, since our ancestors were running about dressed in skins and eating raw flesh—perhaps eating each other, as some allege—as ignorant of their A B C's as of the theory of evolution or the nebular hypothesis, when these Chinese were printing books and sailing ships by the compass. If my English readers will not be too greatly startled at the illustration, I will suggest that the conduct of China and its results suggest a danger for them which their statesmen should not be slow to perceive and remedy. England once stood as much in advance of other Western nations as China did in comparison with other lands, and she has apparently rested till now with equal complacency in the belief of her superiority. It is fast passing away. The English-speaking race throughout the world no longer looks to the parent land for political guidance, for instance, where Britain once reigned supreme. What English-speaking community would now study her antiquated political devices, her throne, her church and state, her primogeniture and entail, her hereditary chamber, unequal representation, or lack of representation rather, except that they might surely learn how to avoid them! Over the day when all English-speaking people turned instinctively to my native land for political example "Ichabod" must be written. They now look elsewhere, follow other ideals, and have adopted other ideas of government and the rights of man.

It is not too late yet, however, for England to regain her proper place in the race if she will only wake up, rub her dear old eyes, and see what the youngsters are about. "There is life in the old dog yet." The world is not done with the glorious little island, nor the island done with the world either. But no nation can indulge in a very long sleep in these days of progress the world over. England must remember,

> " *To have done*, is to hang
> Quite out of fashion, like a rusty mail
> In monumental mockery."

Recent events have undoubtedly awakened the foremost minds of China to the fact that they have been asleep, not twenty years only like our Rip, but twenty generations. They have recently begun to build steamships, a line of telegraph is authorized, postage stamps are being printed, and, best of all, for our comfort, at the principal cities there is generally at least one dealer who adheres to fixed prices for his goods. A daily paper is now published in Chinese at Shanghai, and the English school there is well patronized. All these things convince me that at last Western civilization is making an impression. The inert mass begins to move, and China will march forward ere long. The most convincing proof of this is found, perhaps, in the fact that the government appropriated in 1872 nearly two millions of dollars to maintain a hundred and fifty students in the United States. These are to be educated in our colleges and afterward employed officially at home. No action could prove more conclusively that China is at last awakening from her long centuries of repose.

But without railroads the material resources of the country can never be thoroughly developed. I fear this will be among the last features of our civilization which China will adopt, although the most important for her progress, because, as before mentioned, a railway cannot be built without desecrating graves by the thousand, and this every true Chinaman would view with horror. Our guide, although a remarkably intelligent man, and favorable to improvements of all kinds, took his stand here, inflexibly opposing the introduction of railways. No matter what material advantages might accrue, nor how much money he might be offered, no earthly consideration would induce him to disturb his ancestors, who have lain in one place in uninterrupted succession for nearly seven hundred years. If my friends Messrs. Garrison, Field and Pullman, who have so skilfully managed to give us elevated railroads without disturbing proprietary rights below, wish to enhance their fame, let them ask a concession in the Celestial Empire for railroads "topside," guaranteed to dodge every grave, and I do not doubt their success. Such inborn superstition as is here depicted dies hard, but it must pass away with the spread of knowledge; it will, however, take time. Nevertheless, China has a great future before it, as it has had a great past, and instead of having passed her climacteric, I predict that she is destined to reach a position of paramount importance in the Eastern world.

———

TUESDAY, December 26.

The Pie Ho is a magnificent ship, and we are delighted at getting under the auspices of a French cook once more, after the experiences we have had in Chinese cookery. No doubt about the preëminence of the French in regard to human food. Whoever sends the raw material, the French send the cooks. The *table d'hôte*, now common in England at the hotels, and the French service found in private houses, all so very different from the practice even since I began to revisit England, show how rapidly the world is bowing to the French cuisine.

We are scudding along before the monsoon, the

temperature that of June, an agreeable change from Hong Kong, where the nights have been chilly. We are out of the region of cold weather now for the remainder of our travels. We reached Saigon, the capital of the French settlement in Cochin China, at six this morning, after sailing forty miles up a branch of the Cambodia. Lower Cochin China belongs to France, and is under the rule of a colonial governor, French troops being scattered through the provinces. It is a low-lying district, celebrated only for growing more rice than any other part of the world. Our ship took on large quantities of it for France, but this is exceptional, the scarcity of freights being everywhere so great that steamers are glad to get anything to carry. The Saigonites are the lowest specimens of humanity we have yet seen—miserable, sickly-looking creatures, and without the faintest regard for cleanliness. Their long, coarse black hair hangs over their shoulders in thick, tangled masses which apparently have never known a comb. Every one chews the betel-nut without intermission, young and old alike, and this so discolors the teeth and mouth as to render them extremely disgusting. We drove about the town for a few hours, but it was so hot we were compelled to return to the ship. This is the God-forsaken-looking region about which France is now disputing with China. I cannot but wish that every deputy had been with me during the few days of my visit, that he might see what kind of a land and what sort of human beings his country expected to derive credit from by superintending.

What I have said previous to the foregoing paragraph was written on the spot, and therefore I cannot be accused of being prejudiced by the recent action of France, which has caused me, as its well-wisher, much sincere regret. Any power acquired by France over this portion of the world can be but illusory—wholly so. The importance even of Saigon is so small that it offers no inducement to any of the regular steamers to call as they pass. The French line alone visits it under a subvention from the home government. A few poor French people manage to exist after a fashion by trading with the ignorant natives, and a few soldiers and a ship-of-war give some semblance of French authority. But just as certain as the sun shines, should any considerable commerce arise in Cochin China, the English will absorb nine-tenths of it, and this by a law from which there is no escape.

When the French people forced the government to withdraw from Egypt they gave us reason to hope that Herbert Spencer's law, which creates pacific principles in proportion that power is held by the masses, had received a significant vindication. Let us hope the republican element will ere long put its veto upon foolish interference in Tonquin.

The night we spent at Saigon the French governor gave a grand ball, five hundred invitations; but out of all this number how many ladies, think you? Society here musters but thirty-five, mammas and grandmammas included, and only three young ladies. Think of it, ye belles of Cresson, Newport and Saratoga (Cresson first, Mr. Printer, is quite correct)! fifteen officers in dazzling uniforms for every lady!

We have on board several English merchants and one American, who are taking a run home for a visit. The latter regrets that his countrymen should be induced to drink green tea abominations, and I console him by stating that a reform is surely near at hand. These gentlemen agree that the American cotton goods are taking the market and driving the adulterated English goods out. The trade is increasing so fast that it was welcome intelligence for them to be advised by the last mail that another large mill in Massachusetts was being altered to make exclusively Chinese goods. I congratulate my friend Edward Atkinson upon this result. But is this new business to be permanent? I think not. The day is far distant, I hope, when either labor or capital in America will have to be content with the return obtained in a populous country like Britain; and unless we have superior natural advantages we cannot hope to compete with her. In cotton manufacture for the East we have not any advantage, as I find that the cheapest way of reaching China from New York is to ship *via* London. England can bring the raw cotton from New Orleans or New York, and send the manufactured goods to market for certainly not more than the cost of transportation from the American mills to market, and therefore England can retain that trade whenever she adopts the latest improvements in mode of manufacture; and this she is as certain to do as the sun shines, and probably to improve upon them.

WEDNESDAY, January 1, 1879.

The clock strikes twelve. Good-bye, 1878; and you, 1879, all hail! Be as kind to us as the departed, and we shall in turn bless your memory. This midnight hour of all the hours of the year is reputed the best for framing good resolutions, but somehow those I have tried at this season hitherto have not been exceptionally fortunate in bearing good fruit. However, I have never "resolved" on a New-Year's night before while suffering from heat and mosquitoes. I conclude to hazard one, so here goes antipodal resolution No. 1. See what you are good for. I record it that it may be the more deeply impressed upon my mind, and, if a failure, that it may in print sternly stare me in the face, and not "down at my bidding."

To-day we make our first acquaintance with punkas. They extend throughout the cabin, ominous of hot weather, which I detest; Vandy, on the other hand, revels in it, and it is his turn now. Vandy handed me to-day a string of Cambodia money, sixty pieces, which cost only two cents, showing to what fractions they reduce exchanges in Cochin China. I have been careful to collect coins in every place visited. Sock No. 1 is now full, and I have had to start bag No. 2. I have some rare specimens; of Japan the set is complete, from the gold cobang, worth $115, oblong, five inches long by about three wide, down to the smallest copper piece. I have some Chinese coins shaped like a St. Andrew's cross, dating before Christ. The mania for coin collecting is another inherent tendency the presence of which has probably never been suspected in my disposition. But collecting the coin of the realm, when one thinks of it, isn't at all foreign to my tastes. The form of manifestation is different, that's all—old coin for new—the "ruling love," to use a Swedenborgianism, being the same; and the ruling love must be acted out, so Aunt tells me, even in heaven. "Oh!" said L., when she heard this, " I wonder what they'll get for Mr. —— to do in the other world ; there are no dollars and cents there ; but there will be the *golden harps* for him to trim and weigh." So he would still handle the siller, and be in his element. Some time afterward, when this was recalled to L., she declared that it was impossible that she could have said it. "Mr. —— trim and weigh ! He would never be satisfied unless he were *boiling it down solid.*"

SINGAPORE, Saturday, January 4.

We reached Singapore at dusk. The drive through the town was a curious one. Nowhere else can such a

mixture of races be seen, and each nationality was enjoying itself in its own peculiar fashion—all except the
Chinese, who were, as usual, hard at work in their little
dens. No recreation for this people. Work, work,
work! They never play, never smile, but plod away,
from early morning until late at night. The Chinaman's
objection to giving his creditor in New York a note was
because it "walkee, walkee alle timee; walkee, walkee,
no sleepee." They seem to me to emulate these objectionable obligations.

We saw in Singapore our first lot of Hindoos,
moving about the streets like ghosts, wrapped in webs
of thin white cotton cloth, which scissors, needle, or
thread have never defiled. The cloth must remain just
as it came from the loom; no hat, no shoes, their foreheads chalked, or painted in red with the stamp of the
god they worship and the caste to which they belong.
They are a small, slight race, with fine, delicate
features.

I went out for a stroll before retiring, and hearing a
great noise up the street, followed and came up with a
Hindoo procession. The god was being paraded
through the Hindoo portion of the town amid the beating of drums and blowing of squeaking trumpets. The
idol was seated in a finely decorated temple upon wheels,
drawn by devotees, many of whom danced wildly
around, while others bore torches aloft, making altogether a very gorgeous display. Priests stood at each side

performing mysterious rites as the cortege proceeded. It was my first sight of an idolatrous procession, and it made a deep impression upon me, carrying me back to Sunday-school days, and the terrible car of Juggernaut and all its horrors.

I have had many experiences in beds, from the generous feather cover of the Germans to the canopy of state couch of England, but to-night my couch was minus covering of any kind. Calling to Vandy, I found he was in the same predicament. Each had instead a long, stiff bolster lying lengthwise in the middle of the mattress, the use of which neither of us could make out. We soon discovered that there was no need of covering at the Equator; but this bolster must have some use, if we could only find it. Upon inquiring next day we ascertained that it is composed of a kind of pith which has the property of keeping cool in the hottest weather, and that it is the greatest relief at night to cultivate the closest possible acquaintance with this strange bed-fellow; in fact, in Singapore, " no family should be without it."

The island of Singapore, which is included in the British Straits Settlements, is nearly seventy miles in circumference, with a population of about one hundred thousand, one-half of which is Chinese, the remainder Malays, Klings, Javanese, Hindoos, and every other Eastern race under the sun, I believe, and a few Europeans. Here the "survival of the fittest" is being fought out under the protection of the British flag, which insures peace and order wherever it floats. In this struggle we have no hesitation in backing the Heathen Chinee against the field. Permanent occupation by any Western race is of course out of the question. An Englishman would inevitably cease to be an Englishman in a few, a very few, generations, and it is therefore only a question of time when the Chinese will drive every other race to the wall. No race can possibly stand against them anywhere in the East.

On Sunday, Major Studer, United States Consul, and his accomplished daughter, drove us to the house and gardens of the leading Chinese merchant of this region, Mr. Wampoo, who received and entertained us with great cordiality. His residence is extensive and filled in every part with curios; but his gardens are most celebrated, and far surpass anything of the kind we have yet seen. His collection of Victoria Regia plants is said to be the best in the world. Unfortunately none were in bloom, but a flower was due, I understood, in about ten years! The kind old gentleman invited us back to see it, and we accepted; but since writing this we have heard, alas! that he has ceased to play his part upon earth.

The newspapers here sometimes give strange local items. Here is one from yesterday's *Times:*

"Tigers must be increasing on the island ; a fine big male one was caught in a pit on Christmas eve at the water-works."

The fellow was probably on the track of a Christmas dinner, and ventured to the very suburbs of the town.

We were driven one day, by the major and Miss Studer, some ten or twelve miles in the interior, passing through groves of cocoa and betel-nut trees, both in full bearing, to a tapioca plantation, where we saw many trees and plants new to us—the fan and sago palms and many other varieties, bananas, nutmeg trees, bread fruit, durion, gutta-percha trees and others. We also saw the indigo plant under cultivation, and passed through fields of the sensitive plant as we walked about, while pine-apples were everywhere. We are in a new world of vegetation here, within a degree of the Equator; but, rich as it is, there is still a feeling of disappointment because it is all green—no bright hues, no coloring, such as gives Florida its charm, or lends to an American forest in autumn its unrivalled glory! It is always summer, and the moisture of the tropics keeps everything green. There is another cause of disappointment to one accustomed to the primeval forest and its majestic trees. These monarchs cannot develop themselves in the tropics, and in their stead we have only underbrush, the "jungle" of the tiger, which does not at all come up to one's expectations.

About one thousand men and women are employed upon this tapioca plantation. Married Hindoos get twenty cents per day, but the greater number are Javanese unmarried men, who get only sixteen cents;

both find themselves. The Javanese are Mohammedans from Java *en route* to Mecca as a religious duty.
They come here and work and save for two years to
get sufficient to pay their passage and return to this
point, when they work a year more for funds to carry
them home. How vital is the creed which brings its
adherents to such sacrifice! This drive gave us an
excellent opportunity of seeing just how the people live
in the country. Dress is confined to the rag worn about
the loins, except that the women wear in addition a small
cloth over their shoulders. The children wear nothing
whatever, but we saw none that were not ornamented
by cheap jewelry in the most extraordinary manner.

The subject of clothes, as we all know from the
days of "Sartor Resartus," lies very closely at the
roots of civilization. I think every thoughtful person
must admit that here the Heathen Chinee shows
that he has reached the best solution of that annoying
question. The every-day dress of the Chinaman
is to-day just what it was thousands of years ago.
As there is no going out or coming in of fashion,
he wears his clothes till they can be worn no longer.
The heavy overcoats which distress Americans and are
a weight even to the Englishman, our celestial friend
escapes by having three or four light coats all of one
pattern and weight. It is a one, two, or a three-coat
day, according to temperature. Again and above all he
escapes the horrid starch entirely, neither shirts nor

collars nor cuffs, sometimes like thin sheets of iron, irritating his skin.

Vandy and I seriously resolved to-day that we would never again tolerate a starched thing about us; no matter what others did, we would discard the vile custom and be free. In revising this I am bound to admit our weakness: neither Vandy nor I have been strong enough to contend against our mothers. I don't know exactly what Vandy's experience was, but I know he fell soon after our return. For my part I fought it out awhile and tried many ways to win ; but my flannel and frieze underwear which I brought from China soon became unwearable, I was informed, from shrinkage, then they had broken into holes, and so on. They were finally missed from my wardrobe, and I compromised by stipulating that I should return to the shirt and collars and cuffs, and agreed they might be all pure white —provided that little or no starch should be used— this is an improvement, but linen is the most uncomfortable material known, used as we use it.

Vandy and I when in the East reduced the time for bathing and dressing in the morning to seven minutes. Of course, we have long since given up the folly of shaving. How one envies the man of the East who has but four articles to slip on, and no pins required: socks and low shoes (no lacing), one; breeches, two; undershirt, three; coat, four; and there he is, ready for breakfast. The coat buttons close to the chin, and has a small upright collar, and a watch-pocket outside; no cuffs, collars or neckties. Why does not some born reformer of our sex devote his life to giving his fellow man such additional happiness in life? Hundreds waste their energies upon objects which, if accomplished, would not be half as fruitful.

Here is a description of a woman's jewelry, as taken from life by Vandy: lobes of ears pierced with holes large enough to allow one's thumb to be inserted; above these holes two small gold-color rivets in each ear; in each nostril two gold pendants, inserted by screwing in; through the centre of the nose a large silver ring; on each wrist four bracelets; higher up the arm more rings; around her neck a necklace; around each ankle a large silver ring; and around her big toe and the next, on both feet, were rings. The smallest children wore many similar jewels. Upon these every penny they can save is squandered, and to secure them they are content to live on a little boiled rice and fish—a bamboo hut of one apartment their only home, and a piece of cotton cloth their wardrobe.

We had the pleasure of meeting, at Major Studer's, Mr. Hornaday, a young gentleman who travels for Professor Ward, of Rochester, New York, whose museum is well known the world over. Mr. Hornaday's department is to keep the Professor's collections complete, and if there be a rare bird, beast, or reptile on the globe, he is bound to capture specimens. He had just returned from spending four months among the savages of Borneo, where alone a supply of orang-outangs could be obtained. He returned with forty-two of these links, shot mostly by himself. He came one day upon two very young ones, and these he has brought here alive. They are suggestively human in their ways, and two better-behaved, more affectionate babies are rarely to be met with. Let no anti-Darwinian study young orang-outangs if he wishes to retain his present notions. The museum, Mr. Hornaday is advised, is now short of dugongs, and he is off for Australia next steamer to lay in a supply. The recital of his adventures is extremely interesting, and I predict that some day a book from him will have a great run.

What an interest is awakened by one who is able to tell stories of his own experience! No wonder that Othello won Desdemona with the recital of his adventures. He was the hero who had been the actor in all the scenes he depicted. Listening to Mr. Hornaday was a source of rare pleasure to-night. His chief regret is that he missed, during his visit to Borneo, the largest mias ever seen on the island. The natives discovered a troop, all of which made off except the leader. He showed fight, but soon ran up a high tree, from which the native weapons were unable to dislodge him. He was beyond their reach and there he sat. It was resolved to cut down the tree and capture him as he fell; but as soon as they came to close quarters with the monster, he proved so powerful, fierce, and courageous that the natives ran away and he got off.

Mr. Hornaday reached the spot just too late. "Why didn't you send for me? Didn't you know my rifle would have reached him?" he asked. They gave him no reason for their conduct, but he suspected that they feared he would not have paid them had he made the capture. Mr. Hornaday is confident this mias exceeded the height stated by Wallace as the maximum.

Mr. Hornaday was more successful with the largest tiger shot in India for years. He was out after cheetahs, and having no more expectation of meeting with the nobler game than of encountering a lion, had not his tiger rifle with him. On coming to the banks of a small stream he was greatly surprised to see a tiger's fresh footmarks—a big foot, too. Making a sign to his attendants to stand motionless, he glanced up the stream, then down, and saw, not far from him, leisurely strolling along the edge of the creek, seeking a convenient ford, the largest tiger he had ever laid eyes upon, although he had shot many. "Shall I shoot with this gun?" he thought. "If I miss he will certainly be upon us. He will attack one of my colored attendants first, anyhow, and I'll get a chance to reload. I'll do it!" A moment after, the monster, having found a ford to his liking, turned his head and looked cautiously down stream before entering the water. Finding all quiet in that direction, he turned to glance up stream.

For this moment Mr. Hornaday had waited. There is one spot only to hit a tiger—right between the eyes. He fired and the beast fell. No other shot was fired, for holes spoil a skin. The animal writhed for several hours, no one daring to approach him, until he finally sank exhausted upon the sand. I think it was fifteen pounds Mr. Hornaday received from Government for this exploit. I have secured the skin of this very beast, properly preserved, full head, open mouth, glaring eyeballs, and all, and I am ready to match tiger skins with any one.

In the absence of other commercial intelligence, I may quote the market in Mr. Hornaday's line: Tigers are still reported "lively;" orang-outangs "looking up;" pythons show but little animation at this season of the year; proboscis monkeys, on the other hand, continue scarce; there is quite a run on lions, and kangaroos are jumped at with avidity; elephants heavy; birds of paradise drooping; crocodiles are snapped up as offered, while dugongs bring large prices. What is pig metal to this?

The climate of Singapore, as of all places so near the Equator, would be intolerable but for the dense clouds which obscure the sun and save us from its fierce rays; but occasionally it breaks through for a few minutes, and we are in a bath of perspiration before we know it. No one can estimate the difference in the power of the sun here as compared with it in New York. Straw hats afford no protection whatever; we are compelled to wear thick white helmets of pith, and use a white umbrella lined with green cloth, and yet can walk only a few steps when the sun is not hid without feeling that we must seek the shade. The horses are unable to go more than ten miles in twenty-four hours, and our carriage and pair are hired with the understanding that this is not to be exceeded. Nothing could exist near the line if the intense heat did not cause evaporation upon a gigantic scale. The clouds so formed are driven upward by the streams of colder air from both sides, condensation then takes place, and showers fall every few hours in the region of Singapore.

One is not only in a new earth here, but he has a new sky as well. As the tropics have nothing to compare with our more brilliant colors in the vegetable world, so the southern sky has no stars to equal ours. Indeed, with the exception of the four in the Southern Cross, two in the Centaur, and two or three others, there is no star of the first magnitude to be seen, and the constellations are poor compared with those of our splendid northern skies. Shakespeare's

"* * * inlaid with patines of bright gold,"

must seem hyperbole to the Australian. I saw the Southern Cross many nights while at sea, and it is certainly very fine, as far as four stars can make a cross; for, as usual, much is left to the imagination. It is really not a cross at all. These long ocean trips furnish the best opportunity for observing the stars, and I have rubbed up my early knowledge on the subject so far as to be able to point out all the constellations and many of the principal stars; but away down here the North Star even is not to be seen, and we have to steer by Orion's belt if the compass varies.

Tuesday, January 14.

We left Singapore to-day at three P.M. by the English mail steamer Tcheran, parting with very sincere regret from Major and Miss Studer, to whom we had been so much indebted for our week's happiness. These partings from kind friends on our way round the world are the sad incidents of the trip. People are so kind, and they do so much to render our stay agreeable, that we become warmly attached, and have many excursions planned, when some morning up goes the flag, boom goes the signal gun, " Mail steamer arrived!" all aboard at sunset! and farewell, friends! We see them linger on the pier as we sail away, good-byes are waved, and we fade from each other's sight; but it will be long ere many faces vanish from our memory.

While still gazing Singaporeward I am recalled to the stern duties of life. These two baby orang-outangs I told you of are going to a naturalist in Madras. What a present! and Vandy and I have promised to do what we can in the way of attendance upon them. The butcher comes to ask me when they are to be fed, and how, and what. This is a poser. I am not up in the management of orang-outangs, but Vandy has skill in almost everything of this kind; at least he is safer than I, there being a good deal of the incipient doctor about Vandy, and I search for him in this emergency. The fact is, while I have had varied experiences in the matter of delicate charges of many kinds, these have generally been of our own species—a youngster to be taken home to his parents, a dowager lady afraid of the cars—even a blushing damsel to be transported across the Atlantic to the arms of her *fiancé* has been intrusted to me before this, but this charge is decidedly out of my line. These fearfully human-looking, human-acting brutes furnish much amusement to the passengers; but at first every lady whom we took forward to watch them was compelled to run away laughing and exclaiming, " Oh, they are so much like babies! It's just horrid to see these nasty, hairy things carry on so!" Confirmation strong, I suppose, of our kinship, so do not let us neglect our poor relations even if the connection be somewhat remote. Bananas are their favorite delicacy, but this morning not even that fruit could tempt them. I gave one to the smaller of the two, but it would not take it. Then I tried the larger one. He took it in his paw, peeled it at one end and put it to his lips, then looking up at me with a sad, puzzled expression, dropped his prize, and resting his head on his paw laid slowly down on the straw, telling us all as plainly as could be that he was sea-sick. Such was indeed the case; but in a few hours the sea fell and he was as sprightly as ever. Monkeys move spasmodically, by jerks as it were; not so these dignified, stately creatures: they are as deliberate in all their actions as staid, sober people. One day a passenger had offered a banana to the little one, but as it put forth its paw, withdrew it. The wee thing stood this several times, and at last laid down on its face and cried like a child—a wicked cry; nor would it be comforted, the banana when offered being petulantly rejected. They are much too human.

We called at Penang, an island on the western shore of the Peninsula, also belonging to Great Britain, and had time to drive around the settlement. The place is not to be compared to Singapore in size, but vegetation is even more luxuriant. It was very hot, and we envied the governor his residence on a mountain peak eighteen hundred feet above the sea, where, it was reported, fires are actually required at some seasons night and morning. Penang exports large quantities of tin, and we took on a lot for New York. This valuable production seems about the only metal America has now to import, but some lucky explorer is no doubt destined to find it in immense quantities by and by. Having got everything else, it doesn't stand to reason that America should not be favored with this also. Nothing unusual occurred upon our run across the Bay of Bengal. Even Vandy enjoyed the sea voyage this time; something he had never before done in his life, nor ever done since. It was smooth and quiet steaming all the way to Ceylon. I had been humming "Greenland's Icy Mountains" for several days previously, about all that I knew of Ceylon's isle being contained in one of the verses of that hymn, which I used to sing at missionary meetings, when a minister who had seen the heathen was stared at as a prodigy.

And indeed the "spicy breezes blew soft o'er Ceylon's isle" as we approached it in the moonlight. We found Galle quite a pretty, quaint little port, and remained there one night, taking the coach next morning for Colombo, the capital. The drive of sixty miles to the railway which extends to Colombo, seventeen miles beyond, is one of the best treats we have yet had. The road is equal to one of our best park avenues, as indeed are all the roads we saw in Ceylon; from end to end it skirts the rocky shores, passing through groves of cocoa and betel-nut trees, and dotted on each side by the huts of natives at work at some branch of the cocoanut business. Every part of the nut is utilized; ropes and mats are made from the covering of the shell, oil from the kernel, and the milk is drank fresh at every meal. These trees do not thrive except near the coast, the salt air laden with moisture being essential for their growth, but they grow quite down to the edge of the sea. The natives have been attracted to this main road, and from Galle to Colombo it is almost one continuous village; there is no prettier sea-shore in the world, nor a more beautiful surf. Every few miles we come upon large numbers of fishermen drawing in their nets, which are excessively long and take in several acres of sea in their sweep. An artist who would come to Ceylon and devote himself to depicting " the fishers of Ceylon's isle " (how well that sounds! and a good title is half the battle) would make a reputation and a fortune. I am quite sure there is no more picturesque sight than the drawing of their nets, several hundred men being engaged in the labor, while the beach is alive with women and children in bright colors anxiously watching the result.

The dress of the Ceylonese women is really pretty: a skirt closely fitting the figure, and a tight jacket over the shoulders—all of fine, pure white cotton cloth or muslin and quite plain, with neither frill, tuck, flounce, nor anything of the kind. Necklaces and ear-rings are worn, but I am glad to say the nose in Ceylon seems to be preserved from the indignity of rings. The men's dress is rather scanty, their weakness being a large tortoise-shell comb, which every one wears; it reaches from ear to ear, and the hair is combed straight back and confined by it. Women are denied this crowning ornament, and must content themselves with a pin in the hair, the head of which, however, is highly ornamented. The Buddhist priests form a strange contrast

in their dress, which consists of a yellow plaid, generally of silk, wrapped around the body and over the
shoulders.

I asked our Ceylonese guide to-day whether he had
ever heard of our most popular missionary hymn.
"Here is the verse," I said, "about your beautiful
isle":

> " What though the spicy breezes
>   Blow soft o'er Ceylon's isle,
>   Though every prospect pleases,
>   And only man is vile !
> In vain with lavish kindness,
>   The gifts of God are strewn ;
> The heathen, in his blindness,
>   Bows down to wood and stone."

"What do you think of that description?" I asked.
He said he thought " the writer was a fool," and asked
if any one in my country believed that there was a man,
woman, or child in Ceylon who did not know better
than to bow down to any power but God. "Yes," I
said, " I once believed it myself, and millions believe it
to-day, and good boys and girls with us save their pen-
nies to send missionaries to tell these heathen who
worship idols how very wrong and foolish it is to do so,
and how very angry the true God is to have anything
worshipped but himself." He said ours must be a very
curious country, and he should like to visit it and see
such queer people. I gave him my address and promised, if he would come to see me, to take him to a great

missionary meeting where he would see the best and most religious people, all greatly concerned about the idolaters of Ceylon.

The truth is there is scarcely in all the world a human being so low in the scale as not to know that the object he sees is only the symbol of the invisible power. What the cross is to the Christian the idol is to the other, and it is nothing more. The worship of both is to the Unknown beyond. I did my best to soothe the wounded spirit of our guide by explaining the necessities of poetic license. Still he would have it that Bishop Heber had wronged his beloved Ceylon and did not know what he was writing about.

The religion of Ceylon is Buddhism; indeed it is now the most strictly Buddhist country in the world. One condition of the cession of the sovereignty to Great Britain was that this religion should be held inviolable with its rights and privileges, its monasteries and temples and all pertaining thereto. In the language of the greatest European authority, " although government support is no longer given to it, its pure and simple doctrines live in the hearts of the people and are the noblest monument to its founder Gautama Buddha. The taking of the meanest life is strictly forbidden, and falsehood, intemperance, dishonesty, anger, pride, and covetousness are denounced as incompatible with Buddhism, which enjoins the practice of chastity, gratitude, contentment, moderation, forgiveness of injuries, patience, and cheerfulness." The priests of Buddha are regularly ordained and sworn to celibacy, and they are required to meet each other every fourteen days for purposes of mutual confession. The lowest caste is eligible to the priesthood, as with the Christian religion.

Ceylon is somewhat smaller than Ireland, and the population is a little less than three millions, but it is rapidly increasing, as are its exports and imports. Of all the places we visited it seems to have suffered least from the wave of depression which has recently swept over the world. This is undoubtedly owing to the fact that the spicy isle enjoys somewhat of a monopoly in coffee and some of the spices, cinnamon especially. Java coffee is generally used, I think, in America, but in Ceylon it is deemed an inferior article; Mocha, in Arabia, furnishes the best, but much called Mocha is really grown here. In the coffee plantations men are paid eighteen cents per day; women, fourteen cents. A disease akin to that which attacked the vines in France some years ago has raged among the plants for two years past; it promises this year to be less destructive, although no effectual cure has yet been discovered. We met several coffee planters, generally young, pushing Englishmen who either own the estates, or are related to those who do. They lead a pleasant life in Ceylon, the climate being good most of the year, and those who are contented declare that a European can live there and enjoy as good health as at home. If the weather prove too warm in the summer there are the mountains to run to. Scientific cultivation of coffee began in Ceylon as late as 1824, and public attention was not directed to it until 1834—only fifty years ago—yet to-day there are more than twelve hundred coffee plantations, and the amount of coffee exported exceeds twenty millions of dollars per annum. Tea cultivation has been introduced recently, and the quality is said to be excellent. There cannot be any doubt of this, because it finds a ready market here. None has been exported. If it were not a remarkably good article the foreign would be preferred, as we all know a domestic article has a world of prejudice to overcome at first. I shall watch the Ceylon tea question with interest, and hope that at some not distant day the production of tea leaf may rival that of the coffee bean.

I have no intention to enter into any political question—certainly not into the merits of Free Trade vs. Protection; but I must own I was surprised to find that one-fifth of the total revenue of the island is derived from taxes upon the daily food of the people, two-thirds of this from a tax upon imported rice, and the other third from native grain.

Ceylon teaches many lessons. The liquor traffic, for instance, is managed throughout the entire island as a governmental monopoly. Distillation is restricted to a few specified distillers who can sell their product at wholesale in open market, but the right to retail is restricted to certain taverns, which are rented year by year to the highest bidders, subject to stringent conditions. Pure arrack only can be sold at fixed prices, and lessees are held to strict account for drunkenness and disturbances. The liquor monopoly yields £170,000, or about one-seventh of the whole revenue, which in 1873 was £1,241,558 ($6,200,000); about ten shillings per head, as against England's two pounds and more.

The main roads of Ceylon are equal to those of Central Park; so they should be, for their cost has exceeded £2,000 per mile. Ten thousand dollars!—we could almost build a railway in the West for this. However, it is not as much as it costs in Britain to get the right to begin to spend money on a railway; so we must congratulate the Ceylonese upon getting a splendid return for their investment. During our brief sojourn in the island (alas! all too short as I write these pages) we travelled over every mile of railway there. This sounds large to one who judges of a railway system by that of the United States—a hundred and twenty thousand miles; there were then only about a hundred miles in all Ceylon—two short lines. To-day there are doubtless a hundred and fifty miles in operation, as the line under construction between Colombo and Galle was expected to be opened in two years more. This brings Japan and Ceylon about even upon the railway question, though the population of Ceylon is only about one-twelfth that of Japan.

————

A railway has been built from Colombo, the shipping port, through the mountains to the coffee-growing districts, a distance of seventy miles, and this enabled us to visit Kandy, more than 1,600 feet above the sea, and the summer capital to which the government repairs in hot weather. It is a beautiful little town, and gave us the first breath of air with "ozone" in it that we had enjoyed since we were on the Sierras. Our hotel fronts upon the square, and is opposite the Buddhist Temple, celebrated as the receptacle of that precious relic, "the sacred tooth of Buddha." A former king of Ceylon is reputed to have paid an immense sum for this memento of the departed. We were too near the temple for comfort. The tomtom has to be beaten five times each day, and as one of these is at sunrise, I had occasion to wish the priest and tooth both far enough away. I wonder the Europeans don't indict this tomtoming at unseasonable hours as a nuisance.

The Botanical Gardens here are rivalled in the tropics by those in Java only, and upon seeing the display of luxuriant vegetation, we fully understood how it had acquired its celebrity; but still all is green. The great variety of palms, the bread-fruit, banyan, jack-fruit, and others sustain this reputation. The chocolate tree was

the most curious to us; it has recently been introduced
in the island, and promises to add one more to the
list of luxuries for which Ceylon is famous. A fine
evidence of the intelligence of the Ceylon planters is
seen in the fact that the association employs a chemist
to investigate and report upon the different soils and
what they are capable of producing; under his supervision various articles are always under trial. Recently
Liberian coffee has been found to thrive in low latitudes
unsuited for the Arabian variety, which requires a
higher district, thus rendering available for this plant a
large area, which has hitherto been necessarily devoted
to less profitable uses. Nothing nowadays can be
thoroughly developed without the chemist's aid, and
the day is not far distant when our farming will be conducted under his instructions as completely as our steel
manufacture is now.

Ceylon is noted for its pearl fisheries and its supply
of rubies, sapphires, and cats'-eyes as much as for its
spices; and from the hour the traveller lands until the
steamer carries him off he is beset with dealers offering
precious stones, worth hundreds of dollars in London
or New York, for a few rupees; but those who purchase no doubt find their fate in the story of the innocent who bought his gold cheap. The government
keeps the pearl fishery grounds under proper regulations, and allows divers one half of all they find, the
the other half going to the State Treasury. I was told

the value of the pearls found last year amounted to
$400,000, but the production seems to be falling off. In
1798 the fishery was rented for £142,000 ($710,000).
Now the government has to work it and the net pro-
ceeds have never exceeded £87,000 in any year, and
have fallen as low as £7,200.

The government employed a naturalist to study the
habits of the pearl oyster. He labored for five years,
but this time scientific investigation seems to have
failed and we know but little more about the subject
than before. Some genius will come, however, to solve
all questions. Science may be rebuffed twenty times,
but it never rests until the truth is known. This much
is certain, that these precious oysters leave their usual
beds for years together. There was no fishery once for
twenty-seven years, from 1768 to 1796, and once before
then it failed for about fourteen years. When they do
visit pretty Ceylon, their main residence is upon the
northwestern coast, sixteen to twenty miles from shore.
It is believed that the oyster reaches maturity in its
seventh year, when the pearl attains full size and lustre.
If the oyster be not secured then, it soon dies and we
lose our pearl. Consider the number of these jewels
which fade away to their original elements in the
depths of ocean: for one we get, a million decom-
posed.

Did the poet know how true his words were when
he said :

> " Full many a gem of purest ray serene
>   The dark unfathomed caves of ocean bear."

The government brings the oysters to the beach and sells them to the highest bidders in lots of one thousand. Can you conceive of a prettier game of chance than this! Imagine the natives at work opening the rough shells, expecting at every turn to find a pearl worth a fortune!

The pearl fishers descend six to eight fathoms forty or fifty times a day, and can remain under water from a minute to a minute and a half. So much for practice. In the course of a million or hundred million years, more or less, each successive generation pursuing this calling, under the law of inherited tendencies, these people might well return to the amphibious state and give us an illustration of evolution, backward.

The pearl oyster is a large, round bivalve, sometimes twelve inches in diameter. If Thackeray felt, as he said when he first tried a Rockaway, as if he were swallowing a baby, what would have been his impressions if he had tickled his throat with one of these monsters? Sometimes a dozen, or even twenty pearls, are said to have been found in a single oyster. I remember hearing in China that a fresh water mollusc is made to grow pearls by the introduction of foreign bodies within the shell. These produce irritation which the shell fish seeks to allay by depositing around them a layer of pearly matter, and thus pearls are formed.

It is a fact that the celebrated Linnæus was paid $2,500 by the Swedish Government for a plan he discovered for doing a similar thing with the oyster. He bored through the shell and deposited sand particles between it and the mantle of fine tissues. It was not a success; but some day the race will produce pearls from cultivated oyster beds as we now get our eggs from chickens; that is, provided the coming man is not to regard jewelry of all kinds as barbaric—"*barbaric* pearls and gold" are Milton's very words, and great poets are prophets. The tendency is certainly in that direction. The more ignorant the natives, the more ornamental jewelry is worn, even if it be immense, heavy glass bracelets from Birmingham. Already one says, how simple, how grandly simple she was, with her hair plain, her ears unpierced, her head and neck without a single ornament, save only a rosebud in the hair. Jewels are to women what wine is to man—not recommended till after forty, and a poor help at any age.

———

Colombo, Tuesday, January 21.

Ceylon was originally settled in 1517 by the Portuguese, who obtained the right to erect a small factory at Colombo for purposes of trade. This soon grew into a fort, and naturally the whole west coast became theirs. The Dutch drove them out a hundred and fifty years later, to be in turn expelled by the English after they had occupied the island for just about the same period. As with all their colonies, the Dutch left their impress upon Ceylon. New industries were introduced, great public works constructed, and, better than all, the education of the people was well cared for. The trade with Holland became a source of much profit. England has been master since 1796, nearly ninety years now, and certainly the work she has to show for the less than a century is marvellous indeed.

The people are not yet done rejoicing at the restoration of their ancient village institutions, which took place in 1871. Europeans had rudely swept these away and substituted courts after their own fashion. After many years trial, they were seen to be unsuited for the country, and the ancient village tribunals were reëstablished, as I have said, a few years ago. It will not do to conclude, as many do, that India, Ceylon, and other of the Eastern lands, are left almost bare of just laws and fair administration, for nothing could be farther from the truth. The village elders, chosen by the people of Ceylon, for instance, administer laws which are the outgrowth of centuries, and as such are far better adapted to the real conditions which exist than any other system of laws, no matter how perfect, which have been found suitable in other lands under conditions wholly unlike. Here in this charming island, as indeed throughout all India, villages, or groups of villages, are authorized to frame rules having the force of laws, and which natives construe and administer.

I am amused at the ignorance of the average Englishman or American upon Eastern affairs. He is always amazed when I tell him that so far as representative institutions are concerned, there is not a village in India which is not farther advanced in this department of politics than any rural constituency in Britain. The American county, village, district and township system is of course more perfect than any other with which I am acquainted, but the English is really about the most backward. The experiment in Ceylon of restoring the native system has been an unequivocal success, even beyond the expectations of its warmest advocates, and in addition to the advantages flowing from the native courts, it is found that the village committees are beginning to repair and restore the ancient tanks and other irrigation works, which, under the curse of centralized and foreign authority had been allowed to fall into disuse.

The new blood of home rule in local affairs has aroused local patriotism and established numerous bodies throughout the country, each a centre from which good influences radiate, organizations into which good impulses flow, to crystallize into works of public utility, while at the same time an *esprit de corps* is created which must tell more and more. Wait till this plan is tried in England and Scotland, and, above all, in unhappy Ireland! I shall never despair of Ireland until at least a generation has had such local institutions as we find in Ceylon's Isle. If that people cannot develop under self-government, they deserve to fall away and give place to a better race; but they will *not* fail.

Caste exists in Ceylon, although it is not so strictly preserved as in India. Still, every calling is a caste, down to the scavenger. The several castes do not intermarry, nor is it practicable for one who has reaped great wealth and has natural tastes and abilities above his caste, to do in this small island what is readily done in India, viz., emigrate and set up in superior style in some other part of the crowded empire. The wealthiest native in Ceylon to-day is a fisherman, and yet he cannot gain admittance to the society of poorer natives about him of higher caste. If he were in India, and socially ambitious, he would change his residence. I was told by several Europeans that the bonds of caste in India are slowly weakening, and that when a wealthy stranger comes to a district it is held wise not to inquire too curiously concerning his birth.

Of all the castes, the tiller of the soil stands at the head in Ceylon; even the skilled worker in iron is away below him. The rural laborer with us must be taught to hold his head up. He is A1 in Ceylon.

The position held by Ceylon in ancient days as the great granary of Southern Asia explains the precedence accorded to agricultural pursuits. Under native rule the whole island was brought under irrigation by means of artificial lakes, constructed by dams across ravines, many of them of great extent—one, still existing, is twenty miles in circumference—but the system has been allowed to fall into decay. I am glad to know that government has resolved to undertake the work of repair. Proper sluices are to be supplied to all the village tanks, and the embankments are to be raised and strengthened through the labor of the village communities. We may yet live to see the fertility of the country restored to that of its pristine days.

We saw the new breakwater which government is constructing here at great expense. When finished it is proposed that the Indian steamers shall call here instead of at Galle, the harbor of which is dangerous. This may be a decided improvement upon the whole, but the tourist who does not see pretty Galle and enjoy the long day's drive through the island to Colombo will miss much.

Iron ore exists in Ceylon in vast deposits and is remarkably pure, rivalling the best Swedish grades. It has been worked from remote times, and native articles of iron are preferred even to-day to any that can be imported. If cost of transportation is to keep growing less and less, it is not beyond the range of possibility that some day Britain may import some of this unrivalled stone for special uses. There are also quicksilver mines, and lead, tin, and manganese are found to some extent.

GALLE, Wednesday, January 22.

We reached here last night upon our return, stopping one night at Colombo. Future travellers will soon miss one of the rarest treats in Ceylon. The railway will soon be completed from Colombo to Galle, and the days of coaching cease forever. We congratulate ourselves that our visit was before this passed away, as we know of no drive equal to that we have now enjoyed twice, and the last time even more than the first.

During our trip down yesterday I counted within forty miles eleven schools filled with young Cingalese. English is generally taught in them, and although attendance is not compulsory, great inducements are held out to parents to send their children. The advantages of knowing the English language are so decided that I am told parents generally are most anxious to have their children taught. The school-houses are simple affairs, consisting only of white plastered walls about five feet high, with spaces for entrance. On this wall rest the slight wooden standards which support the roof of palm-leaves, so that all is open to our view as we drive past. The attention paid to this vital subject, evidences of which are seen everywhere, is what most delights us. In 1874 there were 1,468 public schools on the island, attended by 66,385 scholars.

We were equally delighted to see numerous medical dispensaries, where the afflicted natives can obtain advice and medicine free of charge. On several huts we saw large placards denoting the presence of contagious disease within. It is a great work that is going forward here under English rule. By such means England proves her ability to govern, and best confirms her sway against domestic revolt or foreign intrigues. The blessings of good government, the education of the people, and careful attention to their health and comfort—these will be found the most effective weapons with which to combat mutiny within, or Russian or any other aggression from abroad. From all we saw in Ceylon we are prepared to put it forth as the best example of English government in the world, England herself not excepted.

SATURDAY, January 25.

At ten to-night we sailed for Madras and Calcutta by the English mail steamer Hindostan, and were lighted out of the intricate harbor by flaming torches displayed by lines of natives stationed at the buoys.

> " Flashes of flambeaux looked
> Like Demons guarding the river of death."

The last sight of Ceylon's isle revealed the fine spires of the Catholic Cathedral, which tower above the pretty harbor of Galle.

INDIA.

MADRAS, Tuesday, January 28.

We arose to find ourselves at anchor in the open sea opposite Madras. There is not a harbor upon the whole western coast of Hindostan. Government is engaged in constructing one, but it is slow work, as the immense blocks of concrete used can be handled and laid only in smooth seas, which seldom occur. Sometimes the mail steamers find it impossible to land passengers or cargo, and are compelled to carry both to Calcutta. The surf often sweeps over the top of the iron pier, which is certainly twenty feet high. Passengers are taken ashore in native boats twenty feet long and five feet deep. Across the boat, on small round poles, sit ten rowers, five on each side; another man steers, and in the bow stand two boys prepared to bail out the water which sweeps in as we plunge through the surf. Fortunately the sea was unusually calm, and we had no difficulty in reaching dry land. When the surf is too strong for even these boats to encounter, natives communicate with ships by tying together three small logs, upon which they manage to sit and paddle about, carrying letters in bags fastened upon their heads. As the solid logs cannot sink, they are safe as long as they can cling to them, and an upset is to them an occurrence of little consequence. We saw many of these curious contrivances, but one must have a good deal of the amphibious in his nature, or full faith that he was not born to be drowned, to trust himself upon them through the Madras surf.

India at last! How strange everything looks! Brahmans, Cullrees and Banians, devotees of the three different gods, with foreheads marked to denote their status, the white sandal-wood paste upon the Brahman's brow. Our first glimpse of caste, of which these are the three main divisions, to one of which all persons must belong or be of the lowest order, the residuum, who are coolies. There are many subdivisions of these, and indeed every trade or calling constitutes a different order, the members of which do not intermarry, or associate, or even eat with one another. Generations pursuing the same calling, and only marrying within themselves, acquire a peculiar appearance, and this effectually creates a caste. Carpenters, masons, merchants, each are distinct, and the occupation of a man can readily be known by his dress or manner.

Caste! what is caste? whence did it spring? and what are its effects to-day in India? Whatever story I tell about its origin, some great authority will flatly contradict it. The beginning of caste, like that of most existing institutions, is lost in obscurity; but the most likely guess to my mind is that which founds caste upon this natural train of reasoning.

Before men travelled much, when the race were serfs and all their needs were supplied by those immediately about them, it was almost inevitable that the son should be put to his father's handicraft. He could be of service there at a much earlier age than if he had to go to a stranger. Besides, he had a chance from his infancy to become familiar with the work, and again, his father's reputation would serve a purpose. Therefore, successive generations remained bakers, smiths, carpenters, agriculturists, laborers, and eventually this developed special aptitudes under the law of inherited tendencies and each occupation became a caste.

Those who were in the highest employments being the best educated, they soon took measures to secure their privileges, and in the past ages nothing could rivet the chains so effectually as the sanction of the gods. Therefore, we need not be surprised that in good time a revelation came to this effect: " When man was divided how many did they make him? What was his mouth? What his arms? What his legs and feet? Brahma was his mouth, Kshatriya his arms, Vaisya his thighs, and Sudra his feet."

This gives four grand divisions for the race, and their duties toward the State and to each other are clearly defined by the part of the "Grand Man " or "God" from which they sprang. The following are a few of the principal items of the code which regulates these classes: To the first, or Brahman, belongs the religious department—he studies and expounds the sacred books, officiates at sacrifices, and is the recipient of the "presents" offered to the gods. These are modern clergymen. To the second, or Kshatriyas, are given the war department, force, and criminal justice. These are our human butchers, the military class, who are yet not ashamed of the " profession of arms." To the third, or

Vaisyas, belong commerce and agriculture, and to the poor fourth estate, or Sudras, are left the mechanical arts and service to the other castes. The first three alone wear the sacred thread.

The Brahman is entitled by primogeniture to the whole universe. He may seize the goods of a Sudra, and whatever, beyond a certain amount, the latter acquires by labor or succession. If he slanders any of the other castes he pays only nominal fines graduated according to classes. Whatever crime he may commit his personal property cannot be injured, but whoever strikes a Brahman even with a blade of grass becomes an inferior quadruped for twenty-one generations. He is the physician for men's bodies as well as for their souls.

The one duty of the Sudra is to serve all the three superior castes "without depreciating their worth." In administering oaths, a Brahman swears only by his veracity—"his honor as a gentleman." A Kshatriya swears by his weapons, a Vaisya by his cattle, while the poor Sudra has to swear by all the most frightful penalties of perjury.

A curious survival of this same idea lingers in England, where the theory is that all men are equal before the law. Nevertheless members of the Royal Family are still released from the suspicion that they would not tell the truth unless they took an oath to do so. They are not required to take an oath before testifying in court. But imagine Herbert Spencer and the average

Prince giving evidence; whose word would go the farther the wide world over? Yet the former would be insulted by being compelled to swear, while the latter would be allowed to testify upon the "honor of a prince," a very scanty foundation as princes have ever been and must ever be. History seems to teach us that it has been difficult to get this class to keep the oaths they did take. If I were an M. P., I would move that this be changed. The Brahman, notwithstanding his superior station, is nevertheless held to be much more liable to pollution than the lower orders, and is therefore required to bathe more frequently, and to be much more watchful against the tempter. Our Brahmans at home might take a lesson from this. A high authority has told us that

> " Life can be lived well,
> *Even in a palace.*"

But Burns has the truth:

> " And certes in fair Virtue's heavenly road
> The cottage leaves the palace far behind."

I have given you the ideal of caste and its laws. Their administration is a far different matter. It is no longer possible for Brahmans to enforce strictly their claims. Caste crumbles away before the progress of the age. Your railway is a "sure destroyer" of all branches of inequality among men. The Press a still greater; but ages will pass ere we have among the two hundred and fifty millions of Hindostan anything approaching that degree of equality and intermarriage of classes which even England possesses, to say nothing of America. The marvel is that caste took such root throughout India apparently in opposition to the teachings of Gautama Buddha. But it is scarcely less strange than that the fighting Christian nations found their system upon the teachings of the Prince of Peace.

Here is the true doctrine of the Eastern Christ: As the four rivers which fall into the Ganges lose their names as soon as they mingle their waters with the holy river, so all who believe in Buddha cease to be Brahmans, Kshatriyas, Vaisyas, and Sudras. The same doctrine is beautifully expressed in the "Light of Asia." Buddha asks for a drink of milk from a shepherd.

> " ' Ah, my Lord,
> I cannot give thee,' quoth the lad ; ' thou seest
> I am a Sudra, and my touch defiles !'
> Then the world-honored spoke : ' Pity and need
> Make all flesh kin. There is no caste in blood,
> Which runneth of one hue, nor caste in tears,
> Which trickle salt with all ; neither comes man
> To birth with tilka-mark stamped on the brow,
> Nor sacred thread on neck. Who doeth right deeds
> Is twice-born, and who doeth ill deeds vile.
> Give me to drink, *my brother.*'"

Our friend in Madras gave us a rare treat by driving us out to see the celebrated Madras tigers, for nowhere else in the world are such tigers kept as here, and indeed I go so far as to declare that until one has seen these grand animals he has no adequate idea of what a tiger is. All that I have seen hitherto—and I do not forget the "Zoo" in London—are but tame mockeries of the genuine monster. I walked up to a large cage, but was startled by such a fright. A tiger was in an instant flat against the cage, and between me and it were only a few small iron rods which rattled like reeds as he struck them. I thought the whole cage was in pieces, and that beast upon me. Such glaring eyes, burning like immense topazes in his head! and then when he found himself unable to get at his prey, such a yell! but I was many feet from him ere this came, I assure you. He had sprung from the back of his cage against the bars, a distance of at least fifteen or eighteen feet, the moment he saw me, and no doubt hurt himself as he dashed against them. The keeper told us this one had only been caught a few months ago. His stripes were glossy black, and his coat not that sickly tawny color we are so familiar with, but a light fiery brown. Compared with the tiger, it is impossible but that even the noblest lion must seem tame and inert. We took no interest in the lions, although there were some fine specimens. In the evening we enjoyed hearing the Governor's band performing on the beach and seeing Madras society congregated there, and for the first time since we left America saw full-sized horses again. Several gentlemen were riding animals that would pass muster in Central Park. Thus far we have found only little ponies in use.

Our races have never been brought face to face with famine, but in India the masses are always upon the brink of starvation ; a little too much, or too little, rain during the monsoon, and the lives of millions are endangered. The miserable wretches—mere skeletons— we saw to-day sitting on the dusty road sides beseeching passers-by for a pittance, are traces which still remain of the terrible famine of the years 1876 and 1877. Both the monsoons of the former year failed, and the season of 1877 was little better, although the government spent more than eleven millions sterling ($55,000,000) in strenuous efforts to supply enough food to render existence possible. More than five million human beings, more than the entire population of the State of Pennsylvania—far more than that of Scotland —were sacrificed from want and disease resulting from the famine of these two years. There is no doubt about the correctness of this startling statement, for it is founded upon the increased death rate in the afflicted districts.

It was while the shadow of this calamity, unparalleled since the beginning of British rule in India, was over the land that the most gorgeous " durbar " ever held in India was ordered for the purpose of gratifying a whim of Queen Victoria, who had induced Lord Beaconsfield to have her proclaimed Empress of India, or, as is far more probable, which he had instigated her to accept. The natives who spoke of this to us were outraged at the act, and quoted it as proof that their lives and sufferings were held as nothing by England. This does England gross injustice, for, as I was able to tell them, English opinion was itself averse to giving the Queen a title in India which they could not be induced to tolerate at home, and only acquiesce dbecause Victoria had really done so much that was good during her long reign that they did not wish to deny her what she had unfortunately set her heart upon; and then after all the poor Queen probably did not know about the famine. Her books show that her interest in life is confined strictly to the petty details of her household and narrow circle of satellites.

To-day our Sunday-school recollections were again aroused by a sight of the terrible car of Juggernaut. It is really an immense affair, elaborately carved in bold relief, and on the top is a platform for the priests. I should say the car is twenty-five feet high and about eight by twelve at the base; it has six wheels, four outside and two in the centre, the former nine feet in diameter and the latter six, all of solid wood clamped together with iron bands, and all at least two feet in width of tread. Such a mass, drawn through the streets by elephants and accompanied by excited devotees, its hundred bells jangling as it rolled along where there was not another vehicle of any kind with which to compare it, or a house more than one small story high, must have appeared to the ignorant natives something akin to the supernatural; and I can now well understand how wretches, working themselves into a state of frenzy, should have felt impelled to dash under its wheels. It is still paraded upon certain festival days, invariably surrounded, however, by policemen, who keep the natives clear of the wheels, for even to-day, if they were not prevented, its victims would be as numerous as ever. Imagine, if you can, with what feelings we stood and gazed upon this car, which has crushed under its ponderous wheels religious enthusiasts by the thousand, and which still retains its fascination over men anxious to be allowed the glory of such self-immolation, at the supposed call of God, who would be a fiend if he desired such sacrifice.

We left Madras on Wednesday morning, and had a fine smooth sail across the Bay of Bengal to Calcutta, the City of Palaces and centre of the British power in India. Coming up the river we pass the shipping in review, and never before have we seen so many large, magnificent sailing ships in one port, not even in Liverpool or London. The trade requires large clippers, and these splendid vessels lie four and five deep for two miles along the river, all in fine trim, flags flying, and looking their best. We pass the palace of the old King of Oude, who was brought here when deposed for his misdeeds. He is allowed a pension of $50,000 per month, which seems a great waste of money, as it is mostly squandered by the old reprobate. His collection of birds and beasts is a wonderful one, for he pays any price for animals; last month he paid $12,500 for two grand tigers, but they escaped a few days afterward and swam across the river.

The first queer thing that strikes you at your hotel is that two natives take you in custody without even saying " by your leave," and never while you are in Calcutta will you be able to get out of sight of one or the other of these officers. One attends in person to your room, brings you your tea and toast at six, prepares your bath, takes your shoes to the proper " caste " man below (he wouldn't black them for the world, bless you !), and plays the valet while you dress. At night you find him stretched out across your door, like a dog on the watch, and there he lies all night, subject to master's call. I hurt my man's feelings one night by gently stepping over his prostrate form and getting into my room and going to bed without his aid. I turned the key when I got inside, and not many moments after I heard him move. Missing the key, he suspected something was wrong, and tried the door several times ; but as he met with no response he finally gave it over, and lay down to sleep. The other attendant is our waiter at table and out-door servant. You find these people curled up and lying at every step through the halls, and are in constant danger of stumbling over them. Every guest generally has two, although the hotel professes to keep an efficient staff of its own. We hear amusing stories told of servants in India, their duties being so strictly defined by caste that one must be kept for every trifling duty. Our friend the Major tells us, for instance, that upon a recent occasion his wife wished to send a note to him at the Fort, a very short distance from his residence. The proper messenger happening to have been sent elsewhere, she asked the coachman to please take it to master, but he explained how impossible it would be for him to comply, much as he wished to do so. Persuasion was useless; but madame thought of a remedy—order the carriage. The grooms prepare and harness the horses, the coachman mounts the box and appears at the door. "Now drive to master's, and, attendant, deliver this note." All right. This brought it within the sphere of his caste. He is bound to obey all orders connected with the carriage. Incidents of this nature are too numerous to recount. It is in India that political economists can best study the division of labor in its most advanced stage of development. My friend Mrs. K. kindly gave me her list of servants and their various duties. They numbered twenty-two, although Mr. K.'s establishment is a moderate one.

We find the Zoölogical Gardens very interesting. Here we saw for the first time monkeys running about unfettered among the trees, and a lion chained to a dog-kennel doing watch duty like a mastiff. We also saw an entire house devoted to the display of pheasants. These birds make a fine collection, for there are numerous varieties, and some exceedingly beautiful. There are here two full-grown orang-outangs and one child, the former even more human than the pets we had recently been in charge of. The huge crocodile in a large pond failed to make his appearance yesterday, and while we were there five natives with long poles and two in a small boat were detailed to stir him up and see what was the matter. It was amusing to see these naked attendants as they waded in a few feet and poked about, ready to jump back at every movement of the water, and sometimes frightened at each other's strokes; but all will agree with me that this business of stirring up crocodiles at twenty cents per day yields no fair compensation for the risks involved. There are good tigers here also, but having seen *the* tiger of the world at Madras, all others are but shadows. It is the same now with peacocks, which in these latitudes are far superior to those with us, but *the* peacock is at Saigon, in Cochin China, and we never see one without saying, one to the other, "How poor!" We are in a few days to see the Taj, and I suppose it will be the same as to buildings hereafter. Even Walter Scott's monument at Edinburgh—my favorite piece of stone and lime—must be surpassed by this marvel of perfection.

I have been considering whether it is more productive of pleasure really to have seen or heard the admitted best of everything, beyond which you can never expect to go, and as compared with which you must actually hereafter be content invariably to meet the inferior, or whether one had better, for the retention of future interest in things, not see the very topmost and unrivalled of each. I have met people whose ears, for instance, were so cultivated as to render it painful for them to listen even to the grandest music if indifferently performed; some who had "atmosphere" and "chiaro-oscuro" so fully developed that copies of even the "Madonna di San Sisto" were only daubs offensive to the eye; others who, having seen Macready in Macbeth, find the tragedy stale in others' hands. Now I don't believe this ensues where the love of the art itself is genuine; and I rejoice to say that having once listened to an oratorio at the Handel Festival with four thousand selected performers, that oratorio becomes forever a source of exquisite enjoyment, performed where or how it may be. If poorly done, the mind floats up toward the region, if it does not attain quite the same height, where it soared at the perfect recital; the distinct images there seen, which Confucius justly gives music the power of creating, come vividly again as the notes swell forth. The priests who call are different, indeed, but the gods who respond are one and the same. So having seen Janauschek in Lady Macbeth, all other Lady Macbeths participate in her quality. Having almost worshipped Raphael's Madonna, all other Madonnas have a touch of her power. It is of the very essence of genius that it educates one to find beauty and harmony where before he would only have trodden over barren sands, and the grand and poor performances of any masterpiece are not a contrast to the truly receptive, but are as steps leading from the lowest to the highest in the same temple. Because one has been awe-stricken by Niagara's torrent, are the other waterfalls of the world to be uninteresting? No; to the man whose soul has really been impressed, every tiny stream that tumbles down in foam is related to the greater wonder, partaking to some extent of its beauty and grandeur. Having seen the Himalayas, are the more modest but not less dear Alleghanies to lose their charm and power? Never! Let me go forward, then, and revel without misgivings in the highest of human and divine creations, as I may be privileged to see or hear or know them. I do not fear that I shall ever become a member of the extensive band we meet in our travels who have become incapable of enjoying anything but the best.

We paid a visit to the river one morning to see the Hindoos performing the sacred rite of bathing, which their religion commands. Crowds of men and women enter the water promiscuously and pray together. What a mercy that Brahma thought of elevating personal cleanliness to the rank of the virtues! What thousands are saved every year in consequence! What this crowded hive of human beings in hot India would become without this custom it is fearful to contemplate. I find our friends all regretting that Mohammed was less imperative upon this point. His followers take rather to sprinkling than immersion, for dipping hands and feet in water is held by them as quite sufficient, and both are not equally efficacious as purifiers in the tropics, however they may be as religious ceremonies.

A Boston clipper ship was being unloaded of its cargo of Wenham Ice as we strolled along the wharf in the warm early morning. The great blocks were carried upon the heads of the naked Sudras, one at a time, and even at this early hour the ice was melting fast, the drops of cool water forming tiny rills on the soiled, dark skins of the carriers, who no doubt enjoyed the rare luxury of something really cold. The exportation of ice to the East was a great Boston industry at that time; to-day it is wholly gone, the artificial being now made and sold at every centre for one-third the price commanded by the natural product. A slight improvement in the mode of manufacture, and, presto! here at the Equator, where the temperature is always at our summer heat, we make ice by the ton and are able to sell it at prices which the poorest population in the world can readily pay. Where are we going to stop in the domain of invention?

One day we visited the temple sacred to the bloody

goddess "Kali," from whom Calcutta derives its name. She took her rise, as many gods have done, from her insatiable thirst for human blood. One powerful giant alone was able for many years to withstand her arts, he being secretly informed by a spirit that when she pursued he had only to stand in water, and if one drop of his blood was spilled, other giants would spring forth and devour "Kali" herself. This secret she divined, however, and one day attacked him even in the water, strangling him and sucking every drop of his blood without spilling one. But her tongue grew so large and red that she was never afterward able to get it back into her mouth, and now she stands fixed in this temple, her big red tongue hanging out, a most revolting sight. So powerful is she esteemed that pilgrims to her shrine, who have spent months in coming hundreds of miles by measuring their bodies upon the dusty ground, are sometimes seen passing through the by-lanes of Calcutta. Lying flat, they mark their length, rise, and lie down again at this mark, and go on this way, never leaving the path day or night, and begging food and water enough to sustain them as they proceed. I was told of one man who travelled eight hundred miles in this manner. Imagine the strength of the superstition which can so blind its dupes. But even this is nothing compared with the self-inflicted torture practised by many "who seek to merit heaven by making earth a hell." It is not rare for fakirs to stand in postures that cripple them for life. One elects to stand on one foot until it becomes impossible for him ever to put the other to the ground. Another determines to raise his arms to heaven, never taking them down. In a short time, after excruciating pain, the joints stiffen so as to render any change impossible, and the arms shrivel until little but bone is left. Some let their nails grow into their flesh and through their hands. The forms of these penances are innumerable, and those who undergo them are regarded as holy men and are worshipped and supported by their less religious fellows. Kali must still have her blood, and hundreds of kids, goats, buffaloes, and other animals are sacrificed daily at her shrine. We saw the bloody work going forward. Crowds of pilgrims, numbering at least three hundred during our short stay, came in bands from the country to propitiate the goddess. Each one presents an offering as the idol is shown. It is the most disgusting object I have ever seen, and a sight of it would, I am sure, frighten children into crying. The business is skilfully managed. A small dark hall, capable of holding about twenty-five worshippers, occupies the space before the idol. This is filled with people and the doors closed; then, amid the murmurs of priests and beating of gongs, two sliding-doors are drawn aside, and the horrible she-demon, with swollen blood-red tongue, comes into view for a moment only, and the gifts are thrown at her. The crowd is excited by fear and awe, but ere the figure can be closely scrutinized the doors close, and the poor ignorant wretches seem stupefied with what has been revealed. They pass slowly out, looking as if they had been almost blinded with a glimpse of the forbidden mysteries, and another batch crowds in to be similarly worked upon. We saw other forms and figures of worship too gross to speak of. Nothing yet seen can be called idolatry when compared with this, and I felt like giving up all hope of improvement in these people; but then when one sees the extent and character of the superstitions of the East he cannot help having doubts of the advancement or elevation of the species. There is, however, this consoling knowledge, that the worshippers, such young girls and boys as we saw to-day excepted, know that Kali is but the symbol of power, not the power itself. Around this fact the forces able to overthrow superstition may be evolved hereafter. The germ is there.

The hundreds of young, pretty, innocent children whom we saw brought to-day to witness such rites by kind, dutiful, religious parents—the most conscientious and most respectable of the native race—were dressed with as much care and pride as a corresponding number of young Christians would be when taken to the rite of confirmation. How could I be otherwise than sad and murmur, " Forgive them, for they know not what they do." Thus far is plain sailing, for every one will agree with me ; but when I denounced to the priests the pools of clotted blood as offensive, even to coarse men, and wholly unfit as a satisfactory offering to any power to whom we can ascribe the name of God, they retorted by saying this is also part of the Christian system : the God of Abraham demands his sacrifice of blood also. It is in vain to intimate that this day is past and that our Father in heaven no longer takes delight in the blood of rams or of bullocks. I shall never forget the malicious inquiry : " Does your God *change*, then ? " " No, certainly not ; but our conceptions of him change year by year as we gain knowledge." They smile, and I am troubled. Let us pause and reflect before we rashly assail any form of religion until we know that what we have to offer in its place is really free from the errors we mourn over in others. In the progress of the race such dreadful conceptions of God must apparently exist for a time. Has not Herbert Spencer himself assured us that,

"Speaking generally, the religion current in each age and among each people has been as near an approximation to the truth as it was then and there possible for men to receive."

I needed all this from the philosopher to restrain my indignation at first and afterward to mitigate my sorrow. Even this was not quite sufficient, but how much an anecdote will sometimes do, and this one the philosopher above quoted told me himself. At times, when disposed to take gloomy views of man's advance, and sickened by certain of his still barbarous beliefs and acts, he had found relief in the story Emerson tells of himself when in similar moods. After attending a meeting—perhaps the one where he was hissed from the platform for denouncing human slavery—he walked home burning with indignation; but entering his grounds, and wandering among the green grass and the flowers, silently growing in the cool moonlight, he looked up at the big trees and the big trees looking down upon him seemed to say: "What! *so hot, my little sir!*" Yes, we must upon our "distemper sprinkle cool patience." If all is not well, yet all is coming well. In this faith we find peace. The endless progress of the race is assured now that evolution has come with its message and shed light where before there was darkness, reassuring those who thought and who therefore doubted most.

General Litchfield, United States Consul, fortunately accompanied us upon this visit, and he knew two of the officiating priests, who spoke English perfectly. These escorted us round and told us about everything. The history of these two natives is most suggestive. They were educated by the government in one of its colleges, and very soon saw the falsity of their religious tenets, but failing to get suitable employment, they had to return to their families, who owned a share in the Kali Temple, which is still profitable property, held like any other building. The revenues are now divided among a hundred priests, and maintain these and their families, all of whom are of the same family. Should another son marry he becomes entitled to a certain share, and so on. They carry this imposture on simply as a matter of business, and laughed at us when we said they knew it was all humbug. If it be true that no religion can long retain vital force after its priests know it to be false, then there is hope for the speedy fall of idolatry in India ; but I fear there will be no lack of men who will, like these hypocrites, continue to preach what they know better than to believe, as long as rich livings are at stake.

In one of our drives General Litchfield pointed out the house where Macaulay wrote some of his essays while here laying the foundations of the law code which has proved such a boon to India. I see one great tribute paid to this monument of his genius : the codification of the law in England is urged forward by pointing to the indisputable success of the Indian code.

India has also great capabilities in regard to another article of the largest consumption—tea. In this it is not improbable she will some day rival even China. We have been travelling for some days with a gentleman largely interested in its cultivation in the Assam district, and learn from him that the tea grown there commands a higher price than the Chinese article. It also prospers in several other parts of India, and the amount grown is increasing rapidly. The total export in 1878 was 34,000,000 pounds, while last year, 1883, it reached, it is stated, 57,000,000 pounds, a large increase, while the tea culture in China is about at a stand-still, the amount exported to England in 1868, £11,000,000, exceeding that in any year since. India, therefore gains rapidly upon China, and prophets are not wanting who assert that as India was the original home of the plant (as some authorities claim), so India is going to furnish the world in future most of its tea. This may all be true and yet the amount grown in India be a bagatelle to the product of China, which consumes at home about nine times the amount exported. Indian tea is pure, while that raised by both the Japanese and Chinese is adulterated. It is also much stronger. I advise all to give the Indian tea a fair trial.

India, you see, has great possibilities. She is distanced in cotton, is a good second in wheat, and has a place in the race for tea, with odds in her favor in the latter as far as export goes. I think this describes her situation fairly.

There are very few really successful equestrian statues in the world, but Calcutta boasts one of these— Noble's statue of General Outram. The artist has taken a bold departure, and instead of the traditional eagle glance of the hero, the general is represented as just checking his impetuous speed and casting a look behind ; the body turned round, and one hand resting on the horse's flank, while the other reins in the horse ;

his head bare, as if in the attack he had outrun his
troops, lost his helmet, and was stopping a moment for
them to overtake him. I liked this statue much, and
wished that some others of which I wot partook of its
merits.

We attended the Viceroy's ball on Wednesday evening, and enjoyed the brilliant scene. The uniforms of
British officers as well as those of the Civil Service are
gorgeous, and set off a ball-room effectively. We saw
more ladies here than upon all other occasions combined during our travels, and their general appearance
was certainly better than elsewhere, showing the
climate to be less severe upon them. Lord Lytton is a
small man of unimposing appearance, and entirely destitute of style, but the Commander-in-Chief, General
Haines, seems every inch a soldier, as do many of his
subordinate officers. Native princes were formerly
invited to these balls, and their presence, attended by
their suites in Oriental costumes, added much to the
brilliancy of the scene, but it was found desirable to
discontinue the practice; they could not partake of
European refreshments nor understand the appearance
of women in public, and especially their dancing, nor, I
fancy, could they look with becoming gravity upon dig-
nitaries so engaged, as they employ people to do their
dancing. I confess it struck me as bordering upon the
farcical to see Lord Lytton, charged with the government of more than two hundred millions, and

General Haines, Commander-in-Chief, with an active
campaign on his hands, Sir Thomas Wade, Her
Majesty's Ambassador to China, and the Lieutenant-
General, all in uniform, and the two former in knee-
breeches, "all of ye olden time," doing "forward four
and turn your partner" in the same quadrille. Imagine
President Lincoln, Secretaries Seward and Stanton, and
General Grant so engaged.

The Viceroy of India has certainly to do his part in
the way of ceremonial. Flaming handbills of an
English circus announce that the performances are
under his direct patronage. "Victoria, the Empress of
the Arena," is to-night to perform her unparalleled
feats in the ring in the presence of His Excellency.
This was the only tribute we saw paid in India to Her
Majesty's spick-and-span brand-new title of Empress.
We attended the performance, which was really creditable, but the natives sat unmoved throughout every
scene ; so different from the conduct of the Japanese,
who scream with delight like children under similar
circumstances. The Indians seem to take their pleasures sadly, like ourselves.

We did not fail to visit the famous banyan tree of
Calcutta, by far the largest in the world. Vandy
and I started and paced it around until we met, count-
ing three hundred and thirteen steps, or, say, three hundred yards; the main trunk is probably about thirty
feet in circumference, but from each main branch roots

have descended to the earth and become supporters of these branches, allowing them to extend still farther. In this way a branch may have in its course three or four supporters at intervals of twenty or thirty feet; the leaves are thick, and much resemble those of the rubber tree in size and character.

We see numerous native barbers engaged in shaving the people. Victim and operator squat down in a corner on their " hunkers," facing each other, and the operation then begins, the utensils being laid out upon a rag on the ground. It seems the most unnatural posture in the world for shaving or hair-dressing, but as it is the custom there must be some advantages in it which we cannot even guess.

One morning we drove to the burning ghat, and from personal examination of cremation, I am able to express my preference for Christian burial. The business of burning the dead—for in India it is a business like any other, and belongs to a low caste—is carried on in the most heartless manner. A building is erected upon the river-bank, about a hundred feet in length and twenty-five feet in width, and open on the side toward the river. The dead are brought there upon stretchers wrapped in a little cloth, and are first shaved by the attendants, who open the mouth and pour down a vial of the water of the sacred Ganges. The body is then bent into a sitting posture, carried out to the middle of the building, and wood built around it. We saw the

14

embers of several piles which had just done their work, and one pile blazing, through the interstices of which parts of the body were plainly visible. It was all horrible to me as conducted here, but I can conceive of the grand funeral piles of the high priests being made most impressive; and so I am told they are, but the cremation of the poor lacks every element of this nature. My heart bled for a poor widow whose husband had just been taken to the pile. She was of a very low caste, but her grief was heartrending; not loud, but I thought I could taste the saltness of her tears, they seemed so bitter; but she has this consolation to comfort her after the outburst, that she insured the eternal happiness of her mate by having his ashes mingled with the sacred river of God. No one will touch or associate with the caste who dress and burn the dead, nor could any one be induced, save one branch of this caste, to furnish the fire which lights the funeral pile, for which sometimes large sums are exacted, in case the relatives of the dead are wealthy.

The absence of women, other than coolies, which has struck us everywhere in the East, is if anything even more marked in India, where, so far, we have scarcely seen one woman of high caste. The Mohammedans do not permit their ladies ever to leave the house, and upon rare occasions, when temples must be visited, they are closely concealed from view and driven in a close carriage or carried in a sedan chair. The Hindoos are not quite so strict, and we have seen a few in secluded streets going a few steps, but closely muffled up and with faces covered.

Do you remember with what laughter the sun-spot theory was received? At least I know I laughed when I first heard of it—but here in India, where the rainfall is the prime condition of existence to millions and the sun is much more powerful than with us, the Meteorological Department has just reported that there is apparently a sure connection between the rainfall and its distribution and the spots upon the sun. When these spots are at the minimum there is a tendency to prolonged excessive pressure over the land and an unusual amount and irregular distribution of rain.

" There is blood upon the moon,"

still stands as a poetic expression; but " there are great spots upon the sun " must pass as presaging famine. There seems to have been an element of truth after all in " the signs of the heavens " of the astrologer, only the great law which governs them was unknown.

THURSDAY, February 6.

We left Calcutta for the Hindoo Mecca, Benares, to-night, and had our first experience of Indian railway travel, which proved to be very comfortable. We had all to ourselves a first-class carriage compartment containing two sofas lengthwise of the car and one across;

above these were three upper berths, to be let down, if necessary, and used as beds. A smaller compartment contained dressing-room, etc., for all of which there is no extra charge. Evidently there is no field here for my enterprising friend Mr. Pullman. Our route lay through the opium-growing district, and the white poppies were just beginning to bloom. I did not know before that only the white variety is grown, but, curiously enough, the red flower is not nearly so productive. This set us to thinking that there may, after all, be something in the Chinaman's preference for a black dog to one of another color. By all means let us have the two kinds analyzed and see whether the blood be just the same. The opium question has given rise to much angry discussion upon which we do not propose to pass an opinion. My readers may safely assume, I think, that the difficulties we encounter in restraining or abolishing the use of liquor among ourselves, also surround the opium question in the East. It is their liquor. China grows most of what she consumes, and I believe would grow it all if the Indian drug was not admitted. Its exclusion by the Chinese would not therefore seriously lessen its use. Still it places England in a false position before the world to enforce its admission by treaty stipulations. The sum involved to the Indian revenue exceeds seven millions sterling per annum ($35,000,000); that is the net yearly profit made out of the growth of the poppy. It would not all be lost, and perhaps not be seriously reduced, were China free to exclude it, for large quantities would be smuggled in, and the people would have it. I wish England's hands were entirely free from all stain in connection with this business. China should not be compelled by England to admit a drug which is considered pernicious.

The total exports this year were ninety-one thousand chests, valued at thirteen millions sterling, most of it to China. The growing of the poppy is a government monopoly in the Bengal province (Calcutta). Each year government enters into contracts with cultivators to devote so many acres to its cultivation—an advance upon the expected crops is made and final settlements at the end of the season according to amount and quality produced. The drug is extracted at two government factories. In the other district, the produce of which passes through the Bombay presidency, the cultivation of the plant is free, but a duty is collected upon the opium.

We are in the dry season, and where not irrigated the vast plains of India are parched. The soil is a light brown clay, and turns readily to fine dust, which seems to blow over everything and make all of one hue. Even the scanty muslin clothing of the people becomes of this dusty color. The houses are only mud huts one story high and roofed with coarse straw; an opening in one side serves as a door, but with this exception the hovel is closed; neither window nor chimney appears, and when fires are made the smoke escapes through all parts of the roof, and when the roof is closer than usual, through the door. This dusty, dirty mud color of soil, streets, houses, dress, and people gives one an impression of a more squalid poverty even than that of the overcrowded Chinese in Shanghai. These latter have more clothing and no dust, and their dirtiness seems a less objectionable form of dirt.

One remarkable difference between these people and the Chinese is that we never see the former eating, while the latter eat frequently. I am told that the Indians have but two meals a day—at noon and at eight in the evening, with a bite early in the morning. As is well known, the Hindoos are strict vegetarians, neither meat, fish, poultry, nor even eggs being allowed. The result of a vegetable diet, if they are to be taken as a fair example, is not such as to favor its general adoption. The Mohammedans, on the other hand, eat everything but pork; like the Jews, they forbid this one article, and I am informed that the Mohammedans are a far sturdier race than their neighbors the Hindoos; but they should be superior, as the advance from Hindooism, with its numerous gods and idolatrous worship, to Mohammedanism with its one god is an immense one. The claims which Mohammed has upon the gratitude of mankind rest upon a solid basis, for he it was who proclaimed to the East that there is but one

God, and announced himself as his prophet only, instead of demanding that he himself should be worshipped as divine; but he performed another great service, for he abolished the abominable system of caste, and thus it comes that the most popular religion in existence hails all its disciples, from the peasant to the Sultan, as of one brotherhood, as Christianity does with hers. There are nearly fifty millions of Mohammedans among the two hundred and fifty millions of India's population, and it is to them we must chiefly look for the regeneration of the native races.

As we pass through the country we are surprised at the crowds of gayly-dressed natives waiting at the crossings to pass the line, and at the stations to take the trains. All the colors of the rainbow are to be seen in their wraps. It is the season of idleness just now, their two months of rest in the country, and the entire population seem to be running about in holiday attire, forming a striking contrast to their fellows in the towns, who sit in their hovels hard at work, one crowding another in his seat. Before England established free dispensaries for these masses the rate of mortality must have been something incredible; even now it is very high, although last year in the two provinces alone no fewer than eleven hundred thousand patients were treated or prescribed for by these institutions, which we rejoice to see scattered throughout the country wherever we go. Nor in all her illustrious record do we know a brighter page than that which chronicles the rise and progress of these truly English organizations.

Manufactures in India are not profitable at present : during the scarcity of cotton, owing to the American war, large quantities were grown here and fortunes made in the business; eventually cotton mills were built in Bombay and jute mills in Calcutta, which prospered for a time, but now that America, under the system of free labor, has demonstrated her ability to supply cheaper and better cotton than India, these enterprises languish. I counted thirty-eight spinning and weaving companies in Bombay, and twenty-one cotton-press companies, the shares of which were quoted in the market, and found that on an average these would not command to-day one-half the actual capital paid in. It is much the same with the seven Calcutta jute companies. Cotton, both as to growth and manufacture, in India, I believe has no future, save one contingent upon the interruption of the American supply, of which there does not appear much danger. But it must be borne in mind that the fall in the value of silver so far is a direct gain to native productions. The planter and manufacturer alike pay in the debased currency and sell the product as far as it is exported for gold, upon which they realize a handsome premium. America needs a continuance of low rates for transportation to counterbalance this advantage of her Indian rival.

BENARES, Saturday, February 8.

We started from our hotel early this morning to see the Hindoos bathing in the sacred waters of the Ganges. Benares is to the pious Hindoo all that Mecca is to the good son of the Prophet, and much more beside, and he esteems himself happy if it is vouchsafed him to die in sight of this stream and this city. Pilgrims flock here from all parts of India, and thousands are carried from long distances, while dying, that their eyes may behold, ere they close, the holy city of God. At the junction yesterday, six miles out, we came upon our first band of pilgrims, for they now patronize the rail freely, men and women, each with the inevitable bundle of rags which serves as his bed *en route* and as a change of clothing, to be blessed by washing in the Ganges. It requires about a month to worship at every temple and do all that the priests persuade these pilgrims to be essential for their salvation, every ceremony, of course, producing revenue for this class. Each Rajah of India has his temple upon the bank of the river, and it is these handsome structures, situated on the cliff which overhangs the river, that give to Benares its unparalleled beauty. In each temple a priest is maintained who prays constantly and bathes every morning as a substitute for his master, the Rajah, but the latter comes in person also for one month each year to perform the sacred rites. We were fortunate this morning in seeing the Rajah of Nepaul at his devotions. He has a small covered boat of his own, and we found him on his knees, in front of it, gazing upon the sun, as we pulled slowly past in our boat, his staff standing behind him in reverential attitudes. For one full month this intelligent ruler, who speaks English fluently and is well informed of the views Europeans hold of his religious ideas, will nevertheless work hard, visiting daily the temples, going through various exercises, and bathing every morning in the Ganges. One other Rajah is here, and others are shortly to come and do likewise. It seems so strange that these men still remain slaves to such superstitions; but how few among ourselves succeed in rising beyond what we happen to have been taught in our childhood! It is very different, I am told, with those who have received English ideas in their youth at the government colleges. They make quick work of the Hindoo idols; but so far every one here agrees with the Rev. Dr. Field when he says: " It needs very little learning to convince the Hindoo that his sacred books are a mass of fable. But this does not make him a Christian. It only lands him in infidelity, and leaves him there." The *Encyclopædia Britannica* says that " the progress of Protestant missions amounts at present to almost nothing." In Dr. Mullen's report, down to 1871, the " whole force of English missionaries—579, and of native preachers, 1,993—had produced a native Christian population of only 280,600. There was probably a much larger number in the south

of India about the middle of the eighteenth century."
I heard everywhere corroborations of this statement.

The wife of the Rajah, we heard, had yesterday performed the most sacred of all the ceremonies under
conditions of considerable popular excitement. The
sacred well, the stairs leading from it to the river, and
the bathing place at the river, were all covered in; the
crowd could only see the sedan chair which carried the
queen to the well, but the spectacle attracted great
numbers. This well is simply a trench about twenty-
five feet long and not more than three feet wide, but it
must be thirty feet below the surface. Broad steps lead
to it from all sides. In this well every Hindoo of good
caste is permitted to wash, and there are always many
in it. The water is foul and offensive, yet such is its
reputed sanctity that no sin can be committed so
heinous that it cannot be washed away by it. The
ceremony, fortunately, is incomplete until one, rising
from its stench, walks to the pure water of the Ganges
and bathes there. I think the ceremony must typify
man before purification, foul with sin, and then cleansed
by bathing in the pure Jordan afterward; but no one
could give me any information upon this point. At all
events it was into this sink that the Rajah's wife
bravely immersed herself yesterday, and it is here, too,
the Rajah himself must come before he leaves—poor
man!

The place where the dead are burned was pointed

out as we drifted past in our boat, but it was then un-occupied. As we returned, however, one body was in the hands of the attendants, who had taken it into the river and were just in the act of pouring the sacred water down the throat preparatory to the final scene. One woman alone sat on the shore weeping, and two small children at her side seemed not to understand why. It was still early morning, and all was quiet. Our guide pointed out some who were evidently friends, in conversation with men on a parapet above. They were bargaining for the sacred fire to light the funeral pile. Government prohibits the burning of the forlorn widow with her husband's body, as was formerly the custom, but it is said many widows wish this privilege even yet, nor can I blame them much. I'm sure I don't see why, beyond the mere instinct of self-preservation, they should have a wish to live on. Those educated people among us who commit suicide have prospects before them which might be called blissful compared with what confronts poor widows in India.

We visited the principal temples and shrines in succession, but I do not propose to rehearse their names and special virtues. There is a great sameness about them, but the Monkey Temple differs from the others in having several hundred monkeys running over it in every direction. Like the rest, this is owned by a number of people, and its shares are marketable property. Dr. Lazarus, the chief of the medical department, tells us that the "river people," a term embracing those who own the temples on the stream—just as we would say the "steel rail" or the "pig metal" people at home—are very much depressed, complaining bitterly that the revenues have fallen away. One owner in the Monkey Temple, probably the most prosperous of all, had some time ago asked what this trouble meant. He was advised to sell his monkey stock as soon as possible, but up to the present day he has found no one willing to invest in the property. One of the high priests of another sacred shrine said to my informant that he had seen in his day three ages—one of gold, one of silver, and now he had reached the age of copper, and was only thankful when he saw a few pieces of that. "The people still come as of old, to worship, which costs nothing," he said, "but they don't pay the gods more than a pittance. I wonder what we are coming to?" While great allowance has to be made for the changed condition of affairs throughout the world, which has seriously affected the revenues of religious establishments everywhere, and which India has had to share, aggravated by the loss of her cotton industry, still it can hardly be doubted that Hindooism as a vital force is crumbling slowly to pieces, and that the priests are losing their sway over the masses. Caste also goes slowly with the tide of change, and Brahmans are now occasionally found taking employment below that of their caste; and while a high-caste Hindoo some years ago would have considered himself defiled if even the garments of a low-caste person touched him, he now rushes into the same railway compartment among the general crowd and struggles for a seat with various castes, and says nothing about it. One stand the English home Government took, in deference to English ideas as opposed to those of the Anglo-Indian authorities, which alone dooms caste, sooner or later, to extinction: it would not permit different classes on the railways to be established for Hindoos or Mohammedans, or for castes of the former. Many residents in India feared that this would prevent the natives from using the lines, but the result has wonderfully belied these fears and vindicated the sagacity of those who ventured to inaugurate this system; and now one sees Hindoos and Mohammedans, high caste and low caste, jostling each other in their efforts to get desirable seats in the third-class compartments, where, by the way, they travel for less per mile than anywhere else in the world, third-class fares in India being uniformly one-half of a cent per mile. First-class fares, with such sleeping-car luxuries as I have before described included, are just about our rates with sleeping-cars not included—viz., three cents per mile.

While Hindooism is thus passing away, but little progress is made with Islam. The fifty millions of Mohammedans stand to-day where they have stood for ages, and cry from their mosques morning and night, "There is but one God, and Mohammed is his prophet."

No idols, no drunkenness, no caste. The contrast between their faith and that of Christians is therefore much less marked, and our guide says to us, with evident pride, "Hindoos believe many gods, worship idols. *I believe like you*, one God, no idols."

India is thus in a state of transition, her caste and religion both passing away. The work before this generation and probably the next is to pull down and destroy. It will remain for those who come after to begin the more difficult labor of building up.

We met at Benares strings of water-carriers, carrying brass vessels on each end of a pole borne over the shoulder. These come here for hundreds of miles on foot, and take back to their customers in the country the sacred water of the blessed river. It is a regular business, and furnishes employment for thousands of men. Upon no account must this water be carried by railway and deprived of its healing powers by being handled by unbelievers. It must be carried by Hindoos of the proper caste on foot, or it has no virtue.

Science invades everything nowadays, and the officials have recently had the water of one of the sacred wells analyzed by a chemist—audacious dog of an infidel—and here he comes with his CO_2 and all the virtue of this water of life is gone. It is found unfit for human use, and the well is ordered to be closed. The chemist, in the eyes of the ignorant natives, has sacrificed spiritual for physical health; preferred the welfare of their bodies to that of their souls, as is the custom with these wicked scientists.

We pass booths in which native jewellers sit hard at work fashioning rings, brooches, and other articles of personal adornment. Their dexterity is marvellous; without elaborate appliances of any kind, with only a small blow pipe and a few rude tools, they will take a gold coin from you and before your eyes shape it into any form selected. But it is said they must have a model to copy from; no original design emanates from them. The booths, or little shops, are curious affairs. They are built of mud, with neither window nor door, the floor on which the artisans sit being about four feet above the narrow street level.

I never was more thoroughly impressed with the position of the European of India than to-day when pushing through the crowded, narrow lanes of Benares. Our native guide went before us carrying a whip which he cracked and brandished among the crowd, calling out "Sahib! Sahib!" and the people, casting one glance behind, at once hurried out of our way, making a clear track for our august person supposed to represent the conquering race. The respectful salaams, as we caught the eye of one native after another, their deferential, not to say obsequious, attitude as we passed—all this tells its story. That "all men are born free and equal" will not enter the Hindoo mind for centuries—not till England has brought it up to the standard of self-government, which it is gradually doing, however, by its schools and colleges.

Benares has been famous for centuries for its manufacture of gold and silver embroideries. I remember that Macaulay speaks of them in his essay on Warren Hastings as decorating alike the court of Versailles and the halls of St. James. We went to the native village and saw the work carried on. How such exquisite fabrics come from the antiquated looms situated in mud hovels it is hard to understand, but they do. We saw one man who had no less than thirty-three different tiny spools to work from in a piece not more than a yard wide. All of these he had in turn to introduce in the web, and pass through a greater or lesser number of threads, the one starting in where the other left the woof, before one single thread was complete from end to end of the warp and could be driven into the pattern. The people of Benares also excel as workers in brass.

To-day we had a unique experience indeed, being carried through the principal streets of Benares on State elephants, kindly provided for us by the Rajah of Benares. Mr. H., of New York, whom we have met on his way round the world, and Vandy and I were the riders. We were driven to the palace, and found there two huge animals, gayly caparisoned, awaiting our arrival, surrounded by servants in resplendent liveries. The elephants very kindly got upon their knees, which rendered a short ladder only necessary for us to mount by. The motion is decidedly peculiar, and, until one becomes used to it, I should think very fatiguing; but we enjoyed our elephant ride greatly, and the Rajah has our hearty thanks.

We are in the land of the cheapest labor in the world. It is doubtful if men can be found anywhere else to do a day's work for as little as they are paid in India. Railway laborers and coolies of all kinds receive only four rupees per month, and find themselves; these are worth just now forty cents each, or, say, $1.60 (6s. 6d.) in gold for a month's service. Upon this a man has to exist. Is it any wonder that the masses are constantly upon the verge of starvation? Women earn much less, and of course every member of a family has to work and earn something. The common food is a pulse called gran; the better class indulge in a pea called daahl. Anything beyond a vegetable diet is not dreamed of.

Before leaving Benares I must speak again of the scene at the river, which far excels any representation I have seen of it or any description I have read. Photographs cannot be made to convey a just idea of its picturesque beauty, because the view is enlivened by such masses and combinations of color as Turner alone could do justice to. Indeed, my first thought as I saw the thousands on the ascending banks—one tier of resting-places above another, culminating in the grand temples towering at the tops—was that I had seen something akin to this in a dazzling picture somewhere. Need I say that it is in the Turner Gallery alone where such color can be seen? He should have painted the "Hindoo Bathers at Benares," and given the world one more gem revealing what he alone, in his generation, fully saw in the mind's eye, "the light which never shone on sea or shore." We have voted this scene at Benares the finest sight we have yet witnessed.

LUCKNOW, Tuesday, February 11.

We reached Lucknow at night. The moon was not yet shining, but the stars shed their peaceful halo around this spot, to which the eyes of the civilized world were so long directed during the dark days of the mutiny. At the hotel upon arrival a lady's voice was heard singing the universal refrain which nearest touches all English hearts in India and expresses the ever dominant longing, " Home, Sweet, Sweet Home."

There is no trace here of the massacres which have made this region memorable. But is the past to be repeated? Who can assure us that these bronzed figures which surround us by millions may not again in some mad moment catch the fever of revolt? This is the anxious question which I find intruding itself upon me every hour. Truly it is a dangerous game, this, to undertake the permanent subjection of a conquered race; and I do not believe that after General Grant sees India he will regret that the foolish Santo Domingo craze passed away. If America can learn one lesson from England, it is the folly of conquest, where conquest involves the government of an alien race.

Our first visit was to the ruins of the Residency, where for six long months Sir Henry Lawrence and his devoted band were shut up and surrounded by fifty thousand armed rebels. The grounds, which I should say are about thirty acres in extent, were fortunately encompassed by an earthen rampart six feet in height. You need not be told of the heroic resistance of the two regiments of British soldiers and one of natives, nor of the famous rescue. Hour after hour, day after day, week after week, and month after month, the three hundred women and children, shut in a cellar under ground, watched and prayed for the sound of Havelock's bugles, but it came not. Hope, wearied out at last, had almost given place to despair. Through the day the attacks of the infuriated mob could be seen and repelled, but who was to answer that when darkness fell the wall was not to be pierced at some weak point of the extended line? One officer in command of a critical point failing—not to do his duty, there was never a fear of that—but failing to judge correctly of what the occasion demanded, and the struggle was over. Death was the last of the fears of these poor women night after night as the days rolled slowly away. One night there was graver silence than usual in the room; all were despondent, and lay resigned to their seemingly impending fate. No rescue came, nor any tidings of relief. In the darkness one piercing scream was heard from the narrow window. A Highland nurse had clambered up to gaze through the bars and strain her ears once more. The cooling breeze of night blew in her face and wafted such music as she could not stay to hear. One spring to the ground, a clapping of hands above the head, and such a shriek as appalled her sisters who clustered round ; but all she could say between the sobs was: "The slogan—the slogan !" But few knew what the slogan was. " Didna ye hear—didna ye hear?" cried the demented girl, and then listening one moment, that she might not be deceived, she muttered, " It's the Macgregors gathering, the grandest o' them a'," and fell senseless to the ground. Truly, my lassie, the " grandest o' them a'," for never came such strains before to mortal ears. And so Jessie of Lucknow takes her place in history as one of the finest themes for painter, dramatist, poet or historian henceforth and forever. I have been hesitating whether the next paragraph in my note-book should go down here or be omitted. Probably it would be in better taste if quietly ignored, but then it would be so finely natural if put in. Well, I shall be natural or nothing, and recount that I could not help rejoicing that Jessie was Scotch, and that Scotchmen first broke the rebels' lines and reached the fort, and that the bagpipes led the way. That's all. I feel better now that this is also set down.

Lucknow, so rich in historical associations, is poverty itself in genuine architectural attractions, magnificent as it appears at a distance. It is a modern capital. About a century ago a king of Oude, in a moment of caprice, I suppose, determined to remove his capital from Fyzabad to Lucknow. Palaces on a great scale were hastily erected of common bricks and covered with white plaster. These look very fine at a distance, but closer inspection reveals the sham, and one is provoked because his admiration has been unworthily excited. Several other kings followed and carried on this imposture, each building his palace and tomb in this untruthful way. What could we expect from kings content to lie in such tombs but lives of disgusting dissipation? A simple marble slab were surely better than these pretentious lies: anything so it be genuine. However, retribution came, and the dynasty is extinct, the present king living as a prisoner in Calcutta.

The bazaars of Lucknow are well worth seeing, with their native jewellers, brass-workers, and other artificers, working in spaces not more than six feet square. We begin to see persons and modes which remind us of scriptural expressions—the water-carrier with the goat-skin filled, " the hewers of wood and drawers of water," the latter usually working in gangs of five. An earthen incline is built, leading up to the top of the wall which surrounds the well ; the well-rope passes over the shoulders of the drawers, and in marching down the incline they raise the bucket. We came to-day upon a lot of women grinding the coarse daahl. Two work at each mill, sitting opposite one another, pushing around the upper stone by means of upright handles fastened into it.

"And two women shall be grinding at the mill, and one shall be taken and the other left,"

saith the Scriptures of old, but our coming revised and corrected edition, I could not help hoping to-day, as I saw this picture for the first time, will note an error, or at least intimate a doubt of the correct translation of this passage ; or, if not, the age may require some commentator "more powerful than the rest " to console us with the hope that while at the first call one was indeed left, there would be a second, yea, and a third, a seventh, and a seventy times seventh call, in one of which even she would participate.

We have been this afternoon among the tombs of heroes—Lawrence and Havelock, Banks and McNeil, Hodson and Arthur—men who fell in the days of the mutiny. Lawrence's tomb is most touching from its simplicity—a short record, no eulogy, only

> " Here lies Henry Lawrence,
> Who tried to do his duty."

"I have tried to do my duty," he said, as he breathed his last, and this is all his tomb has to say of him ; but isn't it enough ?

One day in our drive we came upon our first elephant and our first camel camp, hundreds of the latter and nearly two hundred of the former being attached to the transportation department of the army. They are said to perform work which could never be done by other animals in this climate. Bullocks are the third class used as carriers: these are taught to trot, and do trot well. I remember one day in Ceylon one of them in a hackery gave us in the mail coach quite a spirited race for a short distance, but it was only to-day that I learned that camels are also so trained and used as mail or despatch bearers where speed is necessary, and the gait of a really good trained camel is said to be quite easy. If development goes forward in this line, our posterity may be using the camel in trotting matches with the horse. He would possess the advantage over that favorite animal which the Chinaman has over the European; he could go longer between drinks, and that counts for much.

The quarters for troops at Lucknow are models; the officers' quarters are surrounded and in some cases almost embowered by vines and flowers; lawn-tennis courts, cricket grounds, ball courts, and a gymnasium are provided for the private soldiers, and are finer than we have seen elsewhere, and serve to make Lucknow, with its beautiful gardens and long shady avenues, the one really pretty rural spot we have seen in India.

We are on our way to Agra by rail, and expect to arrive in time to drive out and see the Taj by moonlight. I have been reading more carefully than before some descriptions of it, and keep wondering whether this gem of the world is to prove a disappointment or not. Most things which have been heralded like the Taj fail to fulfil expectations at first, and how can stone and lime be so formed as to justify such fulsome praises as have been bestowed upon this tomb? One writer, for instance, exclaims, "There is no mystery, no sense of partial failure about the Taj. A thing of perfect beauty and of absolute finish in every detail, it might pass for the work of genii, who knew naught of the weakness and ills with which mankind were afflicted." The exact and prosaic Bernier had to express doubts whether "I may not be somewhat infected with 'Indianisme,' but I must needs say I believe it ought to be reckoned amongst the wonders of the world." Bayard Taylor exhausts eulogy upon the Pearl Mosque, calling it "a sanctuary so pure and stainless, revealing so exalted a spirit of worship, that I felt humbled as a Christian that our noble religion had never inspired its architects to surpass this temple to God and Mohammed;" but when he comes to the Taj itself he is lost in rapture. There is nothing, however, which the critics—those men who have failed in literature and art—will not venture to attack, and I thought it advisable to tone down my expectations by taking a dose of carping criticism. Unfortunately for me, however, when I had got fairly in with a writer who assures me " the design is weak and feeble," the " shadows are much too thin," this misleader left me in a worse condition than ever, for succumbing at last to the sweet overpowering charms of the structure as a whole, and apparently ashamed of himself for ever having dared to say one word against its perfections, he adds—just after he had bravely done the " design " and the " shadows "—" but the Taj is like a lovely woman : abuse her as you please, the moment you come into her presence you submit to her fascinations." Pretty criticism this for one who wishes the faults of this beauty clearly set forth ! I put this lover of the Taj aside at once and try another writer, who does indeed give me a page of preventive, well suited to one in my condition, but upon turning over the page he too falls sadly away, for here is his last line :

" The rare genius of the calm building finds its way unchallenged to the heart."

Well, then, gentlemen, if all this be so, what's the use of your petty criticism? If this marvel, before whose spell all men, even you yourselves, must bow, has a " rigidity of outline," an " air of littleness and luxury," a " poverty of relief," and if " the inlaid work has been vulgarly employed," and the patterns are " meagre in the extreme," wasn't it the highest aim that its builder could probably have had in view, to entrance the world and give to it a thing of beauty which is indeed a joy forever? and doesn't the Taj do this so far beyond all other human structures that no one thinks of naming another in comparison? And should not this incontrovertible fact teach you a lesson—just a little bit of modesty? No, gentlemen; it isn't the Taj that must be changed, either in its outline or shadows, to conform to your canons of criticism, but your canons of art that must be changed to embrace the Taj, or rather to set it apart, as a stroke of original genius, and consequently above and beyond the domain of criticism; for criticism, like science, works solidly only upon what is absolutely known, formulating its fixed decrees upon the past. All great geniuses have encountered the critics of their day. How Shakespeare violated the unities! and didn't Napoleon win battles which he should have lost? Let these people then be silent, and know that when a transcendent exhibition of original genius wins success beyond the reach of measurement by their plumb and line and square and compass, the higher law governing the seeming miracle will be duly revealed: and the Taj is just such a miracle, from all I can learn of its power.

The evidences of the intense summer heat are seen everywhere. The railway carriages have false tops, leaving an air space of a foot between the roof and the cover. Awnings cover the windows outside, and there are posted up directions for the use of the cooling apparatus applied to each first-class compartment; the frames for punkas are seen in the railway waiting-rooms, and we notice in the army regulations that during the hot season soldiers are required to stay in-doors between the hours of eleven and three. We are told of revolving fans being used to cool rooms, and that it is very common to fill doors and windows with thick mats of scented grass, which are kept constantly wet; the wind, passing through these, is cooled to about ninety degrees, and large banana leaves furnish a cool bed in extreme cases, from all of which, "Good Lord, deliver us!" We thank our stars every day that we are doing India when the heat, though great at midday, is not unbearable. We are five hundred and fifty miles north of Calcutta, and find the temperature much cooler. The people look stronger, and necessarily wear more clothing, which means that another piece of coarse bagging is wrapped around their shoulders. We are at the best hotel in Agra, and I notice as remarkable, in the printed list of prices, that a man to pull the punka in one's bedroom all night can be obtained for the sum of three annas, or six cents in silver. Washing costs two cents per piece, but while these strike us as cheap, the next item tells us that each guest during the hot season is chargeable with twenty cents per day for ice used at table etc. It is very sparingly used, but yet the little bit of ice you see costs as much as the labor of three men all night. All the employees of the railways in

India are required to join the volunteer forces, and to drill under the supervision of regular army officers, appointed by the government for this purpose. An excellent auxiliary force numbering many thousands is thus secured at trifling expense. One significant announcement posted at stations attracted my attention, and gave me an insight into one department in which India is in advance of us. This placard set forth that certain employees having been found under the influence of liquor while on duty, the district court had sentenced them to six months' imprisonment. This betokens a decided step forward, I take it, and one which it would be advisable for us to follow. A captain, pilot, engineer, railway conductor, or any one directly charged with the care of human lives convicted of being drunk while on duty should be held guilty of a criminal offence and punished by the State.

I have been admiring all through India three magnificent vines, now in full bloom. One, the Begonia, resembles our honeysuckle, but the flower is larger and hangs in large clusters; the second, called the Bouganviella, is purple in color and like our morning-glory, and the two are often seen climbing together up tall trees almost to their very tops, covering them with a mass of flowers. The third favorite, Poinsetta, is a leaf of rich magenta color. These three are the special glories of India. Some of our own flowers do tolerably well in this region, and the inherent love of the English for flowers and plants is seen in the numerous pretty plots and gardens.

Life in India is only rendered tolerable by the opportunity people have to enjoy things which would be beyond their reach at home without fortunes. All residences have grounds connected with them, more or less extensive, and laid out in fine gardens. Lawn-tennis and croquet grounds are the rule. Horses and carriages, or at least a vehicle of some kind, are indispensable, and no one who strolls around the European quarters in early morning and sees the large staff of servants lounging about the spacious verandas, awaiting the call of "Sahib" or "Mem Sahiba," can be at a loss to account for the disappointment often experienced by those who, after years of longing, at last go home to enjoy themselves in their fancied Elysium. Alas! ten times the sum that supports them here in style would not suffice in England. Here Sahib awakes and drawls out, "Qui hi" (you of my people who are in waiting). There is a stir among several servants who have lain the whole night long at his door, to be in readiness, and the moaning reply comes, "S-a-h-i-b," and he is surrounded by those who minister to his slightest wish all day, leaving him again at night only to repeat the performance on the morrow. When he drives his gig to town one servant stands at his back to wait upon him, and Madame appears in the afternoon upon the Mall in her grand equipage, two on the box and two standing behind, as if she were a duchess. As a European walks the streets he is salaamed by every native he chances to look at. He moves about, one of a superior race and rank. As he approaches a crowd, to look at a passing sight, a clear lane is made for him; and if he steps into the post-office to ask for letters, the natives instinctively fall back until Sahib is served. All this spoils a man for residence at home, where " one man is as good as another and a good deal better," unless a tremendous fortune is at one's back to purchase precedence, which nowadays is scarcely obtainable at any price even in England where traces of by-gone days linger longest : and so it falls out that many who have prayed for long years for the day to come for their return to England, find the coveted change but Dead Sea fruit when it is gained at last. A few even return to the land they had so long prayed to be allowed to leave, and take up their final abode among the hills. For these people I cannot help feeling deeply sorry. It is impossible that their lives can be full and rich to overflowing here. A tone of sadness, of vain regret, must pervade the mind. The prize so ardently struggled for has been found unsatisfactory, and at best their lives must draw to a close tinged by a sense of partial failure.

How many human beings can the land maintain to the square mile? About three hundred and fifty in Europe say the authorities, provided the soil is fertile and climate good. This is close upon the English and Belgian standard; but some parts of India are cursed with more than double this number; indeed one district has nearly eight hundred to the square mile. This seems to be the limit even for India, as population does not increase beyond it, and female infanticide begins to protrude its monstrous form whenever population becomes so dense. In the Punjaub, for instance, the males exceed the females sixteen per cent.—a fearful revelation; but it is just the same in many parts of China. All authorities agree that male children are tenderly cared for, and even desired. This is especially so in China, for no greater evil can befall a Chinaman than the absence of sons to keep unbroken the worship of ancestors. Death is nothing if he passes away with dutiful sons around his bedside ready to perform the sacred rites. To die without these is to send his soul forth a wanderer without claims upon his gods. The commercial aspect, however, has mostly to do with the question in India. Where is food for the little mouths, to come from, and how can a girl be reared by a family who live from day to day upon the brink of starvation, even when every member labors like a slave?

One morning we drove to the jail—one of the sights of India—and were fortunate in meeting the Inspector-General, Mr. Walker, an authority on all matters relating to prison discipline, and Dr. Tyler, the Chief for Agra. These officials kindly conducted us through the vast establishment. The prison labor is not, as generally with us, contracted out—a vicious plan which necessitates the intercourse of outsiders with the criminals and invariably leads to bad results. Here the prisoners deal with none but their keepers; but what pleased me most was the admirable system of rewards and promotions for good conduct which has been established. Marks are given and worn upon the clothes which shorten one's sentence from one day up to several, and it is possible for a prisoner in this way to acquire marks enough to take as much as one tenth from his imprisonment. The best behaved of all can rise to the position of wardens. Several hundreds have reached this prize, and are distinguished by better clothing, and also by ornamental badges. These wardens are placed over the other malefactors, and there is no difficulty experienced in enforcing the strictest discipline through them. Foremen of shops and of the various departments are all appointed from among the prisoners themselves, and, with the exception of the one in charge of the complicated machinery, there are no others employed in such capacities. The armed guards are, however, not of this class. In ordinary years the cost of maintenance per person is one rupee a month (40 cents gold); clothing 75 cents a year, including cost of supervision and all expenses of the jail department; prisoners in India thus cost only about $14 per year each. This prison maintains itself by the labor of its inmates, and last year showed an actual profit of about $40,000. Twenty-three hundred prisoners were confined within its walls when we were there. The total number of inmates of the jail in this and the Northwest Province is just now 39,000; but last year, owing to the famine, the number rose to 42,000. This seems a great number, but I am informed that, taking the population into account, it is not quite up to the average in England. We saw the prisoners working the celebrated Agra jail carpets and rugs, for which there is such demand that orders given to-day cannot be filled for many months. A new building has just been erected and filled with looms to increase the supply. Native dyes and materials alone are used, and one can thus rest assured that a carpet obtained here is genuine throughout. France takes the finest qualities, and we saw some so fine that the day's task of men sitting as close as they could the entire width of the web was only one inch per day. These carpets, which are really works of art, cost here $10 gold per square yard, and certainly not less than double that when retailed in Paris. Of the inmates about one hundred were women, their special crime being that of child-stealing, which is very common in India, the ornaments worn by the little ones being a strong temptation. We saw two young lads sentenced for life for this crime. They had stolen and robbed a child, and afterward thrown the body into a well. We left Messrs. Walker and Tyler strongly imbued with the feeling that we had seen the model prison of the world in Agra jail.

India gives us valuable hints upon the land question. There is no private tenure; at least it is not general, for when one speaks of a continent with two hundred and fifty millions of people possessed of different customs it is unsafe to say that anything does not exist. Speaking generally, the land of India belongs to village communities in which every family has its right. The State first taxes a certain portion of the produce. Akbar the first Mogul fixed it at one-third of the gross amount, which the head man of each village was required first to set apart for government. The remainder was divided among the community. For untold generations these village communities have preserved intact their traditions, which neither anarchy nor conquest have abolished. Unfortunately the English in the early days were disposed to introduce their system of landlord and tenant, and in the Bengal province this has led to infinite trouble. Men had arisen there who undertook the collection of the land tax of a district and paid the government an agreed-upon sum. They were in fact contractors (Zemindars); this was certainly the easiest mode for the British Government to obtain the revenue, but in recognizing these contractors it raised them virtually to the position of landlord. The poor cultivator could not reach the government at all. He was in the power of the Zemindar, who alone dealt with the authorities. As was to have been expected, the result was just as it has been found in Ireland. The Zemindars squeezed every penny out of the poor farmer which he could be made to yield, until finally the government was compelled to embark upon that perilous sea, land legislation, tenant rights, judicial rents, and all the rest of it.

In the Bombay presidency, however, wiser councils have prevailed. The cultivator deals directly with the government; has a lease as it were subject to revaluation every thirty years. In time the poor cultivator will no doubt rise to the advantages of this system by a process of natural selection. It was certain that many unfit occupiers would be found, and this has been the case so far. The plan is bound, however, to develop and sustain the most competent, and this means that it is the right plan. The land yields the government twenty-two millions sterling per annum ($110,000,000). Had the land owners of England not released themselves while acting as M. P.'s of the tax under which till then land was held by them, England would be in position to-day to remit many taxes which bear heavily upon the people.

We had a talk to-day with an officer of the forest department of India, which vainly strives to save the forests from wandering tribes who practice nomadic agriculture, reaping indeed where they sow, but rarely sowing twice in the same place, which is the difficulty. These tribes inhabit the hills of India, and depend for food solely upon crops grown in the forests. They make a clearing by burning the timber and scatter the seed, rarely taking the trouble to turn up the soil, although some tribes scratch the surface with sticks. The virgin soil yields forty and fifty fold of rice as a first crop. This is gathered and off go the gypsies to another locality for next season. The destruction of timber upon these small clearings is nothing, as our friend explained, compared to that caused by the spread of the fires. The government imposes heavy penalties upon these nomads, if discovered, but vast tracts remain where no restraint is possible. He was on his way to solitude among the hills, which he preferred to even the plains with their crowds. But England, England some day! was his dream. Ah, poor fellow! the chances are that he will fall and lie in his Indian forest; or, sadder yet, should fortune reach him and he realize his dream, that he would find life in England intolerable and return to die here a disappointed man. We have met several such, and for no class am I so profoundly sorry. Never to realize one's life dream is bad enough, but to have it sent you and then find it naught—that seems to me the keenest thrust which can enter the soul of man.

Among the attractions of Agra are the palaces and tombs of the Great Moguls, and we have been busy visiting them day after day. This was the capital during the most brilliant period of that extraordinary family's reign. The founder, Baber, lies buried at Cabool, which was the chief place before the invaders penetrated farther south. Six of these Moguls reigned, and no dynasty in history has six consecutive names of equal power to boast. Hereditary genius has strong support in the careers of these illustrious men; besides this, Baber was a lineal descendant of Tamerlane himself, on his father's side, and of a scarcely less able Tartar leader on his mother's side. So much for blood.

The greatest of the six was Akbar, who proved to be that rare combination, soldier and statesman in one. He, Mohammedan by birth, dared to marry a Hindoo princess as an example for his people to follow, but which, unfortunately, they have failed to do. It is strange to remember that the Moguls were seated on their thrones only three hundred years ago, Akbar being contemporaneous with Henry VIII., and ruling India when Shakespeare was still on earth.

Six successive generations of great men, like the Great Moguls, cannot be matched, I think, elsewhere; but it would not be fair to attribute this unbroken line altogether to the doctrine of hereditary genius. Much lies in the fact that upon each of these rulers in turn, depended the maintenance and success of his empire. The Moguls were real powers, indeed the only powers, and not only reigned but governed. Had the doctrine of the divine right of kings been overthrown in India during the reign of even the ablest of the six, and the heir to the throne been debarred the exercise of power;

taught from his infancy that his rôle was to be wholly ornamental, a sham king whose chief end and use was the opening of fancy bazaars or the laying of foundation stones, he too would have developed into something suited for the purpose in view, just as heirs apparent have done elsewhere. It was the continual exercise of high functions which made the race great and kept it so. To *play* the part of king when one knows himself the political valet of his prime minister, would soon have taken manhood out of Akbar himself, if we can imagine such a man willing to play the part.

I am not going to give a catalogue of what is to be seen in Agra, having no notion of writing a guide-book or of filling notes with long passages from such sources, as I see many writers have done; but I must speak of three or four structures which have pleased me most.

The " Fort " is a most impressive pile of masonry, a Warwick Castle upon a large scale, the ramparts being one and a quarter miles in circumference. This was Akbar's principal palace, or rather series of palaces, for it embraces the Pearl Mosque, Public Audience Hall, and Jessamine Tower, all of which are within its walls.

The tomb of her father, built by that rare woman, Noor Mahal, she who sleeps in the Taj, is a marble structure of exquisite proportions, and quite unlike others because of the great number and extent of the perforated screens of marble of which it is principally composed. Up to the time we had seen this I think I liked it the best of any; but then Noor Mahal had built it for her father, and I was predisposed to like this proof of her filial devotion.

There is one romantic and perfect love story concerning her in the annals of the Moguls. Akbar's son, the future ruler, fell desperately in love with a young lady, but for reasons of state she was not eligible, and the emperor quietly provided a husband for her in the person of one of his generals. The young heir only knew that she was married and he condemned to take to wife the woman provided for him. Two years after he had become emperor the husband of his first love died, and although she was then a middle-aged woman, he, the emperor, sought her out and not only married her (she could have been his slave), but raised her to the throne with himself, stamping her image with his own upon the coin of the realm. Such an unbounded influence did this capable and high-spirited woman acquire over not only her devoted husband but the circle of the court, that she became the constant adviser in all important affairs; and that she might not be less thoroughly feminine, I am glad to see it recorded that she introduced improved modes of dress and manners among her ladies. The emperor told his priests one day that until he had married this paragon he had not known what marriage meant. But her grandest achievement is yet to be told. The emperor had previously been dis-

solute, probably from his first pure dream of love having been so cruelly dispelled—who knows?—but Noor
Mahal lifted him into higher regions, and made him a
better man. She loved him fervently, and, on more
than one occasion, when the emperor was attacked, she
imperilled her own life to save his. As they grew old
they became more and more to each other, and at her
death was it any wonder the emperor ordered that a
tomb should rise excelling all previous tombs as much,
if possible, as Noor Mahal excelled all other women?
This tomb, the Taj Mahal (Diadem Tomb), is said to
have cost more than two millions sterling, which is
equal to an expenditure of fifty millions of dollars with
us to-day. Truly a costly monument, you say. No
doubt, but if it has given to mankind one proof that the
loftiest ideal can be wrought out and realized in practice, the Taj would be cheap even if its erection had
emptied the Comstock lode; and there are men—wise
men too—who affirm that it performs this miracle and
inspires them with the pleasing hope that in the far
ages yet to come the real and the ideal may grow closer
together. The emperor built no tomb for himself, as
was customary, but as the kind fates decreed, he was
placed side by side with her who had been to him so
much, and they rest together, under the noblest canopy
ever made by human hands. Taking into account the
degraded position accorded to women, and remembering
to what Noor Mahal raised herself, I think she must be

allowed to rank as the greatest woman who ever reigned, and perhaps the greatest who ever lived, for no one has climbed from such a depth to such a height as she, as far as I know. Assuming that Cleopatra was all that Shakespeare has made her for us, a human being of whom it could be truly said

"Age cannot wither nor custom stale her infinite variety,"

yet the Egyptian was born to the purple, a queen recognized by her nation, and entitled to rule from the first. What was this general's daughter in India? A woman, to begin with, which in India meant an inferior being, and yet she rose to equality with the Mogul and was consulted upon affairs of state—not simply because she was, in a bad sense, the ruler's favorite, but by the inherent force of her own abilities.

Akbar's Tomb amazes one by its gigantic size, which dwarfs all other tombs. The amount of inlaid work, composed of jasper, carnelian, and other precious stones, seen at every step, inclines one to believe that it cost the fabulous sum stated. It should be remembered that it was the custom among these monarchs always to erect during their lives a palace in which great ceremonies took place while they lived, and which became their tomb at their death. A similar custom prevailed in Egypt, where each ruler began a pyramid when he began his reign. It was in this way that so many splendid structures were built. Akbar did not live to see this vast building completed, but his son carried on the work. The stern simplicity of Akbar's tomb, which is in the centre of the building and under ground, pleased me. It is a plain solid block of marble, without one word upon it, or mark of any kind; as if it would say to all time, What need to tell the world that the great Akbar lies here?

Speaking generally, the palaces and tombs of Agra are far finer than I had imagined them to be, and the relief experienced in getting away from the plaster shams of Lucknow—cheap magnificence, to genuine grandeur at Agra—can be easily imagined.

Our train having been delayed in reaching Agra, we had arrived too late to visit the Taj by moonlight; and in deference to the strong remonstrance of every one we have met here, we have not yet attempted to see the wonder. "Oh! don't think, please don't think of seeing the Taj until the very last, because, if you do, every thing else will seem so coarse," has been in substance the exclamation of every friend. But now we are through with all else, and we start, two o'clock P.M., February 14th, 1879. Vandy has just come to announce that our carriage is ready. Good-bye! Am I to be disappointed? Of course I am. I have made up my mind to that, and having just had tiffin, and drank a whole pint of bitter beer, I feel myself quite competent to criticise the Taj with the best of them, and especially well fitted just now to stand no nonsense.

We met an American who was travelling as a matter of duty, and had found, as far as travel was concerned, I suspect, that he belonged to the class represented by the grumbler in paradise, whose " halo didn't fit his head exactly." He had found nothing in India, he said, but a lot of rubbish, but checked himself at once, "except the Taj. Now that building—that is—perfectly satisfactory," as if he had ordered a suit of clothes from his tailor and had nothing to find fault with. On the other hand, I have just come across a statement " that stern men, overpowered by the sight of it, have been known to burst into tears." It is this miracle of inanimate matter we are now to see. But here cames Vandy again. " Come on, Andrew ; carriage waiting." I'm off—particulars in our next.

FRIDAY NIGHT, February 14.

We have seen it, but I am without the slightest desire to burst into rapturous adjectives. Do not expect me to attempt a description of it, or to try to express my feelings. There are some subjects too sacred for analysis, or even for words, and I now know that there is a human structure so exquisitely fine, or unearthly, as to lift it into this holy domain. Let me say little about it; only tell you that, lingering until the sun went down, we turned in the noble gateway which forms a frame through which you see the Taj in the distance, with only the blue sky in the background,

around and above it, and there took our last fond sad
farewell, as the shades of night were wrapping the
lovely jewel in their embrace, as if it were a charge too
sweetly precious not to be safely enveloped in night's
black mantle, till it could again shine forth at the dawn
in all its beauty to adorn the earth. Full in its face we
gazed. How kindly it seemed to look upon us! And as
one parts for the last time from one whose eye glistens
at his glance, we turned never to look upon the Taj
again, hiding our eyes as the carriage rolled away, lest
by any mischance a partial view should intrude to mar
the perfect image our mind has grasped to tarry with
us forever. We had been so deliciously sad, and at the
same time so thrillingly but yet so solemnly happy for
hours, and now came pain alone, the inevitable finale to
all our joys on earth—the parting forever. But till the
day I die, amid mountain streams or moonlight strolls in
the forest, wherever and whenever the mood comes,
when all that is most sacred, most elevated, and most
pure recur to shed their radiance upon the tranquil
mind, there will be found among my treasures the
memory of that lovely charm—the Taj.

We had engaged to meet some friends at the club
as we drove homeward, but was it any wonder that
neither of us remembered this until the stoppage of the
carriage at our hotel awoke us from our reveries! What
was to be done? Vandy's reply expressed our condition exactly: " Go out to enjoy myself when I feel that

I want to go and put on mourning! I couldn't do it." And we didn't. Our friends will please accept this intimation.

In reading these pages at home so long after the visit one can bring one's self to be a little prosaic in regard to this marvel, and tell his readers just what the Taj is. As before stated, it is the structure erected by the Emperor Jehanghir in memory of that paragon Noor Mahal. That a tomb should be erected at all for a woman in India is of itself significant, to begin with, and the Roman Emperor who put his horse's head upon the coin and who is supposed to have consulted him in political affairs did not take a much wider departure from custom than did this true lover when he put upon the coin a woman's image with his own.

The Taj is built of a light creamy marble, so that it does not chill one as pure cold white marble does. It is warm and sympathetic as a woman. One great critic has finely called the Taj a feminine structure. There is nothing masculine about it, says he; its charms are all feminine. This creamy marble is inlaid with fine black marble lines, the entire Koran in Arabic letters, it is said, being thus interwoven.

The following description is condensed from Fergusson : The enclosure, which includes an inner and an outer court, the whole about a fifth of a mile wide, extends along the banks of the Jumna River one-third of a mile. The principal gateway, opening into the inner court, is a hundred and forty feet high by a hundred and ten feet wide. The mausoleum stands in the centre of a raised marble platform, eighteen feet high, and exactly three hundred and thirteen feet square. At each angle of this terrace rises a minaret, a hundred and thirty-three feet high, and of exquisite proportions, "more beautiful, perhaps," says Ferguson, "than any other in India." The mausoleum itself is a square of one hundred and eighty-six feet, with the corners cut off to the extent of about thirty-four feet. In the centre is the principal dome, fifty-eight feet in diameter, and eighty feet high, and at each angle is a smaller dome surmounting a two-story apartment, about twenty-seven feet in diameter.

The light to the central apartment is admitted through double screens of white marble trellis-work of the most exquisite designs. In any climate but that of India this would produce darkness within, but here, in a building constructed wholly of white marble, it serves to temper the glare of the blinding light. No words can express the chastened beauty of that dim religious light, the unearthly effect of the subdued sunshine, sparkling now and then upon the brilliant stones of which the graceful mosaics, vines and flowers are composed. Twenty thousand workmen are said to have been employed upon this marvel for twenty-two years. I would think the time and labor and money bestowed upon it well spent had it been twenty times—aye, a hundred times—as great.   There is no price too dear to pay for perfection.

The mosaics of the interior are exquisitely graceful. Flowers and fruits are represented by precious stones, formerly genuine stones, but these having been stolen by the Jats and others, have been replaced by glass, colored to represent the originals.   In the centre of the dome lie Noor Mahal and Jehanghir side by side, this being, I believe, the only instance where any emperor of India has condescended to be buried by the side of a woman.   The sweetest echo in the known world answers a call at the side of this tomb.   Of course the architect could not have had this attraction in view when he planned the structure, and the natives who throng this unique gem of architecture do well to ascribe this apparent voice from heaven to the continual presence and approval of the good gods who like to linger over the tomb of true lovers.

The guide steps forward without a word of warning and raises the cry, "Great is God, and Mohammed is his prophet! Allah! Allah!" At first three distinct musical notes are heard in the echo; I mean different notes upon the musical scale, as distinct from each other as " do, sol, do."   These reverberate round the dome and ascend until they reach the smaller dome, where they reunite and escape from the temple as one tone.   Some readers may recall the echo in the baptistery at Pisa, as we did when we heard this new delight in the Taj, but that echo compares with this, well, say as the Taj compares to Milan Cathedral—and now I repent me for comparing the Taj to any other material structure. It is not proper to do so. We shall say as the piano compares with the organ.

If I am ever sentenced to hard labor for life for some unlawful outburst of my wild republicanism, I will make one request as I throw myself upon the mercy of the court : Let me be transported to India, and allowed to perform my daily task in beautifying and preserving the Taj. This would be a labor of love, and I should not be unhappy with my idol to worship, doing my part to hand it down untarnished to future generations.

The Taj is really a very large temple, yet such is its grace, its exquisite proportions, its unapproachable charm—it never occurs to the beholder that it is of such great size. It is neither big nor little, nor heavy nor light—it is simply perfect. You can't tell why it is perfect, and you don't want to. You stand and look at the gem through the great gateway which serves as a frame for the picture, for the Taj is directly in front of the arch, probably five hundred yards distant. A narrow walk, lined on both sides with the choicest Indian plants, leads to it, but it is many minutes before you can be induced to advance. Never before have you gazed upon stone and lime which you deemed worthy of being called beautiful. All you have seen becomes mean, coarse, material; this alone is entirely worthy. There is grace and beauty brought down to us from above, the realization of the ideal ; it really seems an inspiration. Vandy and I separated instinctively without a word. You want to be with the Taj alone, for it leads you captive and invites to secret communion. I wandered around many hours, gazing at every turn, deliciously, not joyously happy ; there was no disposition to croon over a melody, nor any bracing quality in my thoughts —not a trace of the heroic—but I was filled with happiness which seemed to fall upon me gently as the snow-flakes fall, as the zephyr comes when laden with sweet odors. I sat down at length in the garden in full view of the Taj, but had not rested long before an Englishman approached, and something in our faces telling that we were both in the blissful state and the worshipful mood, he came and sat down quietly, without speaking a word, but with a slight and slow nod of recognition, and broke out without one word of introduction —partly as if talking to himself—as follows :

"I stayed away from this in England as long as I could. It is seven years since I was here before. I have been here for two weeks wandering about the grounds ; I must tear myself away to-morrow and my great grief is, that I know that I cannot take and carry with me a perfect image—of *that*—and so I may have to return again." I said that my feeling was the reverse, for I felt that its image could never leave me.

He envied me that, he said.   I have often regretted that I did not get the name and address of this worthy devotee, but under the spell of the spirit neither he nor I cared much for other companionship; but should this ever meet his eye surely he will address me and perhaps we may shake hands in silence over the memory of our idol.

It began to grow dark at length, and I thought of finding Vandy to tell him—for no apology seemed necessary—that I could not possibly resist the spell which had carried me away even from him all the afternoon.   I was at once relieved, for I found him in the archway.   He was first to speak.   " A. C.," he said, " I'm very sorry.   I know I ought to have looked for you long ago, but really I could not leave this spot. Look! there is no place like this." So it was all right. When one is called upward by the spirit, even the dearest of humanity must be left behind.   But Vandy was in the right place certainly for one to take his farewell.   If ever an inanimate object spoke to man, the Taj did to me when I said farewell; the tear was not alone in the eye of the beholder as he took his last fond look, for that spiritual face of the Taj seemed to beam kindly in return.   It said—yes, smile, reader, if you will— I know it said, " This is not farewell, for we understand each other."   There never is a farewell between souls completely sympathetic.   They live forever in the bonds of a sacred friendship which separation cannot break.

DELHI, Sunday, February 16.

Delhi at last—the Rome of Asia! Baber established his capital in Agra, a hundred and forty miles south, and therefore farther into India, but his son Humayun returned to Delhi because the summer heats of Agra were found to be insupportable. But it had before been the principal seat of the Pathans or Afghan kings, and, back of them, of several Hindoo dynasties. There are ruins of palaces and forts here dating to one hundred years before Christ, and for eighteen hundred years we have the ruins of the structures of the kings of Delhi and their most noted subordinates, comprising prime ministers, favorite slaves, barbers, architects, etc. For eleven miles along the Imperial Way, on both sides, these ruins stretch, ending in the Kuttub Minar, the glory of Delhi, as the Taj is of Agra. This is a tower standing alone, two hundred and forty feet in height, fifty feet in diameter at the base, and tapering to nine feet at the top. But pictures and photographs have made all familiar with this superb monument. It and the tomb of Humayun, father of the great Akbar, alone remain vividly impressed upon my memory. A ruin now and then is acceptable, but eleven miles of them in one or two days are rather embarrassing, and it is impossible to examine them in detail and retain interest in the work; besides this, a great similarity pervades the mass. It seems to me the entire population must have been oppressed to the last degree, and every surplus penny secured in some way to be expended in the erection and maintenance of these palaces, and for the support of the classes who occupied them.

One most important department of government in the management of a conquered race is that of its police and intelligence bureau, and this is admirably administered in India. A special department was organized years ago, and specially gifted officers of the army placed at its head. To the present chief, Major Henderson, whose face we see in all the photographs of the Prince of Wales's party, we are deeply indebted for Indian items. This department has almost succeeded in stamping out the Thugs, and it is very seldom that murders are now committed by these religious fanatics. Their goddess Kali demanded blood, but she was fastidious; nothing but human blood would meet her tastes, and so her devotees strangled and waylaid and shot the victims marked out for sacrifice. Some Thugs confessed to between seventy and eighty murders, and one to the incredible number of one hundred and ninety-two (what saints they would make!). The members of the sect were classified into spies, stranglers, and grave-diggers, the spies being in the first stage and not ranking with the two more advanced degrees. Assuming usually the garb of merchants or pilgrims, they often craved the protection of their intended victims. Their favorite instrument for strangulation was a handkerchief, in the use of which they were most expert. The secret that these wretches were linked together as a religious fraternity, bound by all the hopes of future bliss and the terrors of eternal damnation as they satisfied or failed to satisfy the craving of their horrible gods for human blood, was not discovered until about a half century ago. The government purchased the secret with the names and address of every member and relative of a member of the sect, arrested them all in 1837 and colonized them at Jubbulpore, where they were taught trades. Their names and those of their descendants remain on the list of persons suspect, and should Thugism ever show its head again, the presence of any member near the scene of the offence would be held almost conclusive evidence against him.

The Major's department has on its records the names and descriptions of more than four thousand of these people, and also of nearly nine thousand professional gang robbers. Murder has been done when the booty did not exceed six cents. But the systematic hunting down of these dangerous classes is fast ridding India of this curse. If a man will murder another for a sixpence he can be induced to betray his fellow-murderers for a moderate sum. Is it not a blessing for the race that evil disintegrates? Only for good ends can men permanently combine; then no feared betrayal works dismay. As great movements, whether for good or evil, require many supporters, society has its safe-guard; nothing really good can be destroyed by conspirators.

The fort at Delhi resembles in its general features that of Agra, but is famous as having been the receptacle of the Peacock Throne, which was valued by a French jeweller at not less than six millions sterling, say thirty millions of dollars. On such a precious pedestal as this the Moguls sat and ruled this land. The throne was plundered of its jewels by the Persians, but its frame is still shown in the local museum. The fort remains in an unusually good state of preservation, making it by far the most satisfactory specimen of the gorgeous residences of the Moguls that we have seen. The walls are of marble, inlaid in the interior with genuine precious stones of various colors worked into the forms of vines and flowers for a height of about six feet. The floors are similarly decorated. The upper portions of the walls have the same patterns, but these are painted, not inlaid. Every part is gilded in the most elaborate manner, and, in short, here alone of all places that I have seen, one could fancy himself wandering through the resplendent wonders of the Arabian Nights.

Of course we did not neglect the many places rendered historical by the mutiny. These are seen upon every side in this district, but none was more interesting to me than the Cashmere Gate. The rebels held the fort, and it was determined to assault it. Here is the record of the men who volunteered to lay the train to the Gate:

" Salkfied laid his bags, but was shot through the

arm and leg, and fell back on the bridge, handing the portfire to Sergeant Burgess, *bidding him light the fuse.* Burgess was instantly shot dead in the attempt. Sergeant Carmichael then advanced, took up the portfire, and succeeded in the attempt, but immediately fell mortally wounded. Sergeant Smith, seeing him fall, advanced at a run, but finding that the fuse was already burning, threw himself into the ditch."

The age of miracles is admittedly past, but it is certain that the age of heroes existed in 1857.

The finest mosque in Delhi, and one of the finest in the world, is the Jumma Musjid. We happened to visit it just as the priests were calling the faithful to prayer, which they do by ascending to the foot of the minarets and turning toward Mecca and there chanting the call. Numerous worshippers came, and having washed in the pool, went to the Mosque and began their worship on their knees. Our guide was a Mohammedan, and I asked him what a good man is required to do daily in the way of external worship. Here is the programme as he gave it to me: Five times each day he washes hands and feet and prays; first in the morning when he rises, and then at one, four, after sunset, and before he goes to bed, repeating the prayer to Allah and some words from the Koran, and touching the ground with his forehead no less than thirty-eight times during the day. This must be done every day, Saturday and Sunday alike. The prayers are simple exclamations reciting the greatness of God and the insignificance of his servants, and *ask for nothing.* How very close to their daily lives must this constant appeal at short intervals, through each day, bring the Unknown, unless, as is said to be the case, it becomes a more matter of form, familiarity breeding contempt.

Saugor, Great Peninsular Railway, February 19.

We are now *en route* to Bombay from Delhi, a distance of about thirteen hundred miles. We have been two nights in our sleeping-car, and shall spend the night on the line and reach Bombay in the morning. General Grant just passed us going toward Calcutta, but there was no chance for us to get at him to shake hands in India. This is the Pacific Railway of India, connecting Calcutta and all the eastern portion with the western coast, upon which Bombay is situated. The time between Calcutta and England has been shortened almost a whole week by its construction. The railways of India, of which there are at present about nine thousand miles in operation, were principally constructed under a guarantee of five per cent. by the Indian Government, and some of them yield more than that already. In a short time there will be none that will remain a charge upon the revenues. The government retained the right, at intervals of twenty or twenty-five years, to acquire possession and ownership of these lines upon certain terms, and at no distant day will enjoy large revenues from its railway property. If the days of guarantees and subsidies be not hopelessly gone with us, here is an idea worth considering by our government. Fancy what the ·ownership of the Union and Central Pacific lines would mean as recompense for the amounts advanced.

The government has established several model farms in different provinces, for the purpose of testing articles thought suitable for cultivation in India, and of diffusing among the natives improved methods of agriculture. Such farms under able scientific management must eventually bring to the country what it is best calculated to produce. The success attendant upon the growth of a substitute for cinchona is significant. India must have quinine in large quantities as a preventive of malaria. Experiments prove that while the genuine article does not thrive here, a kindred species, possessing nearly the same properties, although to a less degree, will grow well. This has been cultivated in large quantities, and I notice that the medical chief orders it to be used in all dispensaries where quinine has hitherto been required, although the medical officers are permitted in extreme cases to order the dearer drug.

We are now traversing a level plain, and as this region was blessed with rain in season, it seems much more fertile than some other portions of the country; but the poorest harvests I ever saw in any part of

America would be rated as abundant. here. We have seen everywhere herds of buffaloes, bullocks, and sheep grazing in fields which seemed to us entirely destitute of everything; not a green leaf of any kind to be seen, and we could not understand how animals could even get a mouthful of food in the brown parched lands. But I am told they do nibble away at the short stalks and roots of corn or sugar-cane left in the ground when the crop was cut, and in this way manage to eke out a scanty existence. They are at best little but skin and bone. When it is merely a question of keeping life in the body, man and beast alike prove that but little is required.

While everything about us partakes of a dusty clayey hue, we must not forget that we see the plains of India in the winter. Let the blessed Monsoon burst, and these fields, now so parched and dead, are covered at once " as if the earth had given a subterranean birth to heaven." As Roderick Dhu's host rose up at the blast of his bugle, vegetation springs forth, and the land we now wonder at is no longer barren, but teems with tropical luxuriance. Then come the snakes and insects to poison and annoy. Last year, sixteen thousand seven hundred and seventy human beings were reported killed by snakes, while eight hundred and nineteen only were killed by tigers.

One has difficulty in imagining such a change in any land as is implied by these startling figures, for to-day as we travel not a fly nor insect of any kind is to be seen. If it were not for the intense heat, which I know I could not endure, I should like to spend a summer in India, snakes notwithstanding, just to see so complete a reversal of conditions, for no matter what reflection may do to tell, as we see India only under winter conditions, we shall always have a bias to rate it as the miserable, barren land it appears to us. Travellers should be on their guard against this tendency, for it leads to many false conclusions. If both sides of a question need to be considered, all seasons of a country must be experienced before a true judgment can be passed upon it. This is especially true of India, where the change is, as it were, from life to death.

We see wood-gatherers entering the cities, each with a bundle of sticks, or twigs rather, on his head, the result of the day's gathering—scarcely one of the sticks thicker than one's finger, and the great bulk of the bundle composed of mere switches, so closely is everything shaven in crowded Hindostan. To-day we stood and looked at a native who had led his goat into the country to pick up a meal. He bent the boughs of small trees one after another so that the goat could strip them of their leaves. The poor skeleton was ravenous. Nothing goes to waste in India, nor anywhere in the East. Garbage and sewage have value, and all is swept clean and kept clean in every hole and corner in consequence. This simplifies life very much. Our elaborate system of underground pipes, our sewers, drains, and modern conveniences of all kinds, and our sanitary arrangements which are of such prime importance to health, and to which we are fortunately giving so much more attention—these the East wholly escapes. We have to cure; they have prevention. Human labor at four or five cents per day (2 to $2\frac{1}{2}d$.) changes the conditions of existence. It pays to do so many things which, under our rates for labor, cannot be thought of. I have mentioned that in Japan the refuse of all kinds from a residence is not only taken away at any hours each day one fixes, but a small sum is actually paid for it, which the servants of the establishment consider a perquisite.

BOMBAY, Thursday, February 20.

We reached this city on time this morning, feeling not in the least fatigued by our three nights in the train. In the evening we were fortunate enough to stroll down to the pier, where the band was playing. Nowhere have we seen so varied a concourse of people. The drive at Calcutta has long been noted as excelling any other scene in the gorgeousness of its oriental coloring, but this of the pier at Bombay surpasses by far what we saw there. Calcutta can boast no wealthy native Parsees, who attend here in large numbers in fine equipages with servants in livery. The Parsee ladies especially are resplendent in jewels and color; and the rich turbaned Mohammedan adds to the variety. The assemblage moved to and fro among the carriages and along the edges of the broad pier chatting gayly, while the music seemed to set everything in motion. Native boatmen in their picturesque garbs passed now and then plying their trade, carrying a Sahib's portmanteau or a lady's bundle. I sat down and imagined myself in the midst of all that I had seen of pretty seaports in grand opera, the ship scene in L'Africaine, the landing of Desdemona in the Isle of Cyprus, the fishermen in Masaniello, and I thought I had never seen anything of this description so pleasing. I lost Vandy in the crowd, and sat drinking it all in till dark. Certainly among the fine things in the East is to be ranked the music upon the Apollo Bunder, Bombay.

Friday, February 21.

We rose early, and were off before breakfast for a drive to the " Tower of Silence." This is the mountain top where the Parsees give their dead to be torn by the vultures. We shudder at cremation, but the sacred fire of the funeral pile as it flames to heaven has something awe-inspiring about it. Man sprung from the dust mingles at last with the purer element of fire, and "vanishes into air, into thin air," leaving no trace behind. But deliberately to throw our dead out to be torn in pieces and devoured by vultures—who can endure the thought! And yet many of the inhabitants here would be most unhappy if denied the consolation of believing that their bodies were to be served in this manner. Nor are these poor and ignorant; on the contrary, next to the English they are the best educated and the principal merchants in the city. It is simply that they have been taught in their youth that the earth must not be defiled by contact with the dead. They cannot bury, therefore, neither can they burn, because fire, one of the elements, is sacred; neither can they cast their dead into the sea, for it, too, is holy. There seems to them no way but this—of getting the birds of the air to come and take the flesh. We were received at the foot of the mound by a Parsee guide, who conducted us through every part. The towers, of which there are five, are approached by long flights of easy stairs. We entered a door at the top, and the first objects which struck our eyes were the vultures. They sat motionless, as close together as possible, on top of the wall of the round tower, with their tails toward us and their beaks toward the centre of the tower where the bodies are placed. The wall is about twenty feet high and fifty feet in diameter. There did not appear to be room for one more bird upon it, every inch of it being occupied, their bodies almost touching each other. What a revolting coping they formed to the otherwise plain round wall. More birds were perched on trees, and on the other towers; and indeed everywhere we looked these disgusting objects met our view. At ten o'clock every morning the dead are taken from the dead-house, rich

and poor alike being previously divested of clothing;
and were we to revisit the spot at that hour, we are told
the quiet stillness which pervaded the grove would
be found no longer. We inwardly congratulated ourselves that the dreaded heat of a Bombay sun had
sent us to this place at so early an hour—ere the repast
began—and rapidly withdrew. It isn't much, yet I
would not be robbed of it—such a disposition of our
dead as would still render it possible for us to say with
Laertes:

> "*Lay her i' the earth;*
> And from her fair and unpolluted flesh
> May violets spring."

Hard times are everywhere, and produce some
strange changes. The Banyan caste of Suerah has just
resolved to abolish caste dinners after funerals, but if a
wealthy Hindoo still wishes to indulge in these affairs
he is permitted to do so after one year has elapsed. I
fear many of the dear departed will never be honored
by the feast after this interval. At marriages hereafter
only one feast is to be given, instead of four, which
were formerly considered the thing. Retrenchment is
the word even where caste customs of long standing are
involved.

I note that yesterday a native was fined ten rupees
for driving a lame horse. What a singular race he must
think these English! Before their day he could have
done what he liked with horse or servant, male or

female, "because he bought them," and now he can't even be the judge when to use his horse. The more I see of the thoroughness of the English Government in the East—its attention to the minutest details, the exceptional ability of its officials as evinced in the excellence of the courts, jails, hospitals, dispensaries, schools, roads, railways, canals, etc.,—the more I am amazed. I had before no idea of what was implied by the government of India. It would have been madness for any other people than the English to undertake it. Not that we have not in America a class of men of equal organizing power, but these have careers at home open to them, and could not be induced to leave their own land. Even if this were not so, America requires an improved civil service to bring its ablest men forward. I am sure no such body of officials exists as that comprising the civil service of India, whether judged by its purity or its ability.

The British army has been reformed of late years in India to a degree beyond popular knowledge of the subject. Every one agrees in attributing the spread of the great mutiny to the fact that there were at two or three critical points superannuated veterans, unable to take before it was too late the most obvious measures for its suppression. In short, it was here just as it was in Washington when the Civil War began. I remember seeing General Scott, the commander-in-chief, when Bull Run was lost, carried or assisted from his carriage across the pavement to his office, he being too old and infirm to walk. There were others scarcely less feeble in charge of departments. It was just so in India; but now mark the change. No man can retain the command of a regiment in the British army more than five years, nor can generals serve longer. These officers retire on pensions, and the next in seniority takes his turn, always provided he passes successfully the most searching examination at each successive promotion. I was told that upon a recent examination only two officers out of thirteen passed. No favoritism is shown, and I have met young men related to the highest officials to whom it has been kindly intimated that another career than the army had better be sought. I have met many officers, and the impression made upon me is an exceedingly favorable one. I do not believe that in case of war now the blunder of those in command would have to be atoned for by the superior fighting qualities of the rank and file, as was notoriously the case during the Crimean War. The promotion of General Wolseley means business. The Duke of Cambridge, because he is a royal duke, is allowed to reign, but Wolseley is to govern.

I was struck with the full length portraits of the real man and the sham in last year's Royal Academy. General Winfield Scott in all his glory was not more brilliant than the duke, military hat in hand with its white waving plumes, booted and spurred, his breast a mass of decorations, "Old Fuss and Feathers" over again. Beside him was a man in plain attire, about as ornamental as General Grant; but this was the man of war, one of those very rare characters who does what there is to do—in Egypt as in Abyssinia—and never fails.

Bombay and Calcutta are again rivals for supremacy. Bombay Island, upon which Bombay City stands, another of the keys of the world, was given to Britain by Portugal as part of the dower of Catherine of Braganza when she married Charles II. Think of a woman giving anything for the privilege of marrying such a wretch! but so little was it esteemed that the government gave it in 1688 to the East India Company for a rental of £10 per annum. It was subsequently made the principal seat of their power, but it had no access to the interior, and Calcutta, which stands at the mouth of a river system of inland transportation rivalled only by that of our smoky Pittsburgh, soon eclipsed it. There was no chance for Bombay against this natural advantage, and she had to succumb; but now, since railways have penetrated the interior, and especially since the opening of the Suez Canal route has brought Bombay so very much nearer to Europe, the struggle for supremacy has begun anew. The European traffic now goes mainly to her, and Calcutta gets her portion by rail through her ancient rival. In 1872 the exports and imports of Bombay were £50,000,000, and those of Calcutta £54,-000,000; so you see it is not going to be a walk over for

Calcutta, though her population still exceeds that of her challenger by about a hundred thousand. It is water *vs.* rail on a large scale, and the result will be looked for with interest. I think the former capital, once dethroned, will eventually regain the crown; but there is plenty of room for both, and the rivalry between them should be a generous one.

Bombay is by far the finest city in the East, but it has been inflated more than any other, and is now undergoing severe contraction. Its public buildings would do credit to any European capital. Government concluded to sell the land fronting on the bay, which had been used as the site of an antiquated fort, and such was the rage for speculation at the time that five million dollars' worth of land was disposed of and enough retained to give Bombay a beautiful little park and a long drive along the beach. Government took the money and erected on part of the land retained the magnificent buildings referred to. We met one gentleman who had bought one hundred thousand dollars' worth of the new lots, for which he admitted he could not get to-day more than twenty thousand dollars. But Bombay is only learning the universal lesson which the world seems to need to have repeated every ten or twelve years. It is fortunate that this city is our last in India, because it so far excels any other. Nowhere else is such oriental richness to be seen. The colors of the masses as they move rapidly to and fro remind you of the combinations of the kaleidoscope. The native women of the lowest order work in gangs, and it is their dress which chiefly brightens the scene. A dark-green tight-fitting jacket, a magenta mantle festooned about the body and legs in some very graceful manner and reaching to the knees, the feet and legs bare to the knees, a purple veil on the head but thrown back over the shoulders—this is the dress as well as I can describe it. The habit of carrying loads upon the head makes them as straight as arrows, and as they march along with majestic stride they completely eclipse the poor-looking male, who seems to have had his manhood ground out of him by generations of oppression, while his companion has passed through subjugation without losing her personal dignity.

It seems homelike to see street railways, of which there are several prosperous lines here. For this enter-prise an American gentleman has to be thanked. All classes ride together, and caste in Bombay gets serious knocks in consequence. From Bombay as a centre civilization is destined to radiate. A palpable breach has already been made in the solid walls which have hitherto shut India from the entrance of new ideas, and through this gate the assaulting columns must eventu-ally gain possession; but it will not be within the span of men now living, nor for several generations to come. The Sailors' Home and the hospitals of the city are highly creditable, and among the charitable institutions

I must not forget the Hindoo hospital for wretched
animals, where some of each kind are tenderly cared
for, to signify the reverence paid by this sect to all
kinds of life, for the meanest form is sacred to them.
We had a curious illustration of this while in Benares
examining the richest specimens of the delicate embroideries for which that city is celebrated. A little
nasty intruder showed itself on one of the finest, and a
gentleman with us involuntarily reached forth to kill it,
but the three Hindoos caught his arm at once, and ex-
hibited great anxiety to save the insect.   One of them
did get it, and taking it to the window set it at liberty.
It was Uncle Toby and the troublesome fly over again,
as immortalized by the genius of Sterne : " Get thee
gone, poor devil ! there is room enough in the world for
thee and for me," quoth Uncle Toby.   And does not
Cowper say—

> " I would not enter on my list of friends
> (Though graced with polish'd manners and fine sense,
> Yet wanting sensibility) the man
> Who needlessly sets foot upon a worm."

Well, these Hindoos wouldn't do it either.   Let them
be credited accordingly, heathen though they be.

It begins to grow too hot here ; I could not live one
season in India—that I am convinced of. The tropical
sun has no mercy, piercing through thick pith helmet,
white umbrella, and driving one into the house. We
are to leave none too soon. This evening we were sur-

prised to see, as we strolled along the beach, more Parsees than ever before, and more Parsee ladies richly
dressed ; all seemed wending their way to the sea. It
was the first of the new moon, a period sacred to these
worshippers of the elements ; and here on the shores of
the ocean, as the sun was sinking in the sea, and the
slender silver thread of the crescent moon was faintly
shining in the horizon, they congregated to perform
their religious rites. Fire was there in its grandest
form—the sun—and water in the vast expanse of the
Indian Ocean outstretched before them. The earth
was under their feet, and wafted across the sea the air
came laden with the perfumes of " Araby the Blest."
Surely no time nor place could be more fitly chosen
than this for lifting up the soul to the realms beyond
sense. I could not but participate with these worshippers in what was so grandly beautiful. There was no
music save the solemn moan of the waves as they broke
into foam on the beach,

> " With their ain eerie croon
>   Working their appointed work,
>   And never, never done."

But where shall we find so mighty an organ, or so grand
an anthem ? How inexpressibly sublime the scene
appeared to me, and how insignificant and unworthy of
the Unknown seemed even our cathedrals, " made with
human hands," when compared to this looking up

through Nature unto Nature's God! I stood and drank in the serene happiness which seemed to fill the air. I have seen many modes and forms of worship, some disgusting, others saddening, a few elevating when the organ pealed forth its tones, but all poor in comparison to this. Nor do I ever expect in all my life to witness a religious ceremony which will so powerfully affect me as that of the Parsees on the beach at Bombay. While I gazed upon the scene I stood conscious only that I was privileged to catch a glimpse of something that was not of the earth, but, as I sauntered homeward, Wordsworth's lines came to me as the fittest expression of my feelings. The passage is too long to quote at length; besides I have to confess I cannot at this moment recall it all. But he tells first how in his youth Nature was all in all to him, " nor needed a moral sense unborrowed from the eye," but later the inner light came; and hear him in his maturer years:

> " For I have learned
> To look on Nature, not as in the hour
> Of thoughtless youth ; but hearing oftentimes
> The still, sad music of humanity,
> Nor harsh nor grating, though of ample power
> To chasten and subdue.   And I have felt
> A Presence that disturbs me with the joy
> Of elevated thoughts; a sense sublime
> Of something far more deeply interfused,
> Whose dwelling is the light of setting suns,
> And the round ocean and the living air,

And the blue sky, and in the mind of man;
A motion and a spirit, that impels
All thinking things, all objects of all thought,
And rolls through all things."

"The still sad music of humanity!"—it was that I heard sounding in the prayers of those devout Parsees and in the moan of that mighty sea. Sweet, refreshing it was, though tinged with sadness, as all our more precious musings must be, "since all we know is, nothing can be known."

In one of my strolls along the beach I met a Parsee gentleman who spoke excellent English. From him I learned that the disciples of Zoroaster number only about two hundred thousand, and of those no fewer than fifty thousand are in Bombay. They were driven from Persia by the Mohammedans and settled here, where they have prospered.

They do not intermarry with other sects, believe in one God, and worship the sun, moon, earth, and stars only as being the visible angels of God, as he termed them. In themselves these are nothing, but are the best steps by which we can ascend to God. Good men will be happy forever; bad men will be unhappy for a long time after death, and very bad men will be severely punished. But I was delighted to be assured that no one will be punished forever, all life being sacred to God because he made it, and all life must eventually be purified, return to its Maker, and be merged in Him.

Parsees cannot burn the dead, because fire should not be prostituted to so vile a use. They cannot bury, because the earth should not be desecrated with the dead, neither should the sea ; and therefore God has provided vultures, which cannot be defiled, to absorb the flesh of the dead. I said to him that the mere thought of violence offered to our dead caused us to shudder. " Then what do you think of the worms?" he asked. This was certainly an effective estoppel. " It comes to this," he continued, "a question of birds or worms." " You are right " (I had to admit it), I said ; "after all, it's not worth disputing about." When I had asked him a great many questions, I suppose he thought turn-about was fair play, and he began to cross-examine me upon many points of Christian doctrine, which I did my best to put in the proper form. We finally agreed that no good men or good women of any form of religion would be eternally miserable, and upon this platform we said good-bye and parted.

On looking around, I saw that we had become the centre of quite a circle of Parsees, Hindoos, and Mohammedans, who had been attracted by our conversation, their earnest bronze faces, surmounted by the flaming red turbans, so very close to mine, forming with the gorgeous colors of their flowing robes, a picture I shall not soon forget. They opened a way of egress, and Sahib passed out of the throng amid their salaams, evidently an object of intense curiosity.

Our excursion to the Caves of Elephanta was very enjoyable. They are decidedly worth seeing. Here is the strongest contrast to the grand open-air worship of the Parsees, for the Hindoos sought to hide their worship in caves which shut out the light of day, and to seek their gods in the dark recesses. The carved figures and columns of the Temple are fine, the principal idol being of great size—a huge representation of the Hindoo Trinity of Brahma, Vishnu, and Siva, which make the three-headed god. The effect of such a monster, seen dimly by the lighted torch, upon ignorant natures, could not but be overpowering. When examined closely there is nothing repulsive in the faces; on the contrary, the expression of all three is rather pleasing than otherwise, like that of Buddha. It is evident that the gods of the Hindoos are good natured, kind, and disposed to forgiveness.

BOMBAY, Monday, February 24.

We sailed at six in the evening by the splendid Peninsula and Oriental mail steamer Pekin. The city was bathed in the rays of a brilliant sunset as we steamed slowly out of the harbor, and we bade farewell to India when it looked the fairest.

And now for something on the great Indian Question, for it would never do for a traveller to visit India and not to have his decided opinion upon matters and things there, and his clearly-defined policy embracing the management of the most intricate problems involved in the government of two hundred and fifty millions of the most ignorant races known, and all founded upon a few weeks' hurried travel among them. There is, however, a much more extensive class who are even more presumptuous, for they have just as complete a policy upon this subject, although they have never seen India at all.

The vast country we know as India, then, is held and governed, not as one country, but district by district. One province, for instance, has a native ruler with whom England has nothing whatever to do except that, by right of treaty, she sends a political agent to his court, supported in some cases, and in others not, by a certain number of soldiers. This Resident is expected to confer with and advise the Rajah, and keep him and his officials from outrageous courses. Especially are they prevented from warring upon neighboring States. In extreme cases, when counsel and remonstrance avail not, the government has had either to depose the ruling Rajah and substitute another, as in the recent affair of the Rajah of Baroda, or to confiscate the province and merge it in the Empire, as in the case of the King of Oude. But what must be borne in mind is that no two native rulers govern alike. Laws and customs prevailing in one province are unknown in another. Land is held by one tenure in one place, and by an entirely different system in another. India is therefore not one nation, but a vast conglomeration of different races and principalities, each independent of the other, differing as much as France does from Germany, and much more than England does from America. Add to this the fact that the people of any one district are not a homogeneous community, but subdivided into distinct castes, which refuse to intermarry or even to eat with one another, and a faint idea of the magnitude of the Indian question will begin to dawn upon one.

It is this mass which England has to rule and keep firmly in order with her sixty thousand troops, and which constitutes the government of India the most difficult problem with which, I believe, statesmen have to deal. The amount of knowledge, statesmanship, tact, temper, patience and resource absolutely put in requisition by the men who rule India equals, I feel sure, that required for the government of the whole of civilized Europe combined; for it is always easy to govern a homogeneous people, the rulers being of the people themselves, and having the good of their respective countries at heart. It seems to me that an unnecessary element of danger arises from the fact that these Rajahs are permitted to maintain no fewer than three hundred thousand native troops, mainly to swell their importance. The question of enforcing reductions in these armaments is now under consideration, I observe, but I should decidedly say with Hamlet,

"Oh! reform it altogether."

I would not allow a Rajah to keep more than one hundred armed troops, except as a body-guard, beyond the number actually required to enforce order. Upon this point I have decided views.

The existence of Rajahs is perhaps a necessary evil. They are maintained in consequence of a well-grounded reluctance on the part of the government to assume the task of governing more territory. It is to be regretted that it has been necessary to extend the sway so far already; nevertheless, the day will come when the petty courts must be swept away, as they have been in Japan and Germany, and the whole country given the benefits of uniform rule. It is estimated that the Rajahs tax the people to an extent equal to the revenues of the government—about \$300,000,000 per annum : of this much is squandered in upholding their state—a grievous exaction from so poor a country. This will soon be one of the burning questions of India.

The Rajah of Jeypoor draws from the people \$6,000,000 per annum, and one or two others exceed this sum. Poor fellow! the other day he had to marry his tenth wife—a sister of two of his previous wives, for whom no suitable husband could be found. There were but two families in the realm, I believe, of the proper rank, and neither happened just then to have a nice young man on hand. The disgrace of having an unmarried woman in the family was not to be borne, and the old Rajah had to husband her, as he had her other sister some time ago. Although so well provided with wives, he has never been blessed with an heir, and at his death his first wife will adopt a son, who will be his successor.

What do I think of India? is asked me every day; but I feel that one accustomed to the exceptional fertility and advantages of America—a land so wonderfully endowed that it seems to me more and more the special favorite of fortune—is very apt to underrate India. We saw it after two years of bad harvests, and a third most unpromising one coming on. Judged from what I saw, I can only say that I, as a lover of England, find it impossible to repress the wish that springs up at every turn, Would she were safely and honorably out of it! Retiring now is out of the question; she has abolished the native system in large districts, and must perforce continue the glorious task of giving to these millions the blessings of order.

Her withdrawal would be the signal for internecine strife, and such a saturnalia of blood and rapine as the world has never known; but were the question whether Britain should to-day accept India as a gift, and I had the privilege of replying, then, " Declined with thanks ; " and yet it is the fashion just now to call India " the brightest jewel in the crown." The glitter of that jewel may be red again some day.

I have heard only two reasons advanced in favor of India as an English possession. The first is, it furnishes official station and employment for a large number who would otherwise have no field; but I think there is yet plenty of unoccupied territory in which these gentlemen can find work if they can hold their own in the struggle for existence. Besides, the official class requires less protection, not greater, than it has hitherto been favored with, if the true interest of England is to be considered.

The second reason is a commercial one, and it is pointed out that the trade of England is thereby extended; to which it may be said in reply that the occupation of foreign countries and the subjugation of foreign races are in no measure required by the demands of trade. The possession of small islands at proper points secures all this. Hong Kong and a small strip at Shanghai and one or two other ports, afford all the facilities required for England to obtain the trade. Penang on the west of the Malay Peninsula, Singapore at the south end, do the same. All of these have the precious silver thread surrounding them, and can be held easily by Britannia against the world without and native races struggling within for independence, as they are bound to do some day.

There is another view to be taken of this question by a well-wisher of Britain which cannot be ignored. She, the mother of nations and champion of oppressed nationalities, necessarily occupies a false position in India; there she must assume the *rôle* of the conqueror. I do not speak of this to disapprove of it, or even of the Press Laws recently adopted; to avert still greater evils she is compelled to go to any length. Nevertheless, it is a false position; the stars in their courses fight against it, and sooner or later England will retire from it. In short, the pole-star of Indian policy is to bend every energy to the sowing of seed which will produce a native class capable at first of participating in the government, and which will eventually become such as can be trusted with entire control, so that England may stand to India as she stands to-day to Canada and Australia. There is one course for England, and one only, and this let her adopt speedily. Let her call around her Indian government the best men of India, explain to them her aim and end, show them how noble her aspirations are; point to Canada and Australia as proofs of her colonial system, and say, To this condition we hope to bring your country. Can you resist our appeal to come and help us?

Since all this was written the Ilbert bill question has arisen. It will be understood at once that such a measure is believed by me to be emphatically a step not only in the right direction, but in the only direction, if grave dangers are to be avoided in India. Let me tell my English readers that, travelling as I did, an American, and not, in Indian parlance, as one of the governing

class—one of the *usurpers*—I had many opportunities
of hearing educated natives speak the thoughts of their
hearts, which to an Englishman's ears would have been
treason. Such trustworthy indications of the forces
moving under the crust should be considered as invalu-
able by the rulers of India. While, therefore, educated
natives give assent to the claims made for English rule,
that it keeps order and enforces justice as far as its
courts can reach, they are yet antagonistic to it. It is
the old story: You have taught people to read, and
placed before them as types of highest excellence our
rebels, Cromwell, Hampden, Sidney, Russell, Washington, Franklin. In so far as a native Indian dwells
contentedly while his country is ruled by a foreign race,
by just so much do we despise him in our heart, for
loyalty to England means treachery to his country, and
one cannot depend upon traitors.

If India were told that the chief delight of England
was not to hold dependencies but to bring forth nations
competent to govern themselves—a much grander mission—and were England slowly, but steadily to introduce, little by little, the native element in government
whenever practicable—and that it is practicable to do
so in every department to a greater or less degree I am
convinced—then I should feel that sufficient pressure
had been relieved to give hope that peace would reign
there. The greatest danger England will have to contend with in every measure taken toward this great end

will be the violent opposition of the Anglo-Indian. It will be difficult to carry reform against the advice of the only class which seems competent to advise, viz., such Englishmen as have had experience of India. I hold such to be totally incompetent as a class to take proper views of Indian problems—such men as Sir Richard Temple are the exception. His articles upon India seem to me most salutary and to denote a statesmanlike grasp of a subject of paramount importance to England. The reason why the Englishman in India is likely to be entirely wrong in his views of Indian government is because he sits on the safety valve of the terrible boiler. He hears every now and then the sharp rush of the confined steam, which startles the ear as it passes. When it is proposed to relieve the pressure and allow more steam to escape he is frightened, and protests that his position would thereby become unendurable.

But we who stand afar off and know the play of the forces in that boiler, as I know them from sources sealed to him, see that the steam must be allowed vent in constantly increasing volume if a terrible catastrophe is to be averted. John Bright, of all English public men of the first rank, seems to me to understand the Indian problem best; hence the interest he takes in it—an interest which every public man would share did he realize the situation England occupies in Hindostan.

I have before referred to the fact that the Anglo-Indian authorities protested against railway travel being conducted without special reference to caste, and that they were overruled by the Home Government. The result is that more impression has been made upon caste, and is made daily and hourly, by the rush of every grade to get the best seats in the same carriage, than by all other influences combined. The Home Office judged more wisely than those who were too close to the problem to get a clear view; and so it must be in every measure calculated to elevate the people of India to a higher stage of civilization. In my opinion England can scarcely move too rapidly in the imperative task of attaching able natives, as these arise, to her side, and giving them power—at least the danger is that she will move too slowly rather than too fast.

The business of colonizing, as a whole, does not appear to me to pay. As a mission there is none so noble or to be compared with it, next to governing well at home ; but beyond this England's share of the material good looks small. If the colony is rich and prosperous it sets up for itself ; if weak and unsuccessful, it becomes a Natal, and calls upon the generous-hearted mother for assistance. The gain to the colonies is obvious ; nothing could be finer for them ; and if it be clearly understood that England elects to play the tender nurse and receive her reward in the consciousness of doing good—all right. Let her continue! But if it be thought that these dependencies enhance her own power and promote her prosperity, the sooner the books are balanced the better. Only one prayer, May heaven keep America from the colonizing craze! Cuba! Santo Domingo! avaunt, and quit our sight!

From another point of view one keeps inquiring whether all the advantages flowing from the introduction of English ideas, as far as these can really be introduced in the government of subject races—whether, after all, the result is, upon the whole, for the real permanent good of these inferior races. To the uninformed man, who has never been beyond his own island, it seems fanciful, perhaps, to raise this question. English civilization, freedom, civil and religious liberty, order, law, Christianity—these not beneficial, think you! Softly, my friend, softly. These may be growths admirable for English-speaking people who can assimilate them, but yet unsuitable for the Hottentot. You press man's food upon babes to their injury, may be. The true evolutionist must regard these attempts with sorrow.

Speaking broadly, I do not believe that it is in the power of England—and of course much less of any other country—to confer upon another race benefits which are not more than cancelled by the evil which usually follows from her interference. Rob even the lowest people in development to-day of the necessity of governing themselves, take this responsibility away from them, as interference does take it away, and the natural growth of that people is not only checked, but it is diverted into channels foreign to it.

If colonization can follow occupation it is a different matter—the interference is temporary, and Australians, Canadians and Americans soon come forth and govern themselves, the native-born soon grow patriotic, and work out their own destiny. In such cases England's share is her glory, a glory of which no other nation partakes, for she alone is the grand old mother of nations, God bless her! It is different with India. No one pretends that our race can ever obtain a foothold there. Conquerors the English are, and conquerors they must remain as long as they remain at all, which I ardently trust may not be long; not longer than the natives are willing to accept the task of self-government. Meanwhile surely no further rash responsibilities should be taken upon herself by England. She can do most good by example. The little islands of Hong Kong and Singapore, and the other Straits Settlements, Shanghai, and even Ceylon, which is not too big—these teach the races of the East what western civilization means, and serve as models to which they can move with such differentiation as circumstances require and without losing the inestimable advantages of thinking and acting for themselves. Even Christianity will make more progress from such examples than if through the efforts of a paid propaganda we try to *force* it upon people. Rob them of this freedom to act, to accept, and to reject, and all that England can give in return will not atone for the injury she inflicts. A nation should have much to offer in exchange, more than I see that any nation has, which stifles in the breast of the most ignorant people in the world the sacred germ of self-development.

The total acreage under wheat in India is not much, if any, less than that of the United States, and the average yield about the same—thirteen bushels per acre. The quality is excellent. America cannot afford to ignore this potential rival. The cheaper labor of India is quite an element in her favor, but cheap labor is not always cheap. One educated Minnesotan, with his machinery, must count for many spindle-shanked Hindoos with their wooden rakes. India's remoteness from Europe and the lack of inland transportation facilities, give America the vantage-ground. The present low price of wheat in Liverpool to-day, however, warns our western friends that there are other great sources of supply. Until 1873, only ten years ago, an export duty was laid upon Indian wheat. The amount exported in that year was valued at only £167,000; last year, 1882, the exports were £8,869,000 ($45,000,-000), more than one-third as much as the United States exported in that year ($112,000,000), to which, however, should be added $35,000,000 worth of wheat flour exported, making the total United States export $157,-000,000. It must be remembered that India has scarcely yet entered the race with us for the supremacy in this department, for while we have 110,000 miles of railway with 55,000,000 of people, she has 250,000,000 of people with only 10,000 miles of rail. This may seem alarming to the untravelled Yankee, but let him possess his soul in patience. It is a very safe wager that notwithstanding this seemingly uncalled-for disparity in railway facilities, the American railway system is still to increase at a far greater ratio than the Indian. Last year only three hundred and eighty-seven miles of line were built in India as against our six thousand, and even my friend, William Fowler, M.P., in his most interesting article in the *Fortnightly Review* for February, 1884, " India, Her Wheat, and Her Railways," to which I beg to refer such of my readers as are specially interested in this subject—even he only suggests that twelve hundred miles should be built every year in India; to secure which he urges the government to give a guarantee upon $50,000,000 per year, in order to obtain the necessary capital, which he admits cannot be obtained otherwise. This the government is not likely to do until the people rule England and sweep away the privileged classes, who live mainly through wars, and would be relegated to obscurity were the resources of England once spent for peaceful development, as those of Republican America are. Friend Fowler will get a vote to add millions to England's burden by an Afghan or Zulu war, or even to squander her means upon worthless members of a more than useless royal family and its dependents of the court long before he will get a pound for his Indian railways. The Republic will hold control of the world's wheat market for a hundred years and more, but prices must rule lower in consequence of India. Beyond that let posterity wrestle with the question.

As to cotton, of which America holds a firmer grasp upon the world's supply than it appears she does of wheat, India is not an impossible second if from any cause the American supply were forced to extreme prices. During the civil war in the United States, cotton cultivation in India, as I have before said, reached an extraordinary development. In 1866 the exports amounted to thirty-seven millions of pounds sterling, $185,000,000; now the average has fallen to about $40,000,000 per year. If the staple were equal to the American, India would be formidable as a rival, but it is not, and consequently the growth of cotton in the South seems sure to increase as rapidly as ever.

After six days' delightful sail we had our first glimpse of Arabia this morning, and are now skirting the Arabian coast. Aden was reached Sunday morning, and we drove out to the native town and saw the tanks said to have been constructed thousands of years ago. It rains only once in every year or two, and a supply of water is obtained by storing the torrents which then flow from the hills. A more desolate desert than that which surrounds the city surely does not exist. Aden itself illustrates how the whirligig of time revolves. Before the discovery of the passage round the Cape of Good Hope it was the chief entrepôt for the trade between Europe and Asia. It fell into insignificance when the stream of traffic left for the new route around the Cape of Good Hope; but now the Suez Canal, which restores the original route via the Red Sea, to its former supremacy, once more raises Aden to her former commanding position. The population, which in 1839 had dwindled to fewer than a thousand, now numbers nearly thirty thousand.

Aden is just one of those natural keys of the world which England should hold, and I doubt not will hold to the last. The town stands upon a narrow peninsula composed of desolate volcanic rocks, five miles long from east to west, and three from north to south, connected with the main land by a neck of flat sandy ground only a few feet high. The town itself is surrounded by precipitous rocks, which really make it a natural fortress impregnable against attack. All that I urge against conquest in general is inapplicable here, and I say let England guard such spots. As long as she does she is mistress of the sea. Her influence at such points is always for good. The thirty thousand natives of Aden, for instance, may now be considered subjects of Britain by their own act. They have flocked to the town attracted by the advantages to be derived from a residence there, just as the Chinese have done at Hong Kong, Shanghai and Singapore. There is no coercion in the matter. One foreigner electing to come under the British flag is worth ten thousand held down by force, whether considered as an element of strength to the Empire, or as conducive to its glory.

This is the market of the world for ostrich feathers. We saw droves of the birds wandering about Aden and its suburbs at home in the sand. The natives keep ostriches as their chief dependence, and we are besieged at every turn with offers of rare feathers—feathers—feathers—nothing but feathers.

Our trip on the Pekin was the most delightful we ever had at sea; even Vandy was well, and gained by the journey. We had very agreeable company on board, and were especially fortunate in our neighbors, Mr., Mrs., and Miss G., of Edinburgh, at table. The ship was crowded with officers and officers' wives and children returning from India to England, for children must be taken home out of the climate of India. Nothing can exceed the discipline and general management of the Peninsula and Oriental ships. Promotion from the ranks is the rule, and they certainly are served by a class of men which it would be difficult to equal elsewhere. The Cunard line is probably the only counterpart of the Peninsula and Oriental line in existence.

This was our first experience of life upon a vessel crowded with various ranks of English people. On the Atlantic our steamer acquaintances are with few exceptions Americans. The contrast is great in one respect:

the tendency of the English passengers is to form themselves into a great number of small cliques. No doubt
this tendency prevails to some extent upon the Atlantic
also, but then congenial tastes and education form the
divisions there and every one is in his proper sphere.
Upon the Pekin we found that rank and position
formed a strong element in the case—regardless of
merit. Vandy and I being republicans, not caring a
rap about either birth or position, and without social
status in England, seemed to be the only cosmopolitans
on board. From the major-general and family down to
the clerk of a mercantile house and his nice wife and
children, we had the free run of the ship. But when we
met intelligent and interesting people in one or the
other grade, and proposed to make them known to
others, as, had both parties been Americans, would
have given much pleasure, and from whose acquaintance mutual benefit would have resulted, we found
that the miserable barriers of artificial distinction stood
in the way.

I wished two young ladies to know each other, for
they were akin in education, manners, feelings, and
accomplishments, and one morning I said to the
one who surely was not the less desirable acquaintance : "You and Miss —— should know each other;
would you not like to make her acquaintance ? If so, I
shall ask her, and I am sure she would be pleased to
make yours. Both will be the gainers."

"Mr. Carnegie, excuse me, but she is a major-general's daughter, the advance must come from her. If she ever expresses a wish to know me, then you come to me and I'll tell you. This is the proper thing, you know."

Happy American young ladies, into whose pretty heads the thought would never enter that another would be so silly as to stand upon position, and if by any chance it did momentarily arise, it would be scouted as inconsistent with one's own self-respect as a woman. England will never be truly homogeneous till throne and aristocracy give place to the higher republican form.

India claims many victims. We had yesterday a young man near us who had been in India only a short time, and who was returning invalided. Poor fellow! He lay in the hatchway in his easy-chair from morning until night, gazing wistfully over the sea toward his beloved England. There he would soon get well. Only last night as I passed to bed I stopped to encourage him, telling him how finely we were dancing along homeward. At dawn I heard the pulsations of the engine cease for a few moments only, but in those moments he had been cast into the sea. Scarcely any one knew of his death except the doctor and a few of the crew; not a soul on board knew anything of him; he was an entire stranger to all. But think of the mother and sisters who were to meet him on arrival and convey him "to the green lanes of Surrey!"

See them hastening on board and casting anxious glances around! No one will know them, but every one will suspect who they are, and what their errand, and in- stinctively avoid them—for who would be the mes- senger to strike a mother down with a word? The death and burial were sad—sad enough; but the real tragedy is yet to be played in Southampton, when the living are to envy the fate of the dead, who, "after life's fitful fever," sleeps so well in the depths of the Indian Ocean.

Suez, Friday, February 28.

We reached Suez at six o'clock in the morning, and anchored within the bay. An enterprising sail- boat captain came alongside and offered to take us across the bay to the town in time to catch the only train leaving for Cairo for twenty-four hours. It was two long hours' sail, but the breeze was strong, and Vandy and I resolved to try it, bargaining with the captain, however, upon the basis of no train no pay. The few passengers on deck at that early hour gathered to give the adventurers a farewell cheer, and we were off. We made it just in time, and grasping a bottle of wine and some bread at the station—for we had had no breakfast—we started for Cairo.

The railway runs parallel to the Suez Canal, which, by the way, was a canal in the days of the Pharaohs, but, of course, much smaller and only used for irrigation.

We saw the top-masts of several steamers above the sandy banks as they crawled slowly through the desert. How great the traffic already is and with what strides it grows is well known. Its capacity can at any time be doubled by lighting it with electricity, but at present vessels are compelled by rule to lie still after sunset. All is dead through the night. In a few years this will be changed; and indeed the canal must be widened ere long and made a double track throughout to accommodate the continual stream of ships plying between the East and the West. At present it is just like one of our single-track railways with sidings or passing places. The distance from end to end is only about a hundred miles, but ships sometimes take three and even four days to squeeze through. This must be remedied. Twenty-four hours seems to be about the proper time-table. When past Ismailia, the line leaves the canal and runs westward through the land of Goshen. After the parched plains of India, it was refreshing once more to look upon "deep waving fields and pastures green." We were within the regions watered by the Nile, and the harvests resembled those of the carse of Gowrie.

We reached Cairo on time, and our first inquiries were about our friends, Mr. H., Miss N., and party, who were expected there from their three months' excursion upon the Nile. Fortunately, we found their dalbeah anchored in the stream, and we drove to it without delay. Sure enough, as we reached the bank, there lay the Nubia, that little gem, with the Stars and Stripes floating above her. We were rowed on board only to find that our friends were in the city. However, we made ourselves at home in the charming saloon, and awaited their return. Unfortunately, some sailor on shore had told them of two strangers going aboard, and there was not the entire surprise we had intended; but if there was no surprise there was no lack of cordial welcome, and we realized to the fullest extent what a world of meaning lies in the quaint simile, " as the face of a friend in a far-off country."

This reunion at Cairo was one of the fine incidents of our tour. Many months ago we had parted from Mr. H. and family, and half in jest appointed Cairo as our next meeting-place. They went in one direction, we in another, and without special reference to each other's movements it had so turned out that we caught them here. It was a narrow hit, however, as they were to leave next day for Alexandria; and had we remained on the Pekin, as all the other passengers did, and not undertaken the sail across the bay, we should have missed them. We grasped hands once more and sat down to dinner, the Nile gurgling past, the Pyramids with their forty centuries looking down upon us, and here was one more happy band drawing more closely to each other since separated from friends at home, enacting over again such scenes as the famous river has witnessed upon its bosom for thousands of years—one generation going and another coming, but the mysterious Nile remaining to welcome each succeeding host; and thus,

> " Thro' plots and counterplots—
> Thro' gain and loss—thro' glory and disgrace—
> . . . still the holy stream
> Of human happiness glides on ! "

To-day sight-seeing was subordinated to the rare pleasure of enjoying the company of our friends, but we all drove through Cairo streets and saw one memorable sight—the great college of Islam, where more than ten thousand students are constantly under preparation as priests of the Prophet. We saw them in hundreds sitting on their mats in the extensive open courts, all busily engaged in learning to recite the Koran to masters, or listening to professors who expounded it. Their intense earnestness soon impresses you. From this centre radiate every year thousands of these propagandists, scattering themselves over Arabia and to the farthest boundaries of Islam, and even beyond, warring upon idolatry and proclaiming the unity of God. No one can fail, I think, to receive from such a visit as we paid a much higher estimate of the vitality of Mohammedanism, and, having seen what it has to supplant, we cannot refrain from wishing these missionaries God-speed. The race rises step by step, never by leaps and bounds. Upon this point

20

I am much impressed by a paragraph from a lecture delivered by Marcus Dodd, D.D., at the Presbyterian College, London, which seems to me to take a wider and sounder view than one usually finds from such a source, and is therefore specially pleasing. He says: "The great lesson in comparative religion which we learn from the connection of Judaism and Christianity is that men are not always ripe for the highest religion; that there is a fulness of time which it may take four thousand years to produce. The Mosaic religion, imperfect as it was, compared with Christianity, was better for Israel during its period and preparation than the religion of Christ would have been." Then, referring to the Mohammedan religion, he says: "It is not denied that this religion did at once effect reforms which Christianity had failed to effect. It accomplished more for Arabia in a few years than Christianity had accomplished for centuries. It abolished at a stroke the idolatry which Christianity had fought in vain." It is to such men as Mr. Dodd that we are to look to keep religion abreast of the age.

Max Müller says: "In one sense every religion was a true religion, being the only religion which was possible at the time, which was compatible with the language, the thoughts, and the sentiments of each generation, which was appropriate to the age of the world." The Brahman has found the same truth. "Men of an enlightened understanding well know," says he, "that the Supreme has imparted to each nation the doctrine most suitable for it, and He, therefore, beholds with satisfaction the various ways in which He is worshipped." In other words, religion is the highest expression of which a people is capable. There is no reason why we should not try to prepare a people for a better one, but note this, *they must be prepared.* To *force* new religions upon any race is a sad mistake. In a late address on missionary methods in India, Rev. Phillips Brooks said: "That which makes people distrust foreign missions is the testimony that the Europeans in India will not trust the Christianized Indian. It is not strange that some poor creature should bring discredit on the religion he professes. He worships in strange houses and in a strange way. He kneels in American-style churches and is taught by men full of American ideas. Christianity will never be the religion of India until it comes there imbued with the spirit of the day. In time there must come forth an Indian Christianity, rich, full of power and goodness. The missionaries want this, and are perfectly aware it must come. The influence that now goes to India carries with it the curse as well as the blessing. Let the divisions of church creeds be kept at home, and *let the Indian religion be developed from within.*"

We visited several mosques, but they are such poor affairs compared to those of India that we took little interest in them. While the other countries we have thus far visited have all appeared stranger than expected, this is not so with Egypt. Everything seems to be just as I had imagined it. We know too much about the land of the Pharaohs to be taken thoroughly by surprise. Perhaps there is something in our having seen so much that our perceptions are no longer as keen as when we landed in Japan. The appetite for sight-seeing becomes sated, like any other, and I fear we are not as impressionable as before. So we decide not to visit Turkey and Greece upon this trip but to take these when fresh. The crowds of squalid wretches who surround us at every turn, clamoring for backsheesh; the mud hovels in which they manage to live, and the coarse food upon which they exist; the mass of greasy, unwashed rags which hang loosely upon them—such things no longer excite our wonder, or even our pity. We have seen so much of such misery before that I fear we begin to grow callous.

Cairo, as a city, is most picturesque, with its commanding citadel, and its hundreds of mosques with their slender spires and conspicuous minarets; while surrounding all this in the desert lie the ruins of older cities and of tombs and temples innumerable. The Desert of Sahara reaches to the very gates of the city on the east. The city lies between that and the Nile; then comes a narrow strip of green about ten miles in width, and after that the boundless Libyan Desert. The Pyramids stand upon the very edge of this desert, so that it is sand, sand, sand! everywhere around the city of the Caliphs, save and except this little green border along the Nile. But indeed the whole of Egypt is only a narrow green ribbon stretching along the river for some six hundred miles, and widening at the delta, where the waters divide and reach the sea by various channels. All the rest is sand. Egypt has not more cultivable soil than Belgium, and would not make a fair sized State with us.

The Khedive Ismail was determined to make Cairo a miniature Paris, and we see much that recalls Paris to us. The new boulevards, the opera-house, circus, cafés, new hotel—all show how much has already been done in this direction; but he is in hard straits just now, and the cry there, as elsewhere, is for retrenchment and reform. The new streets are Parisian, but it is in the old, narrow streets of the city that one sees oriental life distinctively Egyptian in its character. Indeed these are sights of Cairo which I enjoy most. Muffled ladies pass by, resembling nothing I can think of so much as big black bats as they sit man-fashion on their donkeys, wrapped in black silk cloaks; men in gorgeous silks, also on donkeys, ride along, while laden camels and asses carrying large panniers of clover slowly pick their way through the crowd. Harem ladies, too (there is the weight which pulls Egypt down), roll slowly by in their covered carriages, preceded by the running

Lyces. I never saw such a miscellaneous throng in any street before.

The great event of a visit to Cairo is Pyramid Day. The Pyramids are eight miles distant, and an early start has to be made to insure a return in season. Yesterday was our day. These wonders do not impress one at first —few really stupendous works ever do ; and even when at their base you think but meanly of their magnitude, so much so that you never hesitate as to whether you will ascend Cheops, the largest. Three Arabs, whose duty it is to assist you, are at once assigned to you by the Sheikh ; two of these take your hands, while the third stands behind to "boost" you up at the moment the others pull. It is a hard climb even when so assisted, and many who start are fain to content themselves with getting up one third the distance. I think I rested three times in making the ascent, and each time I found my feeling of disappointment growing beautifully less ; while by the time the shout came from my Arabs announcing that they were on the top stone, I was filled with respectful admiration for Cheops, I assure you, and whatever one may say about the equator, I feel sure no one will ever hear me speak disrespectfully of the Pyramids.

They are without doubt the greatest masses ever built by man. Cheops is four hundred and fifty feet high, and covers thirteen acres at the base, tapering to the top, which is only about thirty feet square, where one false step would be certain death, as, contrary to my opinion at first, I saw that one in falling could not possibly rest on any of the layers of projecting stone. I do not like high places, and I felt, while on the top, I would give a handsome sum just to be safe on level ground again. But I got down, or rather was taken down by my three attendants, without much difficulty, and after luncheon we went into the centre of the pile—a work of considerable trouble—and saw the sarcophagus. Attempts have been made to invest the Pyramids with some mysterious meaning, but, I take it, there will be no more of this, since an explanation is now given which meets every objection. They are simply the tombs of various kings, and differ in size because the kings ruled for different periods of time. The mode of procedure was this: When a king came to the throne he began to build his tomb; perhaps this was an excellent way of keeping before him the fact that he also must surely die, and that ere long ; successive courses of stone were built around the pile, one course per year, and when the king died the building ceased, his successor taking care to finish the course under progress at the death of his predecessor ; hence the great size of Cheops, for the monarch who constructed it reigned forty-two years and built his forty-two courses. This Pyramid is either sixty-five hundred or five thousand years old, according as you decide for one or another mode of computation. Either date will, however, en-title it to the honors of a hoary old age. The old Arabian proverb, "That all things fear Time, but Time fears the Pyramids," holds good no longer, for "the tooth of Time" is slowly but surely disintegrating even these masses. The entire finishing course of huge stone blocks, from top to bottom of Cheops, has already crumbled away, and lies in dust at the base. This is also the case with the second in size, except that a portion still clings around its top; this will fall some day, and leave it stripped like its greater neighbor.

Our Arab guide told us, as he pointed to the numerous monograms carved on the top of Cheops, that a lover who cuts the initials of his adored there, and calls upon Allah to prosper his suit, is certain to win her. Would you believe it, soon after this I saw Vandy secretly carving away.

The Sphinx—the mysterious Sphinx—which has baffled all inquisitive inquirers for centuries without number, stands in the sand only a short distance from Cheops. Imagine, if you can, with what feelings one gazes upon it. It is as old as the Pyramids, perhaps older, and there it still looks out upon the green and fertile banks of the Nile with the Libyan Desert behind. Its countenance has the same benignant cast, but it tells neither of sorrow nor of anger, neither of triumph nor of defeat. It tells you of no human passion, and yet seems to tell you of all—*the end of all* —and yet it is not a sad face. It is every thing and yet nothing. I never was so utterly unable to vivify an image with at least some imaginings. It could be made one thing or another, but no sooner had I thought it indicated one sentiment than a second look made the idea seem absurd. Like so many countless thousands before me, I gave it up. You cannot extract anything from that face. I thought the lesson might be in its position, and I pleased myself with drawing one from that. There this mystery stands, gazing only upon what is rich and fertile and instinct with life, the life-giving Nile rolling before it, and the fields of golden grain in view. Its back turned resolutely to the dreary sandy waste of death behind; and so it said to me as plainly as if it could speak, This is your lesson: let the dead past bury its dead; look forward only upon that which has life and grows steadily towards perfection. It is upon the bright things of life we must fix our gaze if we would be of use in our day and generation.

When in Alexandria we visited with deep interest the site of the famous Alexandrian Library, in which lay stored the most precious treasures of the world. Had it escaped destruction, how many questions which have vexed scholars would never have arisen, and how much ground which it has been necessary for genius to reconquer would have come to us as our heritage!

The Cleopatra's Needle now in New York, the counterpart of the one in London, was still in Alexandria when we were there. Seventeen hundred years before

Christ this huge monolith, which is cut out of solid rock, was erected at Heliopolis, and it was transported thence several hundred miles to its present site. It measures sixty-eight feet in height, and is not less than eight feet square at its base—one solid shaft of granite; but this is exceeded by the one still at Thebes, which is a hundred feet high. It struck me as a notable coincidence that the ingenious Frenchman who first proved the truth of the supposed hieroglyphic alphabet should have done so by assuming that the name repeated so frequently upon a certain stone extolling the virtues of Ptolemy Soter, must be that of the famous Cleopatra, and so it proved. Thus this extraordinary woman, who filled the world with her name during her life, and for centuries after, once more renews her tenure by linking herself with the world's history two thousand years after her death.

The museum in Cairo is said to comprise more Egyptian antiquities than are possessed in the world besides. It is filled with mummies, sarcophagi, jewelry, coins and statues, one wooden statue shown being no less than four thousand six hundred years old. Anything less than five thousand years of age one gets to consider rather too modern to suit his taste. Upon some of the lids of the tombs the inscriptions are as fresh as if cut yesterday. Egypt furnishes the earliest records of our race, because the dry sands of the desert on each side of the Nile, blowing over the cities of the past until these were completely buried, hermetically sealed them, and this preserved them from decay, and would have done so for ages yet to come. Is it any wonder that this narrow strip, filled with buried cities, should have given rise to a body of men who devote themselves to the search for rich spoils of the past and to deciphering the inscriptions? You meet occasionally an Egyptologist, and seem to know him instinctively.

But grand as is Egypt's past, and varied as her fortunes have been, it may surely be said that never during all her misfortunes has she occupied a position as deplorable as that which saddens the traveller of to-day. If any one wants to see what personal rule in its fullest development is capable of producing, let him visit Egypt. The condition of its finances is notorious, but we did not expect to witness such convincing proofs of insolvency.

The Khedive has been maintaining a standing army of sixty thousand men, but it has not been paid for more than two years. Retrenchment having been insisted upon by England and France, it was resolved to reduce the force to some eight thousand, and orders of dismissal were accordingly issued. But about two hundred officers who were in Cairo and had not yet been paid, entered the Prime Minister's chambers a few days before our arrival in the city, clamoring for their dues, and refused to leave until paid. Some slight violence was even used toward that functionary, and the English agent, who came manfully to his assistance, was roughly pushed about. It was finally arranged to pay all dismissed soldiers two months of their arrears. The train upon which we travelled from Cairo carried many of these men to their homes. While the army is not paid, we see on every hand unmistakable proofs of the Khedive's reckless personal extravagance. Here lies his grand steam yacht rotting in the harbor. In the station we noticed the imperial cars stowed away; on the river his large summer boat; and every other remarkably fine house in Cairo seemed to be one or another of the Khedive's palaces or harems. The man does not seem to have had the faintest idea of what was due to his country, or, even worse, what was due to himself. But take the greatest and best man in the world, surround him by people who assure him morn, noon and night that he differs from other men, and has a born right to their obedience—make a khedive, or czar, or king out of him—if kind nature has not made a fool of him at the start, men will do it, and if he has brains, brutality will soon be added to his folly. If he hasn't brains, then he becomes the fool pure and simple. George Washington himself would have been spoiled by royal notions in less than six months—good as he was and sound republican to boot.

One becomes indignant with a people so supine as to endure such waste and oppression. Everything is taxed, and the masses of the people are ground down to the lowest stage compatible with mere animal existence. England and France have been compelled recently to take strong measures in order to prevent impending ruin. The Khedive not long since dismissed the only one of his ministers who seemed to comprehend the state of affairs, but I see the faint remonstrance of these powers has sufficed to reinstate him; in other words, the Khedive has been told he is a figure-head, to reign, not to govern, and we may hope for an improvement in consequence. The population is only five millions, and it is estimated that at least two millions more could be supported by the country; so it seems that only good government is required to restore Egypt to prosperity.

The tenure of land is an important question just now, and men's minds are disposed to give the subject consideration. Mr. George's exciting book has attracted surprising attention. "Thou shalt not sell the land of the Lord thy God for ever," seems likely to prove correct. Egypt has a land history of much significance. Anciently the land was the property of the priests, and of the king and the military class. Although there were no castes, still the fact that the son usually followed his father's occupation, served the purpose of caste. Even Joseph did not purchase the land of the priests when he bought all the rest. Before the time of Mehemet Ali, say up to about a hundred years ago, a kind of feudal system prevailed, but by the massacre of the Mamelukes the feudal system was destroyed. Mehemet Ali seized almost all the landed property, and gave the owners pensions for life. There is scarcely such a thing as private tenure of land now in Egypt.

This little bit of cultivated land has actually borrowed in the last fifteen years no less than £80,000,000 sterling ($400,000,000). Twelve hundred miles of railway have been built, and numerous canals, harbors, and lighthouses constructed; but the amount spent in useful works bears but a small proportion to that squandered. The greatest item of all, however, is the discount paid upon the five successive loans by which funds were obtained. None of these loans cost less than 12 per cent. per annum, while the one for railways cost 26 per cent. per annum. These rates, I believe, are calculated upon the issue prices; what commissions the bankers received is unknown. A report upon the finances states that the Government received only about one-half the amount of the loans.

I have referred to the discontent which had shown itself in the army during our stay in Cairo. How rapidly events have travelled since then! The rise of a popular leader, Arabi, who possessed the confidence, or at least, who was accepted by the people as their only instrument of reform,—effectually put down by the English Government, which surely was misled by its agents in Egypt.

Now that England has been so foolish as to interfere,

but two courses are open. She must either rule Egypt as she does India, or, what would be infinitely better both for Egypt and for England, retire, and allow the people of Egypt to undertake the management of their own affairs. This would be unfortunate for the bondholders, no doubt, but it would sooner or later secure for Egypt those institutions for which she is suited. I am convinced that England is to see the day, and that ere long, when she will bitterly repent ever having thrown her power in the scale against men who revolted at a state of affairs against which revolt was meritorious, and gave to the world the best proof that sufficient sound timber existed in Egypt to form the nucleus of firm national institutions. England's position in Egypt is all wrong. She of all nations should know that there are stages in the life of nations where oppression can be overthrown only by violent means. Ah! John Bright proved himself here once more the true statesman. Had his advice been followed, how different might have been the result! But ere the Egyptian question is settled we may see stranger events still than those which have surprised us.

The cry from the moment you set foot in Egypt until the steamer sails is " Backsheesh! Backsheesh!" Give! give! give! Crowds surround you at every place, and from child to withered eld it is an incessant chorus. If one is weak enough to give a piastre he is done for; the crowd increases, and the roars of the beggars with it.

There is no place in Egypt which can be enjoyed, owing to this nuisance; even on the top of the Pyramid the evil is unabated. Travellers must be to blame for such an annoyance. For our part we resolved never to give anything to a beggar, and adhered strictly to the rule, which preserved us from many a fierce attack; but the objects begging were sometimes piteous-looking enough to haunt one.

The surest means of obtaining a livelihood as a beggar in Egypt is to feign idiocy, which, I am told, is frequently done. Idiots are regarded as saints, and are never restricted in their movements, maniacs alone being confined, and they are often met with in the streets. My Swedenborgian friends might account for the absence of sense being held proof positive of the saintly character by urging that idiots were certainly free from one of the worst evils of this generation denounced by the Swedish Seer as " self-derived intelligence."

The never ending work of creation is finely illustrated in the remarkable depression of the northern shore of Egypt, which is continually going on, notwithstanding the vast deposits from the many mouths of the Nile annually discharged upon it, while on the southern shore, near Suez, a contrary phenomenon is observable. The consequence of this movement is seen in the ruins of places on the Mediterranean shore, and the drying up of large portions of the Gulf of Suez.

Indeed the bed of the Red Sea may be traced for miles north of the town of Suez, which is now at the head of the gulf, and places far north of the town were on the coast in historic times. An equally remarkable change is observable in the level of the Nile. Two thousand years B.C. it is found that at Semneh the mean height of the famous river was twenty-three feet greater than it is to-day. Imagine what results would flow from a change of the level of the Mississippi twenty-three feet higher or lower than now! It would change the continent. While such startling changes are found right under our own eyes, surely we do not require the " doctrine of catastrophes " to explain the creation of this little ball—the earth! The silent, irresistible, unchanging laws of Nature suffice.

We arrived too late to get a run up the Nile, as the boats had ceased to ply for the season. There remained but Cairo and Alexandria to visit, and a few days spent at each place exhausts the sights; but we concluded that nothing could be more enjoyable than a three-months' sail upon the Nile, in one's own boat, breathing the remarkably pure and dry air as it comes from the desert, moving day by day from one to another scene of the far past, and at night enjoying the unequalled sunsets, when it seems, as some one has beautifully said, that " the day was slowly dying of its own glory." This is the trip of trips for an invalid, or for one overtaxed by work or oppressed with sorrow; and for a bridal tour—to give the lovers plenty of time and opportunity to become thoroughly acquainted with each other—it can be highly recommended.

The rapid rise of our western rivers is very different from the gradual swelling of the Nile, which begins at Khartoum, at the junction of the White and Blue Niles, as early as April each year, but which is not felt at Cairo until after the summer solstice, while the greatest height is not reached till autumn. A good flood gives a rise of forty feet at the first cataract, and about twenty-five at Cairo; a scanty rise is when only between eighteen or twenty feet occurs at Cairo. The inundation is good if it is between twenty-four and twenty-seven feet; if beyond the latter it becomes a destructive flood. Upon such a narrow margin—the rise of a few feet more or less in the Nile—depends the entire crop of Egypt! Once for a period of seven years (A.D. 457–464), the rise failed and seven years of famine ensued. A great engineering work, designed to regulate the inundation by means of a *barrage* across both branches of the river below Cairo, was begun some years ago, but, I believe, has been abandoned. When Egypt reaches good government from within herself, not through foreigners, one of its first works should be to complete the barrage. Surplus water will then be allowed free escape, and inundations prevented. When the flow is scanty, egress at the river mouths will be retarded, and thus Egypt will be secured regular harvests.

We watch men at work everywhere raising water from narrow ditches to higher levels, that all parts may be irrigated from the fruitful Nile. We could get no estimate of the amount of water which one man can raise in a day; but when human labor is so cheap, we guessed that it was, upon the whole, an economical mode. At all events a complete revolution in the management of land, and probably of its tenure, must precede the general use of machinery for this purpose. The "shadoof" of to-day is the same in form as that used by the ancient Egyptians. Two columns of mud, or brick, erected at the side of the ditch, support a beam of wood, across which is a pole with a weight at one end, and a rude wooden bowl-shaped bucket, suspended by a stick, at the other. A man stands under the bucket and pulls it down into the water. The weight helps him to push it up to the ditch above, where it is emptied. The operation is very quickly performed, and the bucket kept constantly going. It would be hard to beat these ancient Egyptian shadoofs by any device requiring human labor where the amount of water required is small. Water-wheels, driven by bullocks or cows, and sometimes by one animal only, are sometimes used. There is also a double shadoof worked by two men, and even steam pumps are used in extreme cases where the volume of water desired is unusually large. Steam, no doubt, is ultimately to drive out the shadoof, ancient as it is.

We had a strange meeting at Cairo upon entering the breakfast-room the morning after our arrival. Whom should we be placed opposite to but my friend the Rev. Mr. D., of Dunfermline, my aunty's minister, nae less! He was *en route* to the Holy Land with his father-in-law; but we had several days together at Cairo, and talked upon many subjects, from theology to town affairs. I had received a telegram the day of his departure which told me my mother was to sail from New York that very day to join me in Scotland, as had been arranged, and we drank her health and wished her *bon voyage* in good style.

Before bidding farewell to the East, I wish to indulge in just a few general reflections. Life there lacks two of its most important elements—the want of intelligent and refined women as the companion of man, and a Sunday. It has been a strange experience to me to be for several months without the society of some of this class of women—sometimes many weeks without even speaking to one, and often a whole week without even seeing the face of an educated woman. And, bachelor as I am, let me confess what a miserable, dark, dreary, and insipid life this would be without their constant companionship! This brings everything that is good in its train, everything that is bright and elevating. I cannot satisfy myself as to what the man of the East has to struggle for, since he has dethroned woman and practically left her out of his life. To see a wealthy

Chinaman driving along in his carriage alone was pitiable. His efforts had been successful, but for what? There was no joy in his world. The very soul of European civilization, its crown and special glory, lies in the elevation of woman to her present position (she will rise even higher yet with the coming years), and this favor she has repaid a thousand-fold by making herself the fountain of all that is best in man. In life, without her there is nothing. Much as the lot of woman in the East is to be deplored, that of man is still more deplorable. The revenge she takes is terrible, for she drags down with her, in her debasement, the higher life of man. I had noted the absence of music as one great want. Not an opera nor a concert—not even a hand-organ. Scarcely a sweet sound in all our journey. When we found an English church or a regimental band, we rejoiced. I went to hear the organ upon every occasion, and was seldom absent when the band played; but were women there as with us, wouldn't music spring forth also! so that even this want I am disposed to attribute to the first cause.

The absence of a regularly recurring day of rest ranks next in importance, I believe, in the list of causes which keep the East down in the scale of nations. With few exceptions, the race is doomed to a life of unremitting toil—from morning till night, and every day without respite; for festival and fête days recurring at long, irregular intervals are no substitute for the one regular day to which labor looks forward with us. The prospect of one day of rest frequently intervening gives a toiler something bright to look forward to, without which his life must stretch before him as one unceasing, unvarying drag. In this one blessed day his slavery ceases, the shackles fall. He is no longer a brute—fed and clothed solely because of his physical powers, his capacity to bear burdens—but a higher being, with tastes, pleasures, friends. Life becomes worth living. The man puts on his best clothes—and there is much in this—the woman gives her cottage an extra brushing up. Something extra is prepared for dinner—there is a great deal in this, too—and, in short, the day is marked by a hundred little differences from those of labor—a stroll in the fields, a visit to relatives, or a meeting with neighbors at church, all in their best; and then the swelling organ and the choir—these things lie closely at the root of all improvements; and if ever the race is to be lifted to a higher platform—and who shall dare doubt it?—the weekly day of rest will prove itself an agency in the good work only second to the elevation of woman.

The best mode of improving its most precious hours for the toiling masses is therefore a question of infinite moment, apart altogether from the question of its divine character, and viewed only as a human enactment of the highest wisdom. It would seem clear that to make this only respite from manual labor a day exclusively set apart for the mournful duty of bemoaning our manifold shortcomings—which must at best give rise to gloomy thoughts—would defeat the purposes I have indicated. I want a compromise—church service in the morning, with a sermon "leaning to the side of mercy," as Sidney Smith suggested, which meant that it should not exceed twenty minutes, for, as one wit says, "a minister who can't strike ile in twenty minutes should quit *boring*"—and then the fields and streams for the toilers who are cooped up in factories and workshops all the week long, or a visit to picture galleries, museums, or to musical concerts of a high order in huge centres—for in London and a village it is not the same question at all—to anything that would tend to brighten their existence. I am now convinced that there is an important change to be made in the mode of keeping our Sundays—the cessation of labor, as far as it is possible, to remain a cardinal point, but better facilities to be provided for cultivating the higher tastes of our poor workers, that the day may be to them indeed "the golden jewel which clasps the circle of the week."

One more observation upon the East and I am done: the work that England is doing there. You know that she has in one way or another obtained the keys to the East. Some islands she owns; some small strips of the mainland she also has acquired and governs; at Shanghai, Hong Kong, and other points in

China; at Singapore, Penang, Ceylon, Aden, Malta, and
indeed all through our journey, we stand now and then
on British soil. And wherever the meteor flag floats,
there you find order, freedom, schools, churches, dispensaries, clean streets, hospitals, newspapers, justice; and
under that flag you will find thousands of Chinamen
and Malays, Indians, Cingalese, Arabs—indeed men of
all races—settled and enjoying the blessings of good
government. No revolution there, no slavery, no arbi-
trary arrest, nor forced levy. As a native lawyer in
India said to me—he talked freely because of our
American look—"There is between natives under English rule perfect justice; but," he added, "every one
must behave himself. There is no war nor plundering
when one settles under them, for these English *won't
stand any nonsense, and they will have peace.*"

England, therefore, has planted throughout the East
small models of perfectly governed little States, enjoying all the blessings of the highest civilization. Daily
and hourly these teach their lesson to the native races,
and when they do acquire this lesson—and who that believes in the progress of mankind can doubt but the
day must come ?—they will look westward with grateful hearts and say, "All this we owe to thee, noble
England !"

But while this is true, there is another phase of
England's work to which I have referred in my remarks
upon India. The source of England's good work

springs from example. It is where the native races are drawn to her standard, as at the many points named, where their freedom is not destroyed, that great results can alone be looked for. This is the very reverse of England's position in India. She stands there as the destroyer of native institutions, and forces her views upon an unwilling people wholly unprepared to receive them, instead of resting, as at Hong Kong, Singapore, Aden, and such places, saying to the natives, "Come, try our system, and, if you like it, remain and share its benefits." Nothing but good can result from the latter, and nothing really good can flow from the former; the injury done must more than absorb any temporary gains. Force is no remedy; and some of these years, unless the ablest natives are induced to participate in the government of India, and soon allowed the chief control, England will rise to a rude awakening.

ALEXANDRIA, Friday, March 14.

Off at nine this morning for Naples, taking Sicily *en route*. The voyage was a smooth one, and we landed at Catania upon the morning of the fourth day. As we stepped ashore we felt in a moment that we were once more within the bounds of civilization. What a difference between this and the East! And there frowned Mount Etna, ten thousand feet above the sea level, thirty miles distant, and yet seemingly so near we thought that we could almost walk over to its base after breakfast. We ascended a small hill in the centre of the city—which, by the way, has a population of a hundred thousand—and there lay Sicily spread out before us in all its wondrous beauty. Lemon and orange groves in full bearing, and fields of vines just budding; and in the town clean paved streets and pavements, which are unknown in the East; people with shoes and stockings on; statues and fountains, and a good old cathedral; harps and violins, and the chime of church going bells. Ah! Western civilization is not a mistake, nor a myth, nor a thing of doubtful value, as we can testify. At least so thought two happy travellers in Sicily that bright balmy morning, as they felt how blessed a thing it was to be once more in a civilized country.

The pretty island of Sicily (Sechelia, as the Italians pronounce it) contains nearly three millions of people—nearly as many as Scotland—and supports them almost entirely by the produce of the land, for manufactures are little known. The olive and the vine are everywhere, and the crops of oranges and lemons go to most parts of the world. An English gentleman told us he had bought oranges in the season for one cent per dozen. There is one item of export of rather peculiar character—sulphur—which is obtained from the volcano. We saw it drawn through the streets in large blocks.

Only two hundred years ago an eruption of Mount

Etna took place, and 27,000 people were buried by the lava. We saw where the stream had rushed down from the crater through part of the town, and far into the sea—almost a mile in width, and thirty miles from its source, bearing destruction to everything in its course, and yet to-day fine new houses stand upon the cold lava, and away up and along the sides of the volcano for miles are to be seen cottages clustering thickly together, the inmates busily engaged in cultivating their vineyards. It was only a few days ago the monster gave a warning and shook these houses; but they still " sit under their vine and sing the merry songs of peace to all their neighbors "—these merry, light-hearted Sicilians!—as if they had Mount Etna under perfect control.

The railway skirts the shores of the island for its entire length—some fifty miles—and a more beautiful ride is not to be seen in all the world. It is a succession of fine old castles, in perfect ruin, upon every petty promontory, and we go through nothing but orange and lemon groves and vineyards. We pass at the base of Mount Etna; but although all was smiling in the valleys below, its top was enveloped in dark clouds and busy with the thunder and the storm.

Messina is a very quaint Italian city. The funeral services of a distinguished lady were in progress when we stepped into the cathedral, which was illuminated with hundreds of candles—I think I might say almost a

thousand—the interior being one mass of light, which
shone with strange effect upon the rich black velvet
with which the walls were draped. A lady in our party
counted the carriages as they passed, and told us there
were fifty-three, most of which would compare favorably with those of New York or London. This will
give you some idea of the richness of Messina, which
we had thought to be an unimportant town.

The Sicilians are strict Roman Catholics and completely under the dominion of that faith. There is
scarcely a trace of dissent to be found. When we were
about to sail from Messina for Naples a priest walked
upon the deck and collected contributions from the devout passengers, for which in return he was expected to
give to our good ship the august protection of Holy
Mother Church. We noticed that all the passengers
contributed and received his blessing with much solem-
nity. Faith is still there. They were going to sea
—probably a first experience to most if not all of them,
and were naturally apprehensive. Should we have a
stormy night, no doubt, notwithstanding their bargain
with the priest, some will resolve with good Dame Par-
tington that under like circumstances if ever she set
her foot on dry land she would never again trust herself " so far out of the reach of Providence." But my
mother remembers well that when a member of the congregation was about to start from Dunfermline to London, a rare event in those days, though not so very long

ago, that his safety was always prayed for in church. I mentioned this to Vandy when he was deploring the ignorance and, as he thought, the impiety of the Sicilians. We are not entirely free from superstition ourselves, and were in the last generation where the Sicilians are in this.

The scene in " The Tempest," the enchanted isle, must have been in the neighborhood of Sechelia, and surely no fitter region in all the world could be found; indeed I found sweet Sechelia so enchanting that I voted it the very spot, and selected my Prospero's Cave on the glittering shore within sight of Mount Etna.

BAY OF NAPLES, Thursday, March 20.

Early morning! Yes, my dear friends, *it is round.* Here stands Mount Vesuvius in full view this morning, making for itself pure white clouds of steam, which float in the otherwise clear, cloudless sky of Italy. No entering the crater now as we did before, for the volcano is no longer at rest. Vandy and I shake hands and recall our pledge made in the crater years ago, and say, " Well, that is now fulfilled, and may life only have for us in its unknown future another such five months of unalloyed happiness (save where the dark shades of death among friends at home have saddened the hours) as those we have been so privileged to enjoy."

It is well never to be without something to look forward to, and speculate upon ; and by a happy chance

Vandy and I have hit upon our next excursion, when we shall have earned another vacation by useful work. The very thought of it already brings us pleasure. And so, all hail, sunny Italia! What a picture this Bay of Naples is! We sail past our former haunts, Capri and Sorrento, and are soon in our hotel at Naples, where we are delighted to rejoin our friends.

From this time forth it is impossible but that a change must occur in the character of these notes. There is a first time to everything, and it is first impressions which I have endeavored honestly to convey; but my first impressions of Europe were obtained years ago. The gloss and enthusiasm of novelty are wanting. The sober second thought is proverbial; but there is a sober second sight as well, and it is this I am about to take. Besides this, Europe is more familiar to everybody than the East. Many know it through personal experience, and I shall therefore content myself with giving the salient features of our homeward progress from this point.

We find Naples, Sorrento, Capri, and all the pretty spots around the bay much improved since our last visit. The people seem to us to be remarkably fine-looking, but perhaps this is mainly owing to the miserable races we have been seeing lately. The museum which contains the principal treasures found at Pompeii and Herculaneum is greatly improved, and one has no difficulty now in determining just how the people of those cities lived. There are even models of the houses shown. The frescoes and sculptures are far finer than I had remembered them, and indeed there are so many articles of furniture and domestic utensils that one cannot help admitting that those who argue that man travels in a circle just as the world goes round, and never advances, have some ground for their theory in these remarkable productions of the first century. We are in the land of music, sure enough! Here is the list of operas to be performed to-night, apart from numerous dramatic performances: "Norma," "Sonnambula," "La Belle Hélène," "Martha." You will please take it for granted that our nights here, with few exceptions, will be spent hearing one or another opera, for of all the pleasures of civilized society which we have missed most in our travels, we rank first after the absence of refined women the total absence of music. We hunger for sweet sounds.

We were fortunate this time in getting into the Blue Grotto—the sea being quite smooth. The reflections upon the rocky roof were not as fine as we expected; but Miss N. pronounced the water "the prettiest blue that ever was," and she is an authority upon color. While at Capri we ascended to the villa of Tiberius, on the edge of a perpendicular cliff nearly two thousand feet high. It was from this rock that ruler was wont to throw his victims into the sea. He found they never troubled him again. And now I write amid the orange groves of Sorrento, where we have been spending a few days.

We have just finished, in company with our friends, a three-days' excursion to Pæstum, embracing the famous drive along the coast to Amalfi. Certainly I know nothing of the kind in the world equal to this road in grandeur, and if any of you ever visit Naples I advise you to let nothing interfere with your going to Amalfi. At Sorrento we joined our friends, Mr. H. and party, and our Windsor Hotel delegation was further and happily augmented by Mr. and Mrs. I. and family. Can you wonder that our daily excursions were de-lightful?

ROME, March 26.

Rome once more! What a change! A miniature Paris has been added to old Rome since we first saw it, and even old Rome itself is modernized completely. Much of the picturesque is lost, but well lost, since it brings us clean streets, improved dwellings, and all the accompaniments of progress; but, notwithstanding its now greater likeness to modern cities, it is not with these Rome vies. Her empire is not of to-day, but over the mighty past she alone holds undisputed sway, and the spirit of ages gone still infuses itself into every-thing in Rome. I thought even modern structures were unlike their fellows elsewhere, as if the mere fact that they stood in Rome invested them with a peculiar halo of classic dignity and importance.   Then Rome still has to boast of so many of the best things which the world has to show.   No other cathedral is so grand as St. Peter's nor so beautiful as St. Paul's; no other "bit of color" is equal to the Transfiguration; no other heroic statue is to be compared with the Augustus; nowhere else is so sweet a girl-face as the Cenci; no other group is to be named with the Laocoon, no other fresco with the Aurora; and where is there another Moses, or Apollo Belvedere, or Antinous, or where is there vocal music so heavenly as that of the Pope's choir?   Nowhere.   And so it comes that the world still flocks to Rome, and must continue its pilgrimage hither to this Mecca for a thousand years to come; and artists by the score, day after day, multiply copies of these wonders of art, the recognized "best" in their various classes which man has yet brought forth.   All these works, and others unmentioned, I returned to with enhanced pleasure.   They all seemed greater and finer to me than when I saw them before. I had not forgotten them, while the mass of mediocre works had left no trace.

It is thus that the true fire of genius vindicates its right to immortality.   Generations may come and go, fashions and tastes may change, but "a thing of beauty" remains "a joy forever."   While the statues and pictures of Rome, therefore, gave me far greater pleasure than before, I have to confess that the historical associations

gave me much less.   When in Rome before I was overflowing with Shakespeare, Byron and Macaulay, and
would wander away alone and recite to myself on the
appropriate sites the passages connected with them.
This time I fear our friends proved too congenial.   We
dwelt too much in the happy present to give ourselves
up to the historical past; but I do not think one gets
the sweetest juices out of Rome unless he gives way to
the melancholy vein now and then, and " stalks apart in
joyless reverie."

Another reason for the difference suggests itself.
One fresh from Egypt, where he has been digging
among the five thousand years B.C., and lost in amazement at what the race was even then producing, must
experience some difficulty in getting up a respectable
amount of enthusiasm for structures so recent as the
time of Christ; the "rascally comparative" intrudes to
chill it with its cold breath.

There is a third reason, perhaps—and reasons do
seem as plenty as blackberries, now that I begin to
write them down—we are so near home the echoes of
business affairs begin to sound in our ears.   We snuff
the battle as it were afar off.   It is impossible to become so entirely absorbed in the story of the Cenci as
to prevent the morning's telegram from home intruding, and so it came about that this time we did less
moralizing than before.   We were fortunate in being in
Rome during Easter Week, which gave us an opportu-

nity to hear the best music; and certainly there is no choir for vocal music which can rank with that of the Pope. It is the only choir I ever heard which I felt the finest organ would spoil. It produces a strange and powerful effect, the music itself seeming to be of a peculiar order unlike any other. One of our young ladies, describing her feelings to a friend, said that at one time she felt she was really in heaven; but when the " Miserere " broke forth, she knew she was only a poor sinner struggling to get there.

We visited, with our friends, the various studios. In painting there does not appear to be a high standard of excellence. The Roman school does not stand well, but in statuary it is better. A young American artist, Mr. Harnisch, seemed to me to be doing the most creditable work. His busts have already given him reputation, and he has a figure now in plaster, "Antigone," which I rate as the best classical statue in process of completion which we saw. This young artist is not probably as good a manager as some of his more pretentious countrymen, and, I fear, we are to wait some time before a Congressional committee can be induced to give him a commission; but in the opinion of real Italian sculptors he is an artist. There are those who have "adorned" our public edifices with huge works to whom certainly no one outside of America would apply the name. We shall hear of Mr. Harnisch by-and-by; he is young, and can wait.

I was highly gratified at making the acquaintance of Dr. Smiles, author of "Self-Help," and that favorite of mine, "The Scotch Naturalist," and other valued works. He is a most delightful companion and a true Scotchman, and hadn't we "a canny day thegether" at Tivoli! Through him I met Mr. William Black, who is a small, young man, with a face that lights up, and eyes that sparkle through his spectacles. Mr. Petty, R.A., and he were doing Italy together, and no doubt we are to see traces of their travels in their respective lines ere long.

FLORENCE, Wednesday, April 9.

We spent a few days in Florence, but it rained almost continually, as indeed it has done all winter. This has been the most disagreeable season ever known in Italy, we hear from every quarter. Sight-seeing requires sunshine : but we nevertheless did the galleries, and were delighted with the masterpieces for which the city is famed. The statuary, however, is much inferior to that of Rome. In the way of painting I was most interested in comparing the numerous Madonnas of Raphael, and seeing how he, at last, reached "the face of all the world" in the San Sisto. He seems to have held as loyally as a true knight to his first love. His Madonnas have all the same type of face. You could never hesitate about their authorship. Emphatically they are one and all " Raphael's Madonnas," and very much alike—even the one which the Grand Duke loved so fondly as to take it about with him wherever he travelled is only a little sweeter than the rest. It is a strange fact that it was not by painting Madonnas at all the master obtained his inspiration. He painted the portrait of a lady, which is still seen in the Pitti Palace, from whose face he drew the lacking halo of awe and sublimity. He idealized this woman's face, and the San Sisto came to satisfy all one can imagine about the Madonna. But the face of Christ! Who shall paint it satisfactorily? No one. This is something beyond the region of art. A divine-human face cannot be depicted, and all the efforts I have seen are not only failures which one can lament, but many are caricatures at which one becomes indignant. I was greatly pleased that a true artist, Leonardo da Vinci, realized this, and painted his Christ with averted head. Every great painter in older times seems to have thought it incumbent upon him to paint a Christ, and consequently you meet them everywhere. As for the "Fathers" (*i.e.,* Jehovah) one sees, these seem to me positively sacrilegious. I wonder the arms of the men who ventured upon such sacred ground did not wither at their sides. To paint old men with tremendous white flowing beards—a cross between Santa Claus and Bluebeard— and call them God! Here is materialism for you with a vengeance. These audacious men forgot that *He* was not seen in the whirlwind, neither in the storm, but never seen at all; only *heard* in the still, small voice.

Of course I visited Mrs. Browning's grave in Florence. I had the melancholy satisfaction of hearing, from one who knew her intimately, many details concerning her life here. Mr. Browning left Florence the day after she died, leaving the house, his books, papers, and even unfinished letters, as they were when he was called to her bedside the night before, and has never returned; nor has he ever been known to mention her name, or to refer to the blow which left him alone in the world. He seems to have been worthy even of a love like hers. We stayed over two days at Milan to see friends, and while there ascended to see once more the celebrated cathedral. It is finer—I do not say grander—but much finer, especially as seen from the roof, than any other building in Europe.

From Milan we went to Turin, and spent a day there, as we had never seen that city. It is prettily situated, very clean, with regular streets, but without any special objects of interest. The splendid view of the snow-clad Alps, and the fertile valley of the Po, as seen from the monastery, fully repaid us for the day given to Turin. We leave Italy in the morning. It is impossible not to like the country and to be deeply interested in its future. While it has made considerable progress since the genius of Cavour made it once more a nation, still its path is just now beset with dangers. A standing army of six hundred thousand and all the concomitants of royalty to maintain, and a large national debt upon which interest has to be paid—these require severe taxation, and even with this the revenues show a deficit. That last resort, paper currency, has been sought, and now the circulating medium—although "based on the entire property of the nation," as our demagogues phrase it—is at a discount of ten per cent., which threatens to increase.

But the chief trouble arises from the religious difficulty—that sad legacy from the past, of which, fortunately, a new land like America knows nothing. The Pope and all strict Catholics stand coldly aloof from the government, ready to give trouble whenever opportunity offers. But I have faith in Italy. She will conquer her enemies, and once again be a great power worthy of her glorious past. All her troubles, however, are not to seek.

————

PARIS, Thursday, May 1.

Now comes somewhat of a return to the more prosaic side of life. We made an excursion to the famous iron and steel works of the Schneider Company at Creuzot. What a concern this is, and how small we all are upon the other side of the Atlantic! Fifteen thousand five hundred men are employed here. We saw fifteen steam hammers in one shop. The mill for rolling only is 1,500 by 350 feet, filled with trains. The giant, however, is the 80-ton steam hammer, with its huge appliances. Masses of steel 35 tons in weight are handled as readily as we move a rail ingot. One ingot of steel weighing 120 tons was shown to us. This monster hammer is required only for armor plate and guns—war material. The happier demands of peaceful industry are met with ordinary machinery. Long may it be, therefore, before America can boast an engine of even half the size. Our visit to Creuzot was both interesting and instructive. Mr. Schneider and his officers were most cordial and attentive to us.

We spend a few days in Paris, which shows even more than the other cities we have revisited the march of improvement. It is farther beyond competition in its line than it ever was. I appreciate its attractions more than I have done upon previous visits; but one must be exceptionally strong who can persist in leading an earnest and useful life here, where so much exists to persuade one that after all amusement is the principal thing to be sought for. Most of the American residents seem to me to sink naturally to the level of thinking most—or certainly talking most—of the newest opera, or even the best ballet, or where is to be found the best *table d'hôte;* but, after all, what can a man do who leaves his own country, and the duties incumbent upon him there, to become a man about town here, with no work in the world to do. Good Americans come here when they die, it is said. I think it would be well for most of them if they did postpone their journey until then.

As we have travelled through France bands of the "Reserves" have been constantly seen repairing to their camps. Every Frenchman now, without exception, must serve as a soldier and drill at least one month every year. No substitutes are allowed. Soldiers! soldiers everywhere! Not a petty town at which we have stayed over night but has its barracks—its troops who parade its streets every morning. The entire male population is being trained so as most skilfully to murder, upon the first favorable opportunity, such of their fellow-Christians who may happen to be called Germans, while in Germany a similar state of affairs is rendered necessary to prevent the success of their "brothers'" intention. You see there was a frontier that was not "scientific," and it was "rectified" a few years ago; but these rectifications, of all things in the world, never remain rectified, and so we are to awake some fine morning to find the "civilized" Christian (!) nations (save the mark!) nobly engaged in butchering each other, even if this is the nineteenth century and we all worship Christ and have the same Father in heaven. That thoughtful educated people, even in England and America, can still deliberately send a son "to the army," to be taught the butchering trade, his victims being human, always saddens me when I think of it. The progress of the world has not only been slow but small, till the profession of arms, as it is called, is held to be unfit except for men of brutal natures.

In Italy it is much the same. She has 600,000 men under arms, and is drilling others, while Russia has just ordered an addition to her hosts exceeding five-fold the entire American army. England's war expenditure this year exceeds that of only five years ago by $30,000,000, which is more than America spends for her army altogether. And so the whole of Europe is armed and arming, as if conscious that a storm is about to burst, or at least that such a stupendous drain upon her productive resources has to be endured to insure safety. Happy America! she alone seems to occupy a position free from grave and imminent dangers.

LONDON.

Our next step brought us to monster London, where we attended the interesting meeting of the British Iron and Steel Institute, and being called upon as the only representative of American iron and steel manufacturers present, I had to venture a few remarks. Whatever England may be justly chargeable with in the past for her neglect of scientific methods and the improvements of the day, it is evident she now occupies the van in this respect.

No one could be present at these meetings without being impressed with the amount and thoroughness of the scientific knowledge now engaged in the iron and steel manufacture of Great Britain. Not less remarkable seemed to me the willingness upon the part of all to report and explain every advance made in the various processes to their fellows. The old idea of trade secrets seems thoroughly exploded, and a free interchange of practice and theory is now seen to be the best for all. I cannot but believe that had the manufacturers of America adopted this policy years ago, many millions squandered in the erection of works at unsuitable locations would have been saved. It struck me as strange that no less a personage than Earl Granville, who has had charge of her Majesty's foreign affairs and been leader in the House of Lords, should have been in attendance and participated in these meetings. The company also had the attendance of two dukes; but these were Lord Granville's compeers only in title. All of the three, however, rightfully claim to rank with us as iron-masters. The Bessemer medal was presented this year to Peter Cooper, of New York, much to the honor of the donors, I think.

For one shilling, any one curious to know something of the sights of this London, can do so by purchasing a good-sized volume—Dickens's London. A look at it will soon satisfy one how true it is that compared to London all other cities are but villages. It will very soon count four millions of people under its sway. Every year one hundred thousand are added to the mass, and not even depressed times seem to limit this increase. The reason for this is patent; there is everything here that there is elsewhere, and much that can be found nowhere else; in every department of life, for earnest work in any special line, or for amusement —for sight-seeing, study, or fashion—it is here that the very best of everything is concentrated; the very cream of all the world is here, because no other place is large enough or rich enough to support it. To know the best that has been said and done in the world of the past is no doubt much, as Matthew Arnold says, but there is also much in seeing and living where the best of to-day is said and done, and if possible in the company of those who have said or done any of the best things in any line. Life with godlike men on earth must be the best preparative for companionship hereafter. This is possible in Britain only in London, for the celebrities and their works are centred here. An unusually large proportion of the population is of the wealthy classes, for the height of the average Briton's ambition is, in addition to the essential estate in the country, to be in possession of a mansion in London. After these are acquired, and his wife and daughters have been presented at court, any after-successes may be regarded as details which ornament the solid edifice of position attained; and truly, as far as I have seen human life in any part of the world, I know of no state which in itself seems capable of affording so much pleasure—were happiness dependent upon external circumstances—as that which rewards successful Britons when with their usual good sense they retire from business.

If the owner of a large estate in Britain with its hundreds of people, who are as it were, under his care, its pretty quaint villages and honeysuckled cottages, its running brooks, its hedge-rows and green fields, all giving him scope for change and improvement—if such a man is not happy and does not enjoy life, let him seek for some more favorable conditions in some other planet than this, say I. I must not attempt to follow our steps through England and Scotland, nor to tell you of the cordial welcomes and thousand kind attentions bestowed upon us. We spent a very, very happy month among dear kind friends, and never enjoyed Merrie England more. My mother and Miss F. joined us in London, and took care of us until we sailed for New York, which we did by the new Cunard steamer Gallia, June 14th, reaching New York on the 24th, exactly eight months from the day we sailed out of the Golden Gate. And now, June 25th, I write these lines at Cresson, on the crest of the Alleghanies, having reached our starting point and earned our right to fellowship with the favored fraternity of globe-trotters.

The voyage round the world should be made sailing westward from London or New York, as this gives the traveller the prevailing winds in his favor; at least after he reaches New York, for the Atlantic is never quite blessed with steady winds from the west. The trade-winds waft the traveller on his way when he goes toward the west; should he take the contrary direction and start via England to the East, he must experience many rough days and nights upon the sea. We saw the steamers from England battling against the monsoon, which only served to push us steadily and smoothly on. Let all my readers make due note of this—westward, not eastward. Another even greater advantage, at least to those who, like myself, are affected by heat, is obtained by taking the westward course: the various countries can be visited in months during which no extreme heat is possible. The best time to start from San Francisco is early in September, so that Japan is reached about the first of October, which is a delightful month in that pretty toy-land, neither too hot nor too cold. A month will enable the tourist to see all that is specially interesting—Yokohama, Yeddo, Kiobe, Kioto, Osaka, Nagasaki, and some of the notable inland sights. This brings him to China (Shanghai) the middle of November. After a few days there, a trip up the Yang-tse, on one of the excellent American style of river boats, some six hundred miles to Hang-Kow, should not be missed, as one gets by this the best possible look at the Chinese at home. Hong Kong, the next stage, is reached, say early in December. Here you do Canton, Macao, and other interesting points, and reach Singapore, almost at the equator, and eat your Christmas dinner directly below your friends at home. If the reports from Java are favorable, a tempting excursion to that interesting island can be made from Singapore; but when we were at Singapore Europeans were being brought there from Java, and hurried north to cool places as the only cure for maladies contracted in that island. Therefore we abandoned our intended trip thither.

The traveller can decide whether to take steamer from Singapore via Bankok, Siam, and do that coast of Asia, and reach Calcutta from the west, or to follow our course via Ceylon. If he has plenty of time, the former may enable him to see more of India; but our experience was that there is more to see by any route than can be properly taken in upon one journey. If the wanderer follow us to Ceylon, we advise him to cross from Colombo to Southern India by steamer to Philipopolis, and go up through Southern India by land to Madras, as this will give him an opportunity to see the strange architecture and many customs peculiar to that region. We did the principal sights of India, but we advise any of our readers who make the journey, instead of returning from Delhi as we did, to go further north to Amritsir, and as far toward Cabool as the rail may extend. Simla upon the hills should also be visited. We often regret that we had not a week or two more to spend in India. We were rather late in the season, and Bombay was getting hot—indeed, it is always rather hot anywhere at the equator—but with the exception of a few hours at midday no great inconvenience was found, and the nights and the mornings were pleasant.

By the time the traveller has reached Egypt, and seen Alexandria and Cairo, he will be disposed, if our condition be any guide, to rest and be thankful, consigning any further extended travels to some future time when he has fully digested what he has gathered in his wanderings, and is fresh. When he touches pretty Catania, on his way west, he will feel for the first time that he is once more, as it were, at home among his own kith and kin, and has been quite long enough among strangers. Going round the world yields one exquisite pleasure which cannot be experienced upon any other tour. Our way over the long seas has not to be retraced. The farther we go, the nearer we come to home; every day's journey away from those we love, is also one day's step nearer to them. I think, also, that no amount of travel in detached portions of the world enables one to contemplate the world and the human race as a whole. One must traverse the ball round and round to arrive at a broad, liberal, correct estimate of humanity—its work, its aims, its destiny.

Go, therefore, my friends—all you who are so situated as to be able to avail yourselves of this privilege— go and see for yourselves how greatly we are bound by prejudices, how checkered and uncertain are many of our own advances, how very nearly all is balanced. No nation has all that is best, neither is any bereft of some advantages, and no nation, or tribe, or people is so unhappy that it would be willing to exchange its condition for that of any other. See, also, that in every society there are many individuals distinguished for traits of character which place them upon a par with the best and highest we know at home, and that such are everywhere regarded with esteem, and held up as models for lower and baser natures to emulate.

The traveller will not see in all his wanderings so much abject, repulsive misery among human beings in the most heathen lands, as that which startles him in his civilized Christian home, for nowhere are the extremes of wealth and poverty so painfully presented. He will learn, too, if he be observant, that very little is required after all to make mankind happy, and that the prizes of life worth contending for are, generally speaking, within the reach of the great mass.

Did you ever sum up these prizes and think how very little the millionaire has beyond the peasant, and how very often his additions tend not to happiness but to misery! What constitutes the choice food of the world? Plain beef, common vegetables and bread, and the best of all fruits—the apple; the only nectar bubbles from the brook without money and without price. All that our race eats or drinks beyond this range must be inferior, if not positively injurious.

23

Dress—what man, or rather what woman wears—is less and less comfortable in proportion to its frills and its cost, and no jewel is so refined as the simple flower in the hair, which the village maid has for the plucking. All that women overload themselves with beyond this range is a source of unhappiness. To be the most simply attired is to be the most elegantly dressed. So much for true health and happiness in all that we eat, and drink, and wear.

If we extend the inquiry to the luxuries and adornments of life, is there any music—which of course comes first—comparable in grandeur to that of the wave, stirring the soul with its mighty organ tones as it breaks upon the beach, or any so exquisitely fine as that of the murmuring brook which sings its song forever to every listener upon its banks, while above birds warble and the zephyr plays its divine accompaniment among the trees! We spend fortunes for picture-galleries, but what are the tiny painted copies compared to the great originals, the mountains, the glens, the streams and waterfalls, the fertile fields, the breezy downs, the silver sea! These are the gems of the universal gallery, the common heritage of man, the property of the humblest who has eyes to see, and as free as the air we breathe. We have our conservatories and spend our thousands upon orchids, but which of nature's smiles ranks with the rose and the mignonette, the daisy and the bluebell, and the sweet forget-me-not blooming for all earth's children, and which grow upon the window-sill of the artisan and which the laborer blesses at his cottage door!

If we go higher still in the scale, we find that the companionship of the gods is not denied to the steady wage-receiving man, for Shakespeare and our Burns and our Scott can be had for sixpence per volume. In this blessed age in which we are privileged to live even the immortals are cheap and visit the toiler. We see the rich rolling over the land in their carriages, but blessed beyond these is the man who strolls along the hedge-rows. The connoisseur in his gallery misses the health-giving breeze which brings happiness to the devotee who seeks the original afield. The lady in her overheated conservatory knows nothing of the joyous rapture of her more fortunate sister who gathers the spoils of the glen. Ah, my friends, ponder well over this truth: the more one dwells with her, the more one draws from her, the closer one creeps to her bosom, the sweeter is nature's kiss. From man's neglect of her for meaner substitutes come most of the disappointment and unhappiness of life. The masses of mankind are happy all round the world because their pleasures are drawn so largely from sources which lie open to all. The rich are not to be envied, for truly "there is no purchase in money" of any real happiness. When used for our own gratification, it injures us; when used ostentatiously, it brings care; when hoarded, it narrows the soul. Nature has not provided a means by which any man can use riches for selfish purposes without suffering therefrom. There is only one source of true blessedness in wealth, and that comes from giving it away for ends that tend to elevate our brothers and enable them to share it with us. Nature is gloriously communistic after all, God bless her! and sees that a pretty fair division is made, let man hoard as he may. The secret of happiness is renunciation.

Another advantage to be derived from a journey round the world is, I think, that the sense of the brotherhood of man, the unity of the race, is very greatly strengthened thereby, for one sees that the virtues are the same in all lands, and produce their good fruits, and render their possessors blessed in Benares and Kioto as in London or New York; that the vices, too, are akin, and also that the motives which govern men and their actions and aims are very much the same the world over. In their trials and sufferings, as in their triumphs and rejoicings, men do not differ, and so the heart swells and the sympathies extend, and we embrace all men in our thoughts, leaving not one outside the range of our solicitude and wishing every one well. The Japanese, Chinese, Cingalese, Indians, Egyptians, all have been made our friends through individuals of each race of whom we have heard much that was good and noble, pure lives, high aims, good deeds, and how can we, therefore, any longer dwell apart, believing our own land or our own people in any respect the chosen of God! No, no; we know now in a sense much more vivid than before that all the children of the earth dwell under the reign of the same divine law, and that for each and every one that law evolves through all the ages, the higher from the lower, the good from evil, slowly but surely separating the dross from the pure gold, disintegrating what is pernicious, consolidating what is beneficial to the race, so that the feeling that formerly told us that we alone had special care bestowed upon us gives place to the knowledge that every one in his day and generation, wherever found, receives the truth best fitted for his elevation from that state to the next higher, and so

"Ilka blade of grass keps its ain drap o' dew,"

and grows its own fruit after its kind. For these and many other reasons, let all thoughtful souls follow my example and visit their brethren from one land to another till the circle is complete.

The unprecedented advance made by western nations in the past and present generations, upon which we continually plume ourselves, is shared by the world in general. Wherever we have been, one story met us. Everywhere there is progress, not only material but intellectual as well, and rapid progress too.

The oldest inhabitant has always his comparison to offer between the days of his youth and the advantages possessed by the youth of to-day. Matters are not as they were. We saw no race which had retrograded, if we except Egypt, which is now in a transitional state, and will ultimately prove no exception to the rule. The whole world moves, and moves in the right direction—upward and onward—the things that are better than those that have been and those to come to be better than those of to-day. The law of evolution—the higher from the lower—is not discredited by a voyage round the world and the knowledge of what is transpiring from New York round to New York again gives us joy this morning as we sum it all up.

The trip has been without a single unpleasant incident. We have not missed one connection, nor ever been beyond the reach of all the comforts of life, nor have we had one unhappy or even lonely hour. Every day has brought something new or interesting. And sitting here in our quiet mountain home this morning, I feel that there is scarcely a prize that could be offered for which I would exchange the knowledge obtained and the memories of things seen during my trip. One of the great pleasures of travel in the East is the unbounded hospitality—excessive kindness—everywhere met with. Will the numerous kind friends to whom we are so deeply indebted—a host far too great to name—please accept this general acknowledgment as at least a slight evidence that their goodness to us is not unappreciated? At every stage of our travels I have been struck with the cheering thought, that notwithstanding the indisputable fact that a vast amount of misery seems inseparable from human life, still the general condition of mankind is a happy one. Even the Hindoo in India, or the Malay in the Archipelago—and these seem to exist under the worst conditions—each of these constantly sees cause to bless his good fortune and render thanks—sincere, heartfelt thanks—to a kind Providence for casting his life in pleasant places, and not in damp, foggy England, or amid American frosts and snows. We have their sincere sympathy, I assure you. Nor is patriotism a peculiarly western virtue. No matter who or what he is, the man of the East in his heart exalts his own country and his own race, and esteems them specially favored of the gods. And indeed it is with nations as with individuals: as none are entirely good, so none are entirely bad. The unseen power is at work in all lands, evolving the higher from the lower and steadily improving all, so the traveller finds much to commend in every country, and seeing this he grows tolerant and liberal, and able more heartily to sing with Burns—

> " Then let us pray that come it may—
> As come it will, for a' that—
> That sense and worth, o'er a' the earth,
> May bear the gree, for a' that ;

> For a' that, and a' that,
> It's coming yet, for a'that,
> That man to man, the warld o'er
> Shall brothers be, for a' that."

In which hope, nay, in the confident and inspiring belief in the sure coming of the day of the Brotherhood of Man, I lay down my pen and bring to a close this record of my tour round the world.

www.ingramcontent.com/pod-product-compliance
Lightning Source LLC
Chambersburg PA
CBHW021723110726
47902CB00005B/1315